Flavours

Susan Mehra

~

© Penrose Publishing Ltd

First Published 2013 by Penrose Publishing Ltd, York House, York Road, Felixstowe
IP11 7QG

www.penrose-publishing.co.uk

ISBN-國際標準書號

978-1-909879-00-3 Chinese/English 平裝版

978-1-909879-01-0 Chinese 電子書 Kindle

978-1-909879-02-7 Chinese 電子書 Kobo

978-1-909879-03-4 Chinese 電子書 PDF

978-0-9576201-6-2 English 平裝版

978-0-9576201-7-9 English 電子書 Kindle

978-0-9576201-8-6 English 電子書 Kobo

978-0-9576201-9-3 English 電子書 PDF

~

Susan Mehra

www.penrose-publishing.co.uk

Chapter One

"You've done what?" Kevin stopped walking and stared at her.

"Joined a dating agency. That new online one that's been advertising a lot lately." She pulled up the neck of her plum-coloured coat, shivering.

"Haven't noticed."

"Their office is just round the corner from work." She was skimming down the messages on her phone. She'd been so busy this morning that this was the first chance she'd had. She looked up, aware that Kevin had gone silent.

"Come on, Kev, it's no biggie. Lots of people do it these days." She pocketed her phone, grabbed his arm and tucked it in her own, dragging him onwards.

"Yes, but not you. Why do you need to join one? You're intelligent, caring..." he cocked his head on one side. "And I suppose you're quite good-looking. If you like that kind of thing."

She elbowed him in the ribs. "Oh, thanks. What's up, used your monthly compliment allowance?" She pushed at the door of the coffee shop with her spare hand, releasing him with a shove once they were inside. "You go find table, hunter man, me go get sustenance. Cappuccino?"

Rebecca fished for her purse as she walked towards the counter. Please don't let it be the oily little bloke serving, she prayed. Tony had employed a couple of temporary staff before Christmas, and one of them gave her the creeps. She kept on hoping his time was up, but he'd still been here yesterday.

Phew, it was the other new guy, the brown-haired one. He had his back to her but that was absolutely fine; Rebecca was happy to admire the view. This one could stay as long as he liked.

"You're still here then," she said as he turned.

"Yep. Week 3." He smiled.

"Wow. Almost a veteran. That smacks of vocation, round here."

His smile faded. "Not for me, I'd like to aim a bit higher. It's convenient for now, and Tony's asked me to stay on." His tone was cool. "What can I get you?"

"Sorry," said Rebecca awkwardly. Her and her dumb remarks. "I didn't mean I thought this was the height of your abilities or anything. I've done my share of waiting tables and serving behind counters. It's just that Tony's Christmas people don't normally stay long."

"Sorry, it's okay. I'm only grumpy because you're about the fiftieth person today who's said something along the lines of 'oh, you're still here then'. His mouth quirked.

"Oh." She grinned. "I can see how that would get annoying. Sorry. I'll have one vanilla latte and one hazelnut, please."

He got busy with the coffee machine and lifted the syrup bottles up high to deliver the shots, doing both cups at once.

Rebecca was impressed. "Wow. You look like Tom Cruise."

He smiled at her over his shoulder. "I don't get told that very often, what with having light brown hair and being 6 foot 1, but thanks."

Rebecca laughed. "No, I meant when you do that thing with the bottles. It's like a scene from Cocktail."

"Ah, right." He turned and put the coffees on her tray. "I did work in a cocktail bar for a while. Another one of my dead end jobs," he said, arching an eyebrow, eyes twinkling.

She held up her hands. "Stop! I feel bad enough already."

"Okay. Truce."

Rebecca paid and he put the change on the tray for her. "Thank you... oh, you've got a badge now!" She leaned forward and looked at it. "Stephen Reynolds."

He shook his head and tapped the badge. She squinted at the smaller writing underneath.

"Oh sorry – 'Call me Steve.' Why don't they just put Steve on your badge, then?"

"Tony got these free when he was considering that franchise deal. It was their company policy. Full name on your badge, even if you never use it, and nicknames across the middle. Mad."

She nodded. Tony had told her about it and she'd been horrified. The individuality of Tony's was part of its charm. "Crazy. Thank God Tony never agreed to it, I love this place exactly as it is." She picked up the tray and did a small curtsey. "Thank you, Call Me Steve. And may your days here be happy ones. And short, if you so desire!"

"Thank you... "

"Rebecca."

"Enjoy your coffee, Rebecca."

"Thanks." She walked carefully to the corner where Kevin sat staring out the window. "Penny for them," she said, plonking the tray down and dropping into the seat opposite.

"Oh you know. Just wondering if this dating agency thing means you've taken leave of your senses and I should call a doctor." He prodded her with a wooden stirrer.

"Oh ha ha."

Kevin sniffed his latte appreciatively and took a long drink. "Seriously, though. You don't need a dating agency."

She smacked her forehead. "Of course! You're right. I've had so many dates lately, I can barely fit in time to go food shopping!"

"The only reason you haven't found The One yet is you work too hard." He wiped foam from his mouth with the back of his hand.

"Yeah. And the reason you haven't found The One yet is that you have the manners of a pig."

"All part of my charm." He smiled winningly.

"Is that what it is? Well save it for someone who cares, pig boy." She made a face. "Now I meant to ask, do you want cake? And if I buy you one, can I trust you to keep your mouth shut while you're eating?"

"Yes I do, and yes you could, but no we can't." Kevin tapped his watch. "Not if you want to go handbag shopping, as discussed in your, ahem, 'urgent staff memo' of yesterday."

"No, I can't be bothered any more. We left late as it was, and I'm sure Fran's wedding won't be a disaster just because my handbag doesn't match my shoes."

"Fair enough. Suits me, I'm shattered." He sat back and stretched his legs out with a sigh, and a companionable silence fell as they both sipped their coffee.

"So what's this dating agency called then?" Kevin asked suddenly.

"What? Oh..." Rebecca looked down into the depths of her cup. "Methodical Matches," she mumbled.

"What?"

"You heard!"

"Methodical Matches? What kind of a name is that?" he exploded.

"Shut up, will you!" she hissed, glancing around. "I know it's not exactly snappy, but I picked them because they work up a really thorough profile on everyone. It's all very scientific. A computer sifts all the variables."

"Ah." Kevin batted his eyelashes. "So you're looking for a man with huge variables, then."

Rebecca whacked him with her purse.

"Ow!"

"I don't know why I tell you anything."

"Come on, I'm only teasing. How does it work then?"

"Well... you know... "

"No, I don't. I've never been on one of those sites myself, and don't know anyone else who has—or admitted to it, anyway."

Rebecca stirred her coffee, avoiding Kevin's eyes. "You answer lots of questions about what you like, what your interests are, your beliefs, what you're hoping for from a relationship. That's your profile. Then the computer compares your profile to everyone else's and generates your ideal matches."

"Don't you get to look at other profiles? I thought you could to look at other people's details, check them out."

"And I thought you said you didn't know how it works." She raised an eyebrow.

He squirmed a little. "You hear stuff about it, don't you?"

"Hmm. Anyway, I think you're right, that's the way they normally work—they suggest matches but you can browse people's profiles yourself and filter them and everything. But this company claim they profile you so thoroughly, and match you so scientifically, that you don't need that stage. You find out about your matches when you message each other or meet—and they say that's good, because it gives you something to talk about rather than knowing everything already. That really made sense to me."

Kevin looked doubtful. "Not sure what a computer knows about compatibility and love, but it's your life I suppose. But why sign up in the first place? And why now?"

She shrugged, sipping her coffee. "I thought it would help me meet people."

He looked at her keenly. "You meet people all the time, Becs."

"Not the right people."

"Oh, the right people." He rolled his eyes.

"Shush, you. This way, at least the people I meet will be—well, pre-filtered. We'll already have a lot in common."

"Yes, if they can find anyone else like you, that is."

Rebecca looked away, feeling pathetic and a bit panicky. Perhaps he had a point.

Kevin put his hand on her arm. "Sorry, only joking. I'm a bit surprised, that's all."

"I just feel I want to be with someone. I don't know why I suddenly feel like that, but I do." Her voice was a bit quavery. What was wrong with her?

"Ah. The old biological clock ticking?"

"I don't think so. That's not how it feels, anyway. I haven't got cravings for the smell of baby powder or anything." She smiled weakly. "I just crave a real relationship."

"You've had real relationships."

"Huh. Mainly with men from Emotionally Damaged Boyfriends R Us. I want to meet someone compatible. Someone nice."

"Ralph was nice."

"Yeah. Nice. But he had issues with his mother, plus he was about as exciting as a picnic rug. And that's an insult to picnic rugs." She was glad the conversation had moved to safer territory. Comparatively, anyway.

"Simon."

"Lovely. Except for going back to his ex-wife every couple of months when she threatened to hurt herself. Had to get out of that one before I started to go the same way."

"Hal. He was okay." He smirked. "More than at some things, I believe."

"But deep, meaningful conversation wasn't one of them, if you remember."

"No. His interests were pretty limited. But if it's scintillating conversation you're after, darling, then I'm your man," he grinned.

"Right. Of course! Silly me."

"Seriously, you know what the real problem is," he sighed, looking sad.

"Come on then, Yoda." She did the voice. "Give me the benefit of your wisdom, you must." She tipped her coffee mug to get the last of the coffee and froth.

"None of them can ever compare to me," he said, leering comically, and slid a hand up her thigh. Rebecca squawked, spluttering froth and latte liberally across the table. By the time she'd cleared up the mess, which took ages because Kevin was being even sillier than usual, they had to settle for a takeaway sandwich. But Rebecca was glad Kevin had made her laugh, and banished that stupid emotional moment she'd been having. It wasn't like her at all.

His teasing hadn't changed her mind though, she thought, as they walked back to work. She was going through with it. Nothing ventured, nothing gained, as her Dad used to say. Maybe she really would find The One.

Or a half-decent date, at least.

Steve glanced at the door again. Would Rebecca be back today? She didn't come in every day, but most days she either popped in for a quick coffee and a pastry, or, more often for lunch. He knew her favourite pastry was Apricot Danish and her favourite wrap was Cajun Chicken. He knew her favourite type of man too, unfortunately, because that tall blonde guy was nearly always with her.

He'd watched them after he spoke to her on Monday, although of course he pretended he wasn't. You got good at that, hiding away behind the counter looking busy. They looked good together. She was a stunner; all that chestnut hair, sometimes lying over her shoulders, shiny and smooth, and sometimes caught up in a barrette at the back of her head, the tendrils that escaped making her look, if anything, more beautiful. Laura had worn her hair that way once, he thought with a pang. Now she couldn't be bothered. With her hair, or anything else.

Rebecca was bright and funny, too, but he was on a road to nowhere there. It was very rare for her and the blonde guy to come in separately; he wondered if they worked together. If they did, seeing so much of each other didn't seem to do them any harm. They seemed very comfortable together but there was obviously good chemistry between them too. Steve had noticed him put his hand on her thigh making Rebecca giggle and splutter her coffee everywhere. He realised he was staring far too blatantly. Feeling guilty, he'd pulled himself together and set about cleaning and tidying everything in sight, this had impressed Tony no end.

So knowing she was off limits, why did he find himself hoping she would come in today? Glancing at the door every other minute? And even worse, asking Neil, the Australian guy working here in his gap year, to swap duties so he could be here now, serving behind the counter? You're a hopeless case Steve, he told himself, just setting yourself up for disappointment.

The door opened and he glanced up. Through the throng of people just leaving, he caught a glimpse of a plum-coloured coat. She was right on time for lunch and there was no sign of her boyfriend. His heart thudded a little faster and he took a deep breath, summoning up his professional here-to-brighten-up-your-day smile as she came towards him.

"Back again?"

"Yep. A regular bad penny, me."

"Vanilla latte?"

"Yes please." She sighed deeply. "And a Cajun Chicken Wrap and a double choc chip muffin. Large."

"Like that, is it?" He hit the button on the coffee machine.

"Definitely. I nearly went to the wine bar instead."

"Phew, that bad? What changed your mind?"

"I've got a meeting this afternoon with some Very Important People, so getting sloshed wouldn't be good."

"I see." He slid her latte across to her and put a biscuit on the saucer.

She looked at it, raising her eyebrows. "Plus the staff here are nicer," she said lightly.

Steve willed his cheeks not to go pink. "You're only saying that because I've given you a free biscuit."

"No, I mean it. Biscuit aside."

"Er... thanks." He smiled politely, putting the wrap and muffin on her tray, but inside his heart had done a little flip. Was she flirting with him? Perhaps she was one of those women who flirted with everyone in sight once their boyfriend wasn't around? He found that idea strangely disappointing, but wasn't sure why. When she just smiled in reply and walked away, he didn't know if he felt relieved or demoralised.

He watched her sit down and start on her lunch, then frowned. Her boyfriend had just come in and gone straight to her table. He didn't come to the counter. Probably a good thing, Steve thought, because he could feel himself glowering.

The kitchen door squeaked behind him. "Earth to Steve, come in Steve."

"What?"

"I said, is this the first tray of croissants we've got through today, or the second?" said Neil patiently. Steve liked Neil. He was good fun to work with, but he wouldn't be here for much longer. He'd planned 6 months earning and 6 months trekking, and he'd been here two months before Steve arrived.

"Sorry. First."

Neil carried the tray over to the counter. "I'll just fill up the tray then, and take the rest back. Sorry to interrupt when you're staring at pretty girls."

"What? I wasn't—"

"Pull the other one, dude, I saw you looking at Rebecca. You think she's well fit."

He grinned.

"What, and you don't?" said Steve defensively.

He shrugged, looking a little awkward.

"Doesn't make much difference, anyway. Well fit but well attached, unfortunately," said Steve, jerking his head in Rebecca's direction.

"She is?" Neil glanced up, frowning. "You think those two are together?"

"They're always in here together, and they seem very close. He put his hand on her leg yesterday. High up."

Neil shook his head. "They were probably just mucking about. They work together at the museum. I think you're barking up the wrong tree there, mate."

"Why?"

For some reason he couldn't fathom, Neil went a little pink. "Cos I've, er, seen Kevin about. Out on the town."

"And?"

Neil turned away, rearranging the croissants, although they looked fine to Steve. "He wasn't acting like he was attached, that's all. A single bloke out on the pull, I reckon."

Steve looked back to Rebecca, laughing at something the blonde guy had just said, and shook his head. "I don't know. Perhaps they've got a very open relationship, but I'd bet you that whole tray of croissants they're together. Not that I'm in a position to care one way or the other."

"Why? Because of Laura?"

Steve shrugged.

"Mate, I think it's time to cut the strings there." He elbowed him, nodding at Rebecca and Kevin. "And if their relationship's so open, you might be in with a chance."

"Cut the strings, huh? Easy for you to say." Steve flipped a cloth over his shoulder and sprayed cleaner on the counter. "And not for me, thanks. I don't share."

"Old-fashioned, aren't ya?" Neil winked at him. "I'll leave you to it then, Granddad."

"Back to the kitchen, galley slave."

Laughing, Neil disappeared back to the kitchen

Steve turned and made a start on cleaning the pastry cabinet, watching his targets surreptitiously over the top. Neil must be wrong; those two were joined at the hip. He was never going to get a date with her. He needed to stop mooning over her and look elsewhere, if he wanted a new woman in his life. But did he?

He looked thoughtfully, not for the first time, at the pile of leaflets on the counter. He picked one up.

'Methodical Matches: "We see Suitability as a Science."'

Dreadful name. Tacky tagline. But everything it said inside seemed to make sense. He folded it up and put it in his pocket.

Chapter Two

No time to go to Tony's today, thought Rebecca, sinking into her chair and wrapping her hands gratefully around her coffee mug. Still, at least she could afford a few minutes sitting at her desk, although it was more tempting to hide under it today.

It wasn't that she didn't love her work. Her parents had both been archaeologists; there was nothing else she'd ever wanted to be, and she couldn't be happier with her current role as Project Leader for GLAMAR – the Greater London Anthropology Museum's Archaeological Research team. But today work had been manic.

Every so often the Museum ran family fun days, either for the general public or for corporations. She enjoyed getting the children involved and knew it was important – if she could get them interested, these kids might be the archaeologists of the future—but it meant her days were hectic as she tried to organise activities for the visitors and keep an eye on the everyday work that went on.

She'd left her group in Kevin and Emma's capable hands for a bit, and as this might be the only break she'd get this morning, she'd better hurry up and reply to the supposedly urgent message that had been on her answer phone when she got home last night. She tapped in the number.

"Good morning! Methodical Matches, Nicola speaking, how can I help you?"

"Hello, you left a message on my answer machine yesterday. It's Rebecca Maynard."

"Oh, Rebecca! Hi! Thanks for getting back to me!"

Rebecca pulled the phone away from her ear a little. Nicola was obviously one of those people who only spoke in exclamations. "You said it was urgent?"

"Yes, I phoned because I noticed your profile is still showing as incomplete! Until you finish it, we can't get on the case and find you some great Methodical Matches!"

Wow. Hardly the end of the world, thought Rebecca. "Oh, right. It's just that—"

Her office door crashed open and Kevin slithered to a halt in front of her. "There's a problem in the Kid's Corner, Becs!" He spotted the phone in her hand and put his hands over his mouth, muttering a muffled "sorry!"

"Excuse me for a moment." She put her hand over the mouthpiece and gave Kevin a cool look. "Where's the fire?"

"One of the kids just peed in a Dig It Sandbox."

She rolled her eyes. "Nicola, something's just cropped up. I could pop in at lunchtime, unless you close then? I'm just round the corner."

"Great! Look forward to seeing you then!" Nicola trilled.

Rebecca slapped the phone down and stood up. "How did a kid pee in the sandbox?"

He spread his hands. "Er, the usual way? He kind of stood up and—"

"They're not meant to get in the box, Kev, they're meant to lean over it! You know that."

"I know, I know. Sorry. I only turned my back for a second."

"Which one was it?"

"Rory – you know, the little one with those dark corkscrew curls and scarily pale blue eyes? Devil child, Emma's been calling him. Not in his parents' hearing, of course."

She stared. "Not which kid. Which sandbox, dumbass."

"Oh... sorry." He looked sheepish. "Roman. He'd got down to the First Invasion era."

She strode past him. "I suppose we need new sand then."

"And a new brooch," he called, hurrying to catch up with her. "That's what you get for using fake artefacts in there, it's gone a really funny colour..."

Six hours later, Rebecca was walking quickly along the street, bitterly regretting her promise to call in at the dating agency. She'd had a hell of a day – Rory had turned out to be a serial pee-er—and hadn't managed to stop for lunch at all. It had been easier to grit her teeth and work through it in the hope of leaving on time. She'd managed that, just about, and now all she wanted was to collapse on her sofa with a large glass of wine, happy in the knowledge that takeaway would turn up shortly. But she would have to wait.

She pushed open the door of Methodical Matches and jumped as it made a loud, discordant two-tone beep.

"Oh, sorry about that. We keep saying we'll get a new one!"

Nicola—Rebecca knew it was her before she spotted the name plate—smiled at her from behind a white desk with arty curved shelves on burnished steel supports, devoid of any paperwork or stationery. She wondered if the sole purpose of the desk was to support Nicola's Tango-coloured arms and scarily long mint-green fingernails, which were resting on it in a glowing triangle formation that resembled a fluorescent road sign.

"Hi, I'm Rebecca Maynard. You phoned about my profile?"

"Yes! We're very keen to get started, and wondered if there was a problem. We can't do anything until the profile's completed! We need the whole picture!" Teeth that could have doubled as a Dulux brilliant white sample flashed in Nicola's face.

"I'm nearly finished, it's just that, er…" Rebecca floundered.

"You're having problems with the website?" Nicola supplied. She tilted her head, a tiny, patronising smile on her lips. "It's not always easy for people who didn't grow up in the internet generation, is it?"

Rebecca had never been completely sure what the phrase 'she bridled' meant when she'd read it in books, but she was pretty sure she was doing it now. Yes. Definite bridling going on.

"I'm perfectly fine with the technical aspects, thank you," she replied, in a tone that could freeze polar bears. "But I only registered last week and haven't had time to complete it yet. It's quite long and the website times out after twenty minutes and loses my information. That's happened twice already."

A tiny furrow appeared in Nicola's otherwise stretchy-smooth tanned forehead. "Timing out? We've not had a problem with that before."

"I've printed out the questions now, so I can rough it out on paper, then just type in my answers," said Rebecca. "But I can't finish it until next week. "

"Next week?" echoed Nicola. She leaned forward and lowered her voice to a supposedly confidential whisper. "We're very discreet you know," she hissed, in a penetrating tone that could probably be heard by iPod-wearing passers-by on the street. "If there's a literacy issue, come into the office and someone can help…"

"My literacy skills are fine, thank you!" she retorted. What a nerve! "But the food diary covers a week and I've only filled out the first four days."

Nicola looked at her blankly. "Food diary?"

It's like talking to a parrot, thought Rebecca. Sorry, parrots of the world. "Yes, in the eating habits section. Under lifestyle."

Nicola looked none the wiser.

"I suppose it's so that lovers of daily fry-ups don't get matched up with people whose idea of a big breakfast is a larger slice of watermelon than usual." Why was she explaining the rationale of the profile to someone from the company that had designed it?

"I wasn't aware of a food diary section." Nicola frowned, distracted. "It wasn't there before."

"Perhaps it's new," said Rebecca after a long pause when the only sound was Nicola's nails tapping on the desk. And possibly cogs whirring, if she'd listened closely. "It's very time-consuming. I'm sure some general questions about what people like to eat would be just as useful. Maybe you should suggest it to whoever designs the questionnaire."

Nicola gave a short, sharp laugh, suddenly all attention again. "Oh, that's a great idea." Her tone of voice suggested she thought otherwise. "If I see him, I'll suggest it."

"Er... right. Thanks—"

"Anything else?" Her glare dared Rebecca to say yes.

"No, that's fi—"

"Hope to see your profile soon then."

"Yes, er..." Rebecca was walking to the door, flustered. "As soon as possible."

Once she was safely outside, her breath whooshed out in a huge sigh of relief. Wow. What a turnaround. What had she said to turn Little Miss Jekyll in there into the Evil Hag Hyde?

And why had she thought this would be simpler than making more effort to socialise and hoping that somehow, eventually, she'd meet a nice guy?

Sunday night. Rebecca stretched out on the settee with her laptop, and opened up the copy of the dating profile. The food diary was finally finished, but there were still blank sections in her profile. This thing went on forever. They might just have well have scooped out her brain and had a good look; it would have been quicker. And probably less painful.

Oh, no! She'd forgotten this part. 'List all albums you possess alphabetically by artist's surname or band name.' What was wrong with 'what genres of music you enjoy?' And did people tell the truth, anyway, or did they get to W and discreetly forget their entire back catalogue of Wurzel albums that had pride of place on the shelf? Luckily—or perhaps scarily, she admitted—she arranged her CDs alphabetically anyway, but she had about 75. Should she confess to Abba?

Twenty minutes later, she'd jotted down a judiciously edited list. Abba had gone the way of Michael Ball, Tangerine Dream and a few others, partly because she persuaded herself they weren't typical of her taste, which was a joke, given how eclectic it was, but mainly because she was worried she'd be matched with someone who owned those albums too. She didn't want to think too hard about what that said about her.

Luckily the reading section was far less detailed, or she'd have been up all night listing books. She owned hundreds; they took up more room than anything else in her small flat, stored on a selection of tall, generally wonky mismatched bookcases. She loved biographies and old dictionaries with archaic words, and had a huge number of books on history, archaeology, anthropology and palaeontology.

But when she was snuggled up in her big armchair relaxing, or chilling out in the bath, she normally chose historical fiction or her favourite—a Jodie Forrest thriller. They normally had some kind of ancient mystery to be solved that connected to a modern conspiracy plot, and helped to satisfy her latent Indiana Jones urges. She filled in 'my all time top 10' and 'the last 10 books I read' and grinned, thinking about her conversation with Kevin about her exes. Hal would never have got to 10 in either of those categories—not without some serious head-scratching, anyway.

The next section made her squirm. Did they really need to know the details of every past relationship? She was as brief as possible. Scoring her exes out of 10 on their attributes – some of which were rather personal – was cringe worthy. Thank God the next section was the last. She whizzed through her 'ethics and beliefs'.

It was midnight when she finished copying her answers into the online submission form. She yawned as she clicked 'send', wondering what these men would be like. Did matching attributes and attitudes scientifically really work, or did it just strip dating or all its romance? Would she still get that fluttering in her stomach, that thrill of instant attraction, when she was meeting men in such a pre-planned way?

She closed her laptop. Hopefully, she'd soon find out.

"So what will it be today, oh queen of the latte? Your usual, or something a little more exotic?" Steve leaned forward conspiratorially. "Don't tell everyone," he hissed, "But we've got a new syrup in. It's just not on the board yet."

"Ooh," Rebecca breathed, making her eyes go wide. "Go on. Tell!"

"It's butterscotch," Steve said, in a comical strangled whisper. He made a show of glancing round, then bent down under the counter and let the bottle quickly peep over the top.

"Yum. I love butterscotch. Where did you get that from?"

He shook his head. "If I told you, I'd have to kill you," he rasped. "That would be an awful shame. Bright girl like you."

"Well if I promise not to ask any more questions, can I have some in my coffee?" she whispered back.

"Yes. But remember—tell no one." He glared at her. "Or else..." he mimed cutting his throat.

"Understood."

"Good. What can I get for Kevin?"

"Nothing. It'll get cold."

"Is he not coming in until later, then?"

"Not coming in here at all today, I shouldn't think. He's working miles away."

"Right. Won't you be lonely having coffee on your own?"

"Not if you have your coffee break now too. Then I could give you a minute by minute account of my butterscotch experience." She gave him a teasing smile and Steve's stomach did back flips.

"Won't Kevin mind?" he blurted.

"What? No, I shouldn't think so. He can have coffee with you another day," she said lightly. Steve gaped as she picked up her tray, trying to figure out if she was deliberately misunderstanding the question.

Perhaps their relationship really was open. Or perhaps other people were just better adjusted to the whole man/woman friendship thing, he thought; he used to have women as friends, but maybe he'd forgotten how to. Since he'd left uni, there had always been Laura. Keeping everyone else at arm's length was desirable at first, then recently, a necessity.

Rebecca's voice cut through his thoughts. "As for the butterscotch, he won't know what he's missing, will he," she grinned. "Because I'm not allowed to tell him!" She walked off to her usual table, leaving Steve staring after her and feeling bemused.

After a moment, he went to the hatch. "Tony!"

"What?"

"Can I take my break now?"

"Now? Is bit early, no?" Tony appeared, a stained bright red, green and white striped apron stretched over his bulging middle. He was nothing if not patriotic, thought Steve.

"What is the matter? Is it so busy out there you are worn out?" He stuck his head through, scanning the shop. "No! Is quiet." Then he straightened with a grin. "Ah."

"What?"

"I see why you want the early break. Is not the when, it is the who, yes?" His eyes were mischievous.

"What? No, I—yes, it's just that the girl who comes in most days—"

"The lovely Rebecca." In true Italian style he managed to pronounce an r in 'lovely' that wasn't even there.

"Er... yes, she—"

"Go, go!" Tony had undone his apron whilst Steve was floundering. He threw it through the hatch, eliciting a squawk of protest from Rinaldo in the kitchen, and pulled a fresh white one from under the counter. "Take long break if you like, and have the shorter lunchtime, my friend."

"Thanks, Tony."

"No problem. Tony was young once too."

As he walked away, he could hear Tony say something to Rinaldo through the hatch that provoked a burst of laughter, and felt himself flush. He stopped himself just as he walked around the counter. Idiot. He hadn't got a coffee. He turned back reluctantly and Tony gave a mocking bow.

"And what is sir's pleasure?"

"I'll have a butterscotch latte please."

"Sorry, sir is mistaken. If he look at board, he will see we do not have the bu—"

"Tony!"

"Alright," he grinned. "I see sir is in a rush." Steve's coffee swiftly appeared. "Is that everything for sir?"

"Yes, thanks."

"Enjoy."

"Thanks."

Steve did enjoy it. Not just the coffee, but Rebecca's company. It was hard to hold her at arm's length, he thought guiltily. She was warm and witty and broke through any reserve he tried to cling to.

He didn't know much about archaeology but when Rebecca talked about her work, she managed to explain unfamiliar terms in a way that didn't make him feel she was dumbing things down for him. The enthusiasm for her work shone out of her.

Her eyes sparkled when she talked about the brilliant days, the disappointing days, and the days when small boys peed in her lovingly prepared archaeological activities. That was when she mentioned Kevin. Neil was right; they worked together, and they'd been at uni together too.

He tried to be polite and not to grind his teeth together at the mere mention of the man's name.

"I knew something was wrong when he ran into my office," she laughed. "He doesn't normally venture in, in case I give him extra work to do, so I should have guessed it was a pee-related disaster."

He grinned. "So what do you normally do, call each other in your separate offices? Do you only talk face to face at break times?"

"Kevin doesn't have an office."

"I see. What makes you the lucky one then?"

"I'm his boss. Kind of." She grinned. "Though don't repeat that to him. I'm more senior, let's put it that way."

"So you get an office to boss people about from."

"Yep, and he doesn't."

"How did that happen?"

"You mean, how did a woman get promoted over a man?" Her eyes twinkled.

"No! What kind of dinosaur do you think I am? I just thought, if you two were at Uni at the same time..."

"Ah, but I was doing my master's—something Kevin hasn't got—when he was just starting his degree. He's a few years younger."

"Right. A masters, eh? Impressive."

"Thanks. Kevin got a good degree, don't get me wrong, but he's not interested in going for his Masters—not yet anyway—and he's happy to jog along where he is. I went to workshops, conferences, specialised training, you name it. I was very keen to deepen my knowledge. Plus—" she raised a warning finger, "and you're not allowed to say anything here, Call Me Steve—I've always been mouthy, always springing up with suggestions whether they're asked for on not."

"Not saying a word," said Steve, staring at her woodenly.

"Good. Kevin's brilliant at what he does, though. He can look at soil in a trench and practically tell you its composition before you can say 'let's get this to the lab'. He's a real expert in that field." Suddenly she giggled, nearly spilling her coffee.

"What's so funny?" Steve passed her a serviette.

"It isn't funny, it's awful. Soil? An expert in that field..."

Steve grinned. "Very funny."

"Ooh, don't be so polite, it was terrible. I'm easily amused, that's all."

"Great, I got a book of one-liners for Christmas. I've been waiting for someone to try them out on."

"Nobody at home to read them too, then?" She seemed to be watching him very carefully as she asked.

"Nobody I know is into one-liners," he said lightly, side-stepping the question, "except Neil, and he gave me the book. But being Neil he read it first, so no joy there."

"Well in that case, it looks like I'm doomed to be your audience."

"Hmm. I think you'd have to be a captive one, literally. I might lock the door one day and not let you out until I've read the entire book to you. Of course you'd have to laugh at them all, as well."

"You strike a hard bargain."

"That's me." He got to his feet. "I'd better get back. Think I've stretched my break as far as I can." Tony saw him coming and disappeared through the door with a meaningful wiggle of his eyebrows. And he's got a lot of eyebrow to wiggle, thought Steve, smiling to himself.

She followed him to the counter with the tray. "I suppose next time it's the comedy lockdown, then, is it?"

Steve walked round the counter and put his apron on. "Either that, or I'm cutting you off." He produced the butterscotch syrup and waggled it just out of her reach. "No more Butterscotch Latte á la Steve."

"Ooh, you're a cruel man. I'll have to make sure I don't come in alone then. If I have to suffer this fate, then Kevin should too."

Steve's spirits deflated like a balloon in close proximity to a rose bush. "Yes, I'm sure he'll protect you," he said lamely. He turned so that she couldn't see his face, pretending to be very busy refilling the chocolate sprinkles. He was sure his feelings were written in inch high letters across his forehead. Come on, Steve, grow up. You can't hate him because he got the girl before you even knew her. Be nice. "So Kevin's speciality is soil, is it?" he asked, trying to keep his voice light.

"Not really, no, it's—"

"No, no, no," he said severely. "You have to say yes, his speciality is soil."

"But it's not, because—"

He sighed. "Please. Just say it."

"Okay. Yes, Steve. Kevin's speciality is soil."

"Well no wonder he's an archaeologist," he said, raising his eyebrows, "he must really Dig It." He took a bow.

Rebecca looked blank.

"Oh come on." He put his hands on his hips. "That was comedy gold."

"What was?" Her face was all innocent confusion.

"Soil? Dig it?—" He stopped, frowning, because Rebecca had let a snigger escape. "Huh."

"Sorry. Very good, especially the presentation. Er, mostly the presentation, actually."

"Thank you. I pride myself on my comic..." he frowned, and stared at the syrup bottles. "Ah yes. Timing." He grinned. "Another butterscotch latte? Since you're such an appreciative audience?"

"No thanks, I should go. My meeting's at three, and I'm got to meet Kevin at the site first."

"Right," he said. "Your knight with a shining spade. You never did tell me what his speciality actually is. What a pity." Despite his best efforts, he sounded sarcastic.

Rebecca gave him an odd look. "Never mind. Perhaps next time," she said, a little coolly.

"Yes." He felt awkward now. "See you then."

"See you."

Way to go Steve, he thought, as he watched her leave. Nice one.

Chapter Three

He knew she was in the minute he opened the door. It was the smell. He pushed the door shut behind him, taking a minute to lean back and take a deep, steadying breath. Right. He could handle this. He slung his rucksack over the hook in the hallway and stopped at the door of the lounge, listening.

Nothing. Maybe she was asleep. He put his hand on the door handle and pushed it down slowly.

"For chrissake, Steve, stop poncing about out there." Laura's voice lashed out into the silence, making him jump.

As he walked in, all he could see of Laura was a hand laying on the back of the couch. Two steps more and he could see the whole sorry sight. She was sprawled along the sofa, feet bare, legs encased in skin-tight jeans that had started life black but were now covered in stains. Her hair was a mess, the blonde waves flattened and dulled by grease and... Well, he didn't want to think what else. She was wearing one of his best t-shirts. Great.

He didn't say anything, just let his eyes wander over the coffee table and the floor. Over the empty glasses, cans and wine bottles.

She followed his gaze. "Yeah. Sorry 'bout that. I'll wash up later, I had a fwew, few drinks."

And that wasn't all she'd had, he thought grimly, judging by all the empty crisp packets that littered the floor. If she'd had an attack of the munchies, you could bet it was more than just alcohol that had got her in this state.

"You had to use all those different glasses, did you?" he asked coldly.

She blinked at him. "Course," she said. "I had wine in that one—" she lurched sideways and jerked a finger down into the nearest, "and those two—" she waved at hand at two on the edge of the coffee table and they crashed to the floor. "Whoops s'okay it they wereempty... I had vodka in those and cider in that one. Had beer too." She picked up a can and frowned at it. "Nice, it was in your fridge, wasssit called..." she ran her finger down the writing, bringing it ridiculously close to her face. "Fosters!" she shouted triumphantly, punching an arm in the air." It's blue. Blue can, not beer." She waggled the can and a spurt of golden liquid leapt out of the can onto the t-shirt she was wearing. His t-shirt. "Oh," she looked like she would cry for a second. "Sorry, this is your shirt... where's mine?" She frowned, turning her head unsteadily. "Tha'sright, spilt wine on mine so I borrowed yours!" She looked up at him suddenly with a dazzling smile, which slid from her face just as quickly. "Eww, shouldn't twist my head round," she said, her eyes suddenly losing focus, "think I'm a bit poorly..."

But Steve was already in the kitchen grabbing a bucket. He got back just in time to thrust it into her lap, then walked out, slamming the lounge door behind him. He ran upstairs, desperate to get rid of that foul smell from his nostrils, and headed for

www.penrose-publishing.co.uk

his tiny ensuite shower room. But the smell seemed stronger than ever. He frowned, noticing Laura's t-shirt in a heap on the floor. He moved it cautiously with his foot and was glad he'd been careful. Laura hadn't just spilt her drink over it. And she hadn't just spilt drink down the toilet, either.

Steve felt his stomach heave and turned on his heel, shutting the door and fighting back tears of frustration. He couldn't deal with this now. In fact, why the hell should he deal with it at all? Sod her. She could clear up after herself later. He grabbed fresh clothes and a Jodie Forrest novel, and headed for the bathroom.

An hour later, the warm bath and a little pure escapism had worked their magic and he felt he could handle Laura and the mess now, though he was still reluctant to get back to the real world. On balance he'd rather be accompanying the novel's hero on his trek through the jungle to find a buried Mayan temple, because it sounded less stressful. But he had to face Laura sometime.

Not without a cup of tea first, though. Sometimes after smelling coffee all day tea was all he fancied. In the kitchen he filled a large mug with strong, sweet tea, and then opened the lounge door. Quietly.

Laura was asleep on the sofa. There was a trail of vomit on the armrest where her head lay and some in a pool on the floor. Thank God for laminate floors, he thought dispassionately, drinking his tea as he took in the scene. Back in the kitchen, he finished his tea in one gulp and armed himself with disinfectant, a cloth, a dustpan and a mop. He pinged on plastic gloves. He had no illusions about her Laura's lifestyle. Best not to take any chances.

He made a start on the lounge floor, trying not to breathe in the rank acid smell. Then he soaked the cloth in disinfectant and started to clean the armrest. At least she wouldn't get any more in her hair when she moved.

As though she'd heard his thought, Laura groaned and stirred. Steve sat back on his heels, keeping his expression neutral. After a few moments her eyelids slowly opened. She stared at him blearily, struggling to focus. A lopsided grin appeared.

"Hi Steve."

He didn't answer her; not because he was giving her the cold shoulder, but because he felt empty, as though he had run out of words to say to her.

"Are you cross with me?"

He sprayed the laminate with disinfectant. Got to his feet and started mopping.

"I know I'm a mess, Steve."

His jaw tightened. Here comes the whiney voice. It was like nails down a blackboard. Just mop and walk away, Steve, because you haven't got this under control at all.

"I've been trying, honestly. I've been really good. I just screwed up last night, that's all."

Steve mopped, willing himself not to respond, but he couldn't help himself. "What went wrong last night then?"

"Mike made me cross. You know, Mike from work."

"You don't go to work, Laura. Not anymore."

"You know what I mean Steve," she smiled, raising her hand to slap him playfully, but missing.

Steve wondered how many versions of him she was seeing right now. He felt like there were at least two inside his head, and neither of them knew how to handle her.

"My old work. You remember Mike."

He remembered Mike, alright. Some friend he had been. Mike was a borderline alcoholic himself, albeit a 'social alcoholic'. But he knew Mike wasn't good to be around when he'd been without a drink for a couple of days. And he also knew that Mike had encouraged Laura in the boozy lunches and after work drinks. And probably other after work indulgences too.

"I remember Mike. I don't think he's good for you."

"Good for me? You make it sound like I'm playing with a naughty child."

"So why did Mike annoy you?"

"Asked him for a favour but he said no." Her eyes slid away.

"Did you ask him for money?" his voice was harsh.

"No."

"Because you should be coming to me for money, Laura. We're meant to sort these things together."

"I told you, I didn't ask him for money! And you don't let me have money, except my JSA. I haven't got a bank card for the main account, have I?"

"No, and you know why."

"Oh yeah. I can only have money if you approve of how I spend it. A really equal relationship."

Steve's grip on the mop handle tightened. "I'm the one who earns it, so I should have some say on how it's spent, particularly when I find myself scraping thirty quid's worth of it off my floor!"

"Don't take it out on me because I lost my job!"

"And whose fault is that?"

"They had no right to fire me!" she stormed, tears gathering in her eyes. "I worked really hard for that company."

""Yes, until your wages started going up your nose," he ground out.

"They didn't! I always did my job properly!" she screeched. "But they threw me out! Hated me, all of them! Bitches. Bastards!"

"Yes, after informal warnings, formal warnings, written warnings, and even offering you counselling on their bloody time and money!" Steve roared. "And you didn't go to half the sessions because you were out your head!"

She started sobbing. "That's not fair! I was ill."

Steve shook his head in disgust, feeling his heart pound against his ribs. He'd told himself he wouldn't get mad at her. It was pointless. They'd been down this road a hundred times before, and it always ended up with her drowning in a welter of self-pity.

How had things gone so wrong so quickly? He'd tried to guide her, not condemn her, when he'd seen her going off the rails. She was a lot younger than him and he didn't want to become some kind of domineering father figure; he wanted to help her, and to do that he needed to keep her trust. But any trust between them had completely degenerated, on both sides, and the love and respect were going the same way.

"I'm going out," he said abruptly.

She rubbed at her eyes. "We haven't had any dinner."

"I'm eating out."

"But what am I going to eat?" she said pathetically, staring at him, all big eyes.

"It's your house too, Laura. You know where the food is. There's pizza in the fridge— if you're really still hungry." He looked pointedly at the floor.

"But I'm not well—"

"But finish disinfecting the floor first, and wash out your clothes before your vomit gets spread everywhere." He didn't look at her, busying himself with putting his jacket on, and gathering his phone, keys and wallet. On an afterthought, he picked up his laptop too, slipping it into its bag.

She started to sob again. "But Ste—"

He slammed the front door. He wasn't usually a door slammer, but today it felt good. Therapeutic. He'd go back to Tony's and spend the evening there. It would be familiar and comfortable, and smell a lot better than home.

He was right. It smelled a hell of a lot better than home. The deep aromas of coffee and warm pastry and the light, fresh smells of the cucumber and salad made him feel better – and hungry!—the moment he walked in. Sipping a cappuccino and tucking into one of Tony's handmade sausage rolls, he felt the stress flow out of him. The café was quiet this evening and Steve set himself up in a corner, facing out, near a radiator. He finished his sausage roll and wiped his hands on a serviette. Time to get busy on the laptop.

If today had shown him one thing, it was that he couldn't keep on living his life for Laura. He felt drained. He had given her all the help he could, but she didn't want to help herself. He'd lived like a monk, devoting himself only to her for too long.

He'd saved the dating site to his favourites the other night after wimping out at the last moment. There were lots of internet dating sites to pick from, but he'd gone with Methodical Matches in the end. Their claim that they matched people accurately and scientifically was appealing, particularly as there had been a rumour at university that some dating sites employed students, who spent their evenings matching clients on a drunken whim and posting the worst of the profile photos on the internet for everyone to see.

The downside was, the Methodical Matches profile form was so long that his session timed out way before he had time to complete it. That interruption that had stopped him in his tracks, giving him time to reconsider. He'd wimped out in the end; convinced himself that he was being irresponsible and uncaring. Laura would come out of this; she was young, it was a phase. She needed him to be around for her, not off with someone else. Hadn't he promised to support her, whatever happened? Signed his name to say he would?

But she needed to be responsible for herself now. If he asked her to move out and she refused, what would he do He had no idea. But he knew he needed to find himself a new life.

He copied the profile form into a new document on his laptop. Now he could take his time, thinking about each question carefully. He drained the dregs of his cappuccino and made a start.

His relationships? Well that was easy. He'd only managed a three month romance in sixth form—with a girl he didn't really fancy, but she was quite good-looking and very keen, so it seemed the thing to do—and spent a passionate if turbulent nine months with a French girl in his first and only year of Uni, before she returned to Paris and he got saddled with Laura. Voluntarily, he reminded himself. Yeah. What a mistake that had been.

He scrolled through the rest of the form. It went on forever, but it didn't matter, he was in no rush to get home. He found the next blank section. Every album he owned? He wasn't sure he could remember them all, sitting here. They were in alphabetical order at home, though, so he could try and think his way along the shelf. Hmm. Should he really admit to Abba?

Chapter Four

She should go home and cook, but she had been on her feet all day and they didn't feel like they belonged to her any more. She already knew there was nothing in the freezer that she could pop in the microwave and leave for ten minutes, collapsing on the settee until she heard the magical 'bing'. Anyway, she had a strong craving for one of Tony's hot Southern Fried Chicken Wraps, full of delicious crunchy bacon bits, and just the thought of it was making her mouth water as she pushed open the café shop door.

Inside there were only a few occupied tables but that wasn't unusual in the evenings, not at this time of the year anyway. A group of girls chatted quietly at a table near the window, there were a handful of couples scattered about and a few people sitting by themselves-

She stopped. What was Steve doing here, in civvies, all by himself? He was the last person she would have expected to see here in the evening, this side of the counter, anyway. He was at the small table with just two seats, usually favoured by couples because it was tucked away between the big supporting column in the wall and the alcove with the tall curved bench seat, giving it a sense of seclusion and privacy.

Obviously Steve wanted the privacy rather than the intimate company, she thought, amused. He was sitting with his back to the wall, and she was guessing it was him who'd pushed the other matching chair just far enough away from his table so that it looked like it didn't belonged there. She should probably leave him alone then, especially since he had a laptop in front of him. He must be busy.

She started towards the counter, one eye still on Steve. He looked good out of uniform. Whoops, lucky she hadn't said that one out loud! Good in his own clothes, she'd meant. That denim blue shirt suited him, the sleeves tighter than his white work shirts, showing that his arms were more muscular than she'd thought. Not that she'd been thinking about it. Particularly.

She risked a direct glance. He was staring into space, which seemed to live on the floor to one side of his table this evening, and idly folding an empty muffin case into smaller and smaller triangles. No, he didn't look busy; he looked thoroughly miserable.

She was surprised to find herself making her way between the tables towards him. The impulse seemed to have gone straight to her legs, completely circumventing her brain.

"Hi."

He jumped. "Oh—Rebecca. Hi."

He closed his laptop quickly, looking flustered, and she wondered what he had to hide. Perhaps he'd been looking at porn, she thought, having a mental giggle. But somehow she doubted it. He didn't seem the type to browse x-rated websites in the café where he worked, even if it was outside his working hours.

"Don't tell me, by day you serve in here, latte-maker-extreme, but by night you work for the Food Hygiene Board or whatever it's called and you're here to investigate."

He smiled, relaxing a little. "You got me."

"Now that must be a conflict of interest. You think they'd send someone else." She smiled back. "Are you okay?"

"Fine, thanks."

"Good. Sorry, by the way, I didn't mean to make you jump. You looked a bit fed up, that's all"—gross understatement – "so I thought I'd come over and say hi."

"That's alright. I don't know why I did it, you're not that shocking." He grinned. "And you know how it is. Working here all day, then spending all evening investigating for the—"

"—Food Hygiene Board."

"Exactly. Tires a man out, after a while." He paused and then blurted, "Can I get you a coffee? Or do you have to get home?"

"No, no! I can see you're busy, I was just saying hi."

"Busy? Oh... that." Steve's eyes flicked down to his laptop and Rebecca thought she detected a little pinkness creeping into his cheeks. "That's nothing important."

"Well even so, I'd hate to distract you from your origami."

"My what?"

She nodded at the folded cake case, which was sitting on the table slowly unfolding, trying to spring back into shape."

"Good point. It might never be a swan, now."

"There you go then," she smiled. "I'd better leave you to it." She turned towards the counter, glad she'd at least been able to put a smile on his face, but he called her back.

"Seriously, would you like a coffee? I could do with the company." He looked suddenly awkward, as though he'd revealed a bit too much. He smiled feebly. "It's a lonely life, being a Food Hygiene Inspector on the evening shift."

"Alright. I was going to grab something to take away and then slob out in front of the TV in my PJs all evening, but you've twisted my arm."

"So you're by yourself this evening then?"

"I'm by myself most evenings," said Rebecca with a theatrical sigh. She saw a small frown cross Steve's face and wondered what she'd said. "I'm going to get a coffee and a wrap, otherwise known as dinner. Do you want anything?"

"No. But take a seat, I'll get it." His eyes twinkled as he got to his feet. "I know the manager, you know."

"Ooh, does that mean I get extra chocolate sprinkles?"

"Maybe si, maybe non."

"Anyway, let me give you some money—"

"I'll pay—"

"No, it's not fair you should pay for my dinner."

"Hey, I'm the one forcing you to sit with me."

"You're not forcing me. You've saved me from an evening of laziness, loneliness and bad TV. All that, and I would still have had to pay for my dinner," she said firmly.

"Fair enough. Coffee's on me though. What do you want?"

"Southern Fried Chicken Salad Wrap, please, and a blueberry muffin."

"Good choice. Butterscotch latte?"

"Mmm, Yes please. You know me so well."

He went a little pink again as he pocketed her money and made for the counter.

Rebecca was soon sinking her teeth into the hot, fragrant, spicy wrap. "Mmm-mmm." She closed her eyes for a second. "Tony's wraps are just the best."

"They're unholy magic," Steve agreed. "He won't let anyone else make them. I'm starting to wonder if they're drugged." Suddenly his face darkened, but Rebecca was mid-bite and before she could ask what was wrong, creamy salad dressing burst from her wrap, some dribbling inelegantly down her chin and the rest landing on her jeans.

"Oh great! Now that's too much sauce, that is. I can't believe I'm saying that because it's gorgeous, but you can have too much of a good thing."

Steve grinned and passed her a serviette. "I'll pass that on to the chef. Less sauce."

There was silence for a while as Rebecca did serious damage to the wrap, but happily, no more to her clothes. "What does he make it out of, or does he buy it in?" she asked, after she'd taken the edge off her hunger.

"He makes it himself. Out of exactly what, I don't know. And even if I did, I couldn't tell you."

"Why?"

"Because I'd have to kill you," said Steve sadly. "That's the way Tony rolls."

"Only if you knock him over," giggled Rebecca.

"Ouch! Meow!"

"Sorry. Bless him, he wouldn't look half so cuddly if he was skinny. It's a shame about the sauce, I'd love to have some at home. A girl needs some incentive to eat salad."

"Not a fan of rabbit food then?"

"Not without some kind of sauce on it, no."

"I'm with you on that one. The creamier, the better."

"Hmm, my taste buds agree with you but my waistline doesn't. I always feel guilty when I put creamy dressings on my salad, because deep inside I know I'm probably making the salad-eating pointless in the first place. I must put the calorie count up by about five hundred percent."

"But you're still getting your fibre," said Steve, nodding wisely. "Very important, fibre."

"True, I hadn't thought of that," she said solemnly. "Thanks, Doctor Steve."

"Any time, any time." He leaned back and gestured around him. "My surgery is always open."

"Yep," said Rebecca, nodding as she swallowed her last mouthful. "You're not kidding." She licked her fingers. That sauce really did get everywhere. "What are you doing here? Don't you have evenings off?"

His eyes darkened and Rebecca cringed inwardly.

"Sorry, none of my business."

"No, it's okay, I just..." He shrugged. "I don't come here every night, believe me. I'm not that sad, but I wasn't having a very happy evening at home and didn't want to stay in. I didn't want to go anywhere full of noise and strangers, so I came here." He looked at her and gave a small smile. "My second home."

"Ah, so it's stuff at home that making you look gloomy." Stop prying right now, Bec, she scolded herself.

"I didn't know I looked so gloomy, sorry. But yes." He picked up his coffee, probably hoping she'd leave the subject there.

She didn't. Rebecca firmly believed that bottling up problems only made things worse. Time to change tack. "Gloomy? You looked like your kitten had died!" She started to laugh, but his face didn't change.

"Oh God, I've put my foot in it, haven't I? Please don't tell me your kitten actually has died? Or your puppy, or—"

"It's okay!" Steve grinned. "It's fine, nothing died. Not even a goldfish. I don't have any pets, dead or alive."

"Phew!" She slumped back in her chair. "Thank God for that."

Their laughter left a small silence behind, but Steve didn't volunteer the real reason for his mood. She decided there was only the direct approach left.

"Do you want to tell me what made you gloomy then, if it's not your mythical kitten? It might help."

"Not really, thanks." He fiddled with his coffee cup. "Sorry."

"That's okay. I just thought, you know, a problem shared..."

"I'm afraid it's one those insoluble, grin-and-bear-it-and-hope-it-improves problems," he said quietly, "So I don't think sharing it would halve it. But thanks for the offer."

"No problem." She felt strangely disappointed that Steve didn't want to confide in her, but she wasn't going to push it. Instead, she looked at the blueberry muffin and sighed. "That seemed like such a good idea. Before I ate the wrap."

"Don't tell me you're full up."

"Not quite. But I don't think the space I have left is blueberry muffin sized. Want to share?" she looked at him hopefully.

"I've already had a muffin."

"Only a small one." She nodded at his 'swan' cake case. "You could only make a cygnet out of that, not a full-grown swan."

He smiled. "True."

"And you bought me the giant size. Wicked man, not thinking about my waistline."

"Alright, anything to help a damsel in distress. Although there's nothing wrong with your waistline," he said with a smile.

"Thanks." Her stomach gave a tiny flutter. Was he flirting with her? Concentrate Rebecca, he's still talking.

"I'll go and get a knife; otherwise it's going to get messy. Actually..." he leaned over. "Talking of messy," he hissed, "Would you like some cream on top? Being as I know the manager, 'n all."

She looked round. "Yes please," she hissed back.

"Okay. I'll get some spoons and plates too."

A very messy but pleasant twenty minutes later, Rebecca looked at her watch. "Oops, is that the time? I should head for home. I've got lots to do before I get my beauty sleep."

"Yes, I'd better be off too." Steve slipped his laptop back inside his case. "Tony will be closing up in a minute, and if I'm still around he might rope me in to help."

"Heaven forbid!" laughed Rebecca. "You'd have to call in the union." She pulled on her coat. "Thanks for the coffee, Steve. And the cream!"

"My pleasure. Thanks for the company."

She looked up at him. Normally there was a certain reserve in his eyes when he spoke to her, but it wasn't there now. In fact, there was a very different look in his eyes that surprised her. "And thank you for your company, too. It was far better than spending the evening by myself." Another impulse circumvented her brain, and she found herself stretching up to give him a fleeting peck on the cheek. For a split second she wanted to stay there rather than rock back on her heels where she could see the look on his face. Why had she done that?

When she did move back, she was relieved to see that he looked startled but not horrified. She didn't want to give him time to say anything, though, or think too much. "I'll see you soon," she said quickly, grabbing her coat and bag as though they were lifebelts and she was drowning in the deep end. Hmm. Maybe you are, she thought.

"Soon? So not tomorrow, then?"

Was she imagining the disappointment in his voice? "Probably not. I need to be on site this week."

"I see. See you when I see you, then."

"Thanks. Night, then."

"Night."

You're a bit of an enigma, Call Me Steve, she thought as she walked towards the door. But definitely one worth getting to the bottom of. She couldn't remember the last time she'd enjoyed being in the company of just one other person so much.

Behind her she heard the kitchen door open and Tony's rumbling voice call out, "Steve? You are going?"

"Yes."

"Here I have two syrup muffins left, you would like to take them home to Laura, si?"

There was a pause. Rebecca paused too, one hand on the door, and her heart seemed to join in. Open the door and stop eavesdropping. It's none of your business.

"No thanks Tony."

"No? Well, you please yourself! They go in bin, then, is terrible waste!" she heard Tony grumble, as the door closed behind her.

It was bitter outside and she turned her collar up, setting off briskly along the road and nearly bumping into someone looking in a show window further along, huddled down under an umbrella. But she paid little attention. She was going over what she'd heard.

There was a Laura? At home? Oh, God. She'd completely misread the signals there then, hadn't she. She couldn't believe she'd kissed him. Okay, only in a friendly way, on the cheek, but still...

And if this Laura lived with Steve, was she the cause of his bad evening at home? It seemed likely. Perhaps they were heading for a break-up. Rebecca realised that a tiny part of her – a selfish, undoubtedly foolish part, that she wasn't particularly proud of—was hoping that was true.

Chapter Five

Rebecca fired up her email and waited for her messages to download, greedily scooping sweet and sour noodles out of a bowl. Her eyes flicked down the screen as the messages popped up, her finger hovering over the delete button to weed out the ones about Viagra, foreign brides, online casinos and PPI. She almost deleted the email from the dating agency; she was so used to deleting the spam invitations from dating agencies that habit nearly took over.

"Great news from Methodical Matches! You have a message from THRILLER-MAN, 32, from FARRINGDON. Click here to read the message from your Hot Match. We already know you two are a great match, so don't hang around!"

"Thriller-man? What kind of a username is that?" she muttered. Did it indicate he was a Michael Jackson fan or that he liked watching Prime Suspect? Although she had to admit, choosing a username that gave the right impression was tricky. She'd spent ages thinking up something suitable and ended up with Digger Girl. It was only later that it occurred to her people might think it indicated she was a gold-digger, only after someone rich.

She logged into her mailbox on the website. There was the message, flashing to show it was unread. Rebecca clicked on the thumbnail of his profile photo, wanting to look at that first. Hmm. Dark blonde hair, glasses, not bad looking.

The message didn't tell her much. "Hello. My name's John and I'm 35. I live in Farringdon. I'm a business analyst in the City. Your profile is showing as a hot match so hopefully we will have much in common. Perhaps we could meet for lunch?"

She gritted her teeth. She knew it was unreasonable, but she hated it when people spelt city with a capital C, it seemed so pretentious. It wasn't a good reason to dismiss John from Farringdon out of hand. If he was her perfect man in every other way, having to put up with his capital Cs would be a small price to pay, she thought, sucking up her last noodle. Who knows, maybe I can train him out of it.

Where should they meet? She wasn't sure she should do lunch on the first meeting. Okay, he looked pleasant enough: tidy (if boring) hair, cheerful expression, plain shirt. But say he had terrible breath or a weird voice that reduced her to fits of giggles? And his email sounded really stilted, although some people did sound very formal when they wrote anything.

She took a deep breath, fingers on the keyboard. Stop being an idiot Rebecca and type the message. "What about starting with a coffee first? Are you free on Saturday morning?"

There, that hadn't been so hard. She only had a few other emails to read, so she flicked through them quickly and was about to shut her computer down, when a reply pinged back.

"What were you doing, sitting on the keyboard?" she muttered crossly, feeling unaccountably like her space had been invaded.

"That's fine. What time? And where?"

Hmm. Too late and it would be difficult to get out of progressing naturally on to lunch. Too early, and it might be awkward to suggest extending it until lunch if she did want to. And she might, she thought, forcing herself to think optimistically. They must have a lot in common and if sparks flew when they got together, then who knew what could happen. Where? Not Tony's, definitely. Too many people there she knew; she'd be self conscious.

"10.30? At Café d'Italia?"

"Certainly. Although can I ask that if we decide to have lunch afterwards, we go elsewhere? I'm not fond of Italian food."

Oh great. She loved Italian. She typed 'yes, that's fine', and then stopped. How should she sign off? Best wishes? Naff. Kind regards? Hmm. All the best? No, that's what salt-of-the-earth-type older men said when they shook the hand of someone whom they hadn't seen for ten years (and probably wouldn't see for another ten years). Damn it! She wouldn't put anything. She typed her name underneath and hit send.

She found herself rushing to the kitchen to boil the kettle, wondering what 'John' would say in reply. Just as the kettle clicked off, she heard the sound that told her a message had been received. She bounded back into the lounge.

"I look forward to meeting you on Saturday. John."

Well that was an anti-climax, Becs. Idiot. What were you expecting? A love poem in return? She giggled to herself. Pathetic. She amused herself by trying to compose a poem about John in her head as she made herself coffee, but she soon ran out of things that rhymed with John and gave up. Now what should she wear to a weekend, mid-morning, first, blind, date? She had no idea.

The rest of the week flew by. Work was manic and by the time her head hit the pillow on Friday night, a mixture of nerves and exhaustion meant that all she longed for was a long lie-in the next morning, followed by a wander through the market and a leisurely late lunch. She resented the thought of having to get up and go for coffee with someone she didn't know. Still, she couldn't back out now.

By 8:30 the next morning she'd had breakfast and was out of the shower, towel-drying her hair with one hand while flicking though her clothes with the other. What impression did she want to give? Fun? Sophisticated? Both? She didn't want to look OTT, but not like she hadn't made any effort at all, either.

She sighed. This had seemed like a good idea, but if she was so desperate for someone to share her life with, why did it feel like a chore now? She faced herself in the full length mirror. "You have to do this," she told herself sternly. "Otherwise you'll end up an old batty woman muttering to yourself as you polish the skeleton you've stolen from the Museum for company."

In the end she chose smart indigo blue jeans, slim-fitting but not skin tight, and a blue, white and lilac check shirt over a white vest top with a funky neckline. She could wear her fitted lilac denim jacket over the top. Not too formal or too trendy; it was only a Saturday morning coffee, after all, although the lilac-tinted fake pearls that dangled by intricately twisted dark silver strands from her ears were more dressy than anything she usually wore for daytime. She hoped it said 'fun and stylish—pleased to meet you but not desperate'.

She used more products on her hair—i.e., some—than she normally would before venturing out on a Saturday morning, applied barely-there make-up and sprayed on a light, fresh fragrance. She hesitated by her jewellery box a few times as she scuttled back and forth gathering her phone, purse and keys, eventually muttering, "no, it's only coffee!" to herself. But when she locked the door behind her, the silver and amethyst bracelet that Hal had brought her was on her wrist. It was fairly flashy, she admitted, but it went well with her outfit and added a little more glamour, something she feared she was sadly lacking.

Outside her front door her nerve nearly deserted her. Should she have told someone where she was going? Don't be daft, it's a Saturday morning and you're going to a busy coffee shop. You won't be alone with him, even if he does turn out to be a psychopath. Despite the stern talking to, her legs felt wobbly in a way they hadn't done for years, and never before a date; she had saved her nerves for exams and her driving test. But then she'd never faced a date with a man she knew so little about. She knew what he looked like – supposedly; it could be a picture of someone completely different, or a 10 year old picture. But if he'd used a false picture, how would she recognise him?

Oh God, perhaps that was the whole point! Luring women to different places and ogling them whilst remaining incognito, getting some weird stalkerish thrill out of it. What was she doing?

The blare of a car horn brought her to her senses. She'd been so busy fretting that she hadn't looked properly as she crossed the road. Come on woman, get a grip. This is worst case scenario stuff. He's probably perfectly normal.

As the coffee shop came into view her mouth went completely dry and she tried to control her quivering legs, determined to walk in looking like a confident, professional woman.

A head swivelled to look at her as she came in. Thank goodness! It belonged to a man sitting two tables back, and he looked as similar to his summer holiday photograph as anyone else would to theirs. She smiled tentatively in his direction and he half rose.

"Rebecca, I presume?"

She nodded, suddenly tongue tied.

"Do join me."

Hugely self-conscious, she attempted an elegant walk, which was difficult for someone who spent most of her life in wellies or walking boots.

He held out a hand which was strangely light and dry when she took it, holding hers for longer than she was comfortable with. "You look even lovelier in real life." His voice was thin, the voice of a far older man, but strangely silky too.

"Thank you." She did her best to smile graciously as she sat at his table, but she already felt repulsed, and the feeling didn't go away when she realised he wasn't taking his eyes off her for a second as he sat down, moving his coffee and reaching for the cake menu with his eyes glued to her face.

"I have been here a while, so I took the liberty of ordering myself a coffee. I hope you don't mind."

"No, not at all."

"In my concern not to be late, I am afraid I was rather too early. But the coffee and cake menu is quite extensive, if bewildering, so I had plenty to reading material to keep me occupied."

She wasn't sure how to respond to that. Say something, Rebecca, for goodness sake. "What did you choose?"

"An espresso. I'm afraid I'm not keen on all these unnaturally flavoured, sweetened, frothy or all-milk coffees." He gave a delicate shudder. "It seems sacrilege to me. The ruination of a perfectly good beverage. I found it hard to believe they had nothing on the menu that was simply labelled 'coffee'."

Oh. My. God. Great start.

He smiled, blinking in a way that was disturbingly reptilian. "What will you have?" He offered her the menu, but Rebecca shook her head. "I'll just have the same as you for now, thanks."

He smiled a smile that met his eyes, yet seemed to be a very different type of smile when it got there. He slid up rather than stood up; there was something snake-like about him that definitely hadn't come across in his photograph. She gave a little shiver.

"Are you too cold, my dear? We will move to a table further away from the door before I order for you."

She raised a hand in protest but he completely misread the cue and took her hand, pulling to her feet. "Let's remove ourselves to the corner over there. It looks far more snug and secluded."

Protesting feebly, Rebecca trailed after him, her hand still firmly in his grasp. Snug and secluded with him was the last place she wanted to be.

He left her briefly to order her espresso and she sat there eyeing the distance to the door. Could she make it without him seeing her? Doing a runner before things could get any worse was very appealing.

Too late. He was back.

"Would you like a cake or pastry? I'm always rather concerned about the hygiene in these places, even at this time of year when there are few flies around, but at least here their patisserie section is covered. Also I see they have tongs to handle the cakes too, so I think you will be safe. I never think gloves are really adequate, do you? Unless one was to remove them and put on another pair every time one touched something new or turned to a different task."

Rebecca gaped. "No thank you, perhaps later," she mumbled.

He gave her a wide smile in return. Argh. She'd said the wrong thing, unwittingly suggesting she was pleased with what she saw so far and planning to hang around! No, she wasn't.

She picked up her coffee and tried to hide behind it, which would have been a lot easier to do if she'd asked for the large, frothy, sweetened, all-milk caramel latte that she'd really craved. Shallow espresso cups weren't really fit for the purpose.

"So Rebecca. What exactly do you do?"

Oh no. She didn't want to tell him. If he knew where she worked, he might turn up, and GLAM wasn't exactly an inconspicuous place to work.

"Sorry, do you mind if I just take my jacket off..." She got up, surreptitiously sliding a hand into her jacket pocket as she turned away.

"Of course not, of course not, dear lady. I want you to be comfortable."

I couldn't be more uncomfortable, she screamed internally, as she slid her thumb across the screen of her Smartphone. Dear lady? What century was this man from? She pretended to drop a tissue and bend down to retrieve it. That gave her time to activate her 'staff meeting 10:50' alarm on her phone, and pop the phone back in the pocket of her jacket which hung on the back of her chair.

"Can we talk about you first?" she asked, trying to smile. "Only my throat's dry. I've had a bit of a cold. Hopefully the coffee will help."

"Of course, of course." He smiled but looked rather anxious, edging away from her a little as he settled back in his chair. Excellent. She faked a cough and he visibly paled.

"What would you like to know?"

"Oh, um... what you like to do in your spare time?"

"Oh yes, of course, of course. Although naturally I get very little spare time, my job keeps me very busy. Very busy indeed." He puffed up his chest and smiled patronisingly.

Naturally, she thought. "But when you do..." she prompted.

"When I do, I like to read. Mostly, the autobiographies of the great movers and shakers of our time. Sugar, Dyson, Brady, Getty, Hiroshi Mikitani, Branson."

"Uh-huh." Fascinating. Yawn...

He looked awkward. "I'm afraid my secret vice is Jodie Forrest novels. I hesitated to admit that on my profile, knowing how it would look. It's far from sophisticated literature, I am afraid, and I don't imagine you're familiar with her work."

"I've read a couple," she mumbled.

"Really?" he looked down his nose at her and she had the distinct impression that far from delighting him, it had made him disappointed in her. Not half as disappointed as I am in you, she thought.

"Her thrillers do have a certain logic to them that I like. The action sequences and drama, however, are completely far-fetched."

Rebecca gulped. They're my favourite parts.

"Sometimes I find myself skipping over the action sequences and dialogue to the sections where the clues are put together and the characters decide their next logical move."

"I see." Ask him something else, Rebecca. Use up the time. "And do you like to, er, eat out with friends or anything?"

"Very rarely. I'm so busy with work that there's little time to socialise."

Argh! I know! You said!

"I do have a small circle of friends but unfortunately, they tend to favour Indian restaurants." He wrinkled his nose.

"You don't like Indian food?" she asked politely.

He shuddered. "Certainly not. My friends know that, yet still choose these places."

Hmm, thought Rebecca. Surprise, surprise.

"Not only do I have reservations about the hygiene standards in these places, I also detest foreign foods."

She knew she was staring, but she couldn't help it. "What, all foreign foods?" she blurted.

"Yes." he wrinkled his nose. "Indian, Mexican, Thai... if only these places would prepare some plainer dishes. Even other restaurants with less spicy dishes—Greek, for instance, or Italian – will insist on adding so many herbs or peppers to their foods that one can barely determine what manner of food forms the basis of the dish! And the French, of course, simply drown everything in garlic."

"Yes, I suppose they do," she croaked.

"I occasionally take Mother to a nearby hotel for a Sunday roast," he added. "But enough about food. It's only purpose is to fuel one through a hectic day, as far as I'm concerned, and of course, you'll be wondering about my work." He put his coffee down and slopped a little on his fingers. He glanced down with a look of distaste, then quickly swept up a serviette and made a meal out of wiping his fingers. "Firstly, I have a job that, in popular conception, is considered boring."

She nodded, still playing the dry throat card.

"I work as a business analyst. I think I may have told you that in my email."

Nod.

"Is business analysis something you know much about?"

Shake.

"It's a fascinating career, I assure you. Only the other day, I was looking at the projections of a third-world company that a client, Messchler and Messchler, is planning to bid for. And what I found was, that despite—"

John seemed was so fond of the sound of his own voice that he needed no interaction from her, and Rebecca's attention started to drift away; very useful, as she gave a genuine start when her phone rang.

"Sorry, do excuse me..." She grabbed the phone and made a show of struggling to hear. "Low signal," she mouthed and walked closer to the window to continue her 'conversation'."

"No, I quite understand." She shook her head. "No. Don't worry, if you need me right now, then you need me right now. Okay. Well I'll see you in ten. Bye for now." She walked back to the table with an apologetic smile carefully arranged on her face.

"I'm so sorry, John, but I'm afraid I have to go. A friend's babysitter has let her down and she's due at an important meeting."

He raised his eyebrows. "What kind of important meeting can a woman who has a baby possibly have? Or is it with Social Services?"

Rebecca gaped for several moments then narrowed her eyes. "It's a business meeting."

"Really? On a Saturday?"

"Well when you run several companies, you know how it is." Her voice was icy and she'd given up all pretence of having a sore throat. She was making up for it in the pretence department with her fictitious, high-flying friend. "In business, as you said yourself, you have very little spare time."

He looked like he'd just been force-fed a Vindaloo. "Won't you at least finish your coffee?" he said curtly. "After all, espressos aren't cheap here. It seems a shame to waste it."

"No, I have to go straight away. But I'd hate for you to be out of pocket," she said smoothly, slapping a £5 note on the table.

"Oh no, my dear I couldn't accept that. The espresso was not quite that expensive."

"Nonsense. My pleasure." She turned on her heel.

"We must do this again. I'll be in touch!" he called after her. She waved a non-committal hand behind her, already at the door. As it closed, she glanced back through the window. He was squirreling the £5 note away in his pocket with alacrity. He was welcome to it. It was a small price to pay for escape.

Chapter Six

Laura was getting worse and Steve had no idea how to help her. She didn't seem to go more than a couple of days now without coming home drunk, high as a kite, or twitchy and aggressive.

He had tried to get her help in the past, but Laura didn't seem to fit into the right categories. Anyway, the message from all the addiction and mental health services he'd contacted had been the same: she had to be willing to seek help herself. Nobody could forcibly step in unless—or until, as Steve thought more likely—she posed a significant danger to herself or others, or committed a criminal act, and then a referral was likely to come from the court. One of the caseworkers at the local addiction centre, a girl who looked about sixteen to Steve, asked what Laura was taking and how often. He admitted he didn't have a clue. He was sure he'd seen a flash of contempt on her face, but perhaps it was his own guilty paranoia.

"If you're telling me she can go a week without a drink, or any withdrawal symptoms then it's alcohol abuse, not dependence, so drying out won't help," advised the tall, burly man from the Alcohol Dependency Drop-in Centre. "It's what's going on inside her head that needs sorting. She's choosing to binge drink, not drinking because she can't do without it." He gave Steve some leaflets on binge drinking. Laura didn't so much look at them as sneer.

The GP had reiterated what everyone else said, although he did call Laura in on the pretext of a 'Young Person's Health Check.' To Steve's amazement Laura had gone along to the surgery without argument, not only on time but comparatively neat and clean; where, when asked, she'd said without batting an eyelid, that she only drank occasionally—"the odd birthday or leaving party, that kind of thing, and I only have a couple" – and that she'd never touched drugs.

"I'm afraid there's nothing more I can do," said Doctor Anderson regretfully.

"What about a blood test?"

"We did the standard one for diabetes, thyroid and cholesterol. I couldn't test for anything else without informing her, that would be completely unethical; and I can't imagine asking her to submit to drugs testing would go down well."

"No, I think you're right there," Steve said heavily. "Thanks for all you've done."

"No problem, only sorry I couldn't do more. You know where I am if you need me."

"Thanks."

Steve had asked Laura to take a drugs test last week. Yelled it at her, in fact. He wasn't proud of it but she'd got under his skin, despite every effort to keep his cool. On Saturday, she'd come home talking gibberish, eyes unfocussed, pupils dilated and her mouth on overdrive. Not alcohol this time, Steve thought. Her behaviour was different and he couldn't smell booze. His best guess, referring to the leaflet Dr Anderson had given him, was cocaine, but it could be something else. Or a mixture.

She was in no state to have a rational conversation, and Steve knew that when she returned to planet earth, she wouldn't want to talk about it. So he tried to stay calm and ride it out. He switched on the TV watched it with her, keeping as much of an eye on her as he did the programme. It had seemed like a good idea, but Laura had embarked on a jarringly loud non-stop commentary.

Steve got her a glass of water. He knew most of the things she might have taken caused dehydration and a dry mouth. She downed the water and kept on talking. Then he brought her sandwiches, but she flipped the top of the sandwich to see what was inside then brought her hand up sharply underneath the plate Steve still held, crashing it upwards into his nose before it fell to the floor, scattering cheese, coleslaw and salad all over the floor.

"I can't eat that shit. Take it away."

Steve's chest felt tight and his nose was agony. "That hurt."

"What did?" She glared.

"You knocked the plate into my nose." He felt his nose and his hand came away bloody.

She stared at his face. "Doesn't look broken, so what are you whining about?"

"It hurts like hell, and you haven't even said sorry. A simple no thanks to the sandwich would have done."

"It wasn't a sandwich, it was shit." She was focussed back on the TV.

With a supreme effort, Steve turned on his heel and walked back to the kitchen because otherwise he thought he might shake her or slap her. He wished he could go out and leave her to it, but how would he feel if she had a bad reaction to whatever she'd taken? He did need to stay away from her though.

He could vacuum upstairs, but there was a watery sun peeping out from behind the clouds and for this early in the year, it was a mild day. Maybe he'd put another layer on and sit in the garden with a book. Just imagining it made him relax a little. But Laura came to find him and wouldn't leave him alone.

He abandoned his book and went to the laptop, expecting her to stay in the garden because she'd finally stretched herself out on their small patch of lawn, and her mouth had slowed down. She looked exhausted. It seemed like a good time to get on with his Methodical Matches profile.

Five minutes later she was at his elbow. "What are you doing?"

"Nothing important." Instantly he minimised the window. "Can you take your boots off, Lor, you're trailing mud everywhere."

"Methodical Matches? Isn't that the dating place that's moved into Cooper's?" Damn it, he must have been too slow.

"I think so." He tried to sound offhand. "I was just seeing what it was all about, because they left leaflets at work."

"So how many dates do you get?"

"No idea."

"Where do the people come from? I mean, do they only pick people from r—"

"I don't know, Laura."

"It's not a hoax, is it? Because Lauren Miller said most of them are hoaxes, the people don't even exist." She was bouncing her legs, letting her ankle bang out a rapid rhythm on the chair leg.

"How would I know? I shouldn't think so, if they've got an office."

"What would happen if-?"

"I don't know! I didn't even get the chance to look, because you won't shut up!" He got to his feet, closing down the laptop.

She stared at him, eyes wide, legs temporarily still. "Ooh, someone got out the wrong side of bed. If you're finished, can I play on the laptop?"

"Fill your boots. Since you can't be bothered to take them off." He turned his back on her. Maybe the vacuuming had been the best idea, after all

He wouldn't normally have considered vacuuming as peaceful, but that's how it had felt. For ten minutes, anyway. Until he heard a rhythmic banging on the doorframe.

He looked up. Laura was leaning on the doorframe, banging her still-booted foot against it, hard.

He turned the vacuum cleaner off. "Finished on the laptop?"

"No, but it's crashed, says I've downloaded a virus or something. Piece of shit, you should get a better one. Just wondering when the hell lunch is, it's already half past one. You do a crap job of looking after me, don't you, Stevie Boy."

That was the point when the last thread of Steve's patience had unravelled with an almost audible twang. He yelled first, but who wouldn't. He wasn't a saint.

He accused her of being high. She swore she'd taken nothing. Then swore some more.

"You know what your problem is, don't you, Steve? You just want me to behave like an obedient little girl all the time, because it suits you. Out of sight, out of mind, not seen and not heard!"

"Of course I don't!"

"You do, because the minute I have different opinions to you and I open my mouth about them, you can't handle it! You can't handle it because I don't live my life like photocopy of yours!"

"You're joking! You haven't got a clue what my life's like, and you sure as hell couldn't live it! You're far too selfish and self-centred to ever put your life on hold for someone else!"

"Oh here we go! Ram it down my throat, what you've given up for me! You know what, I didn't ask you to, and I wish you hadn't. Then you wouldn't hate me so much for screwing up your life!"

"I don't hate you Laura, don't be so stupid!"

"I am stupid, remember? I must be, because I didn't go to uni, did I? After all that effort he put in I let Stevie down by finally not jumping through one of his hoops!"

He shook his head. "I'm not doing this. You don't know what you're saying, it's the drugs talking." He went to leave the room, but she blocked the doorway.

"That's what you'd like to believe, isn't it! The perfect excuse! God forbid little Laura might actually think these things for real!" She was right in his face now. "I don't TAKE drugs!"

"Bloody well prove it then!" he yelled back, face inches from hers. "Let's book you a blood test, shall we? Right now! I bet Dr Anderson could fit us in!"

"I don't have to prove anything to you, you wanker!" she screeched, and fled.

Steve had stood there for a while, breathing heavily, trying to calm himself down. He could hear her banging about and swearing. Then he heard the front door slam. After a while, he went to check what she'd taken. Not much. Some of her clothes, and her day-to-day toiletries. He wandered to the kitchen in a daze and fixed himself lunch. With no small sense of irony, after a minute's hesitation he'd pulled a can of lager out the fridge too. Then he'd grabbed his book and headed to the garden.

Laura had turned up two days later, looking fine and acting as if nothing had happened. Steve felt wrong-footed. He had no idea how to react. She hadn't answered any of his calls to her mobile, ignoring his voicemails.

He'd been worried sick and on the verge of calling the police and reporting her missing. She'd seemed on an even keel since then. Not that she'd done much to clear up after herself or keep the house clean, and there was no sign she was looking for work. But for now, things were calm, so Steve was letting things ride. He knew he was just sticking his head in the sand though, and he felt a constant tension, as though a thunderstorm was brewing.

He tried to be glad she was back. That she seemed okay. Tried to convince himself it had just been a phase, and now it was out of her system. She would find work soon, get back on her feet, and gain some self-esteem, wouldn't she. Perhaps it might all happen in time for Steve to feel confident applying for uni this year; after all, he wouldn't go for another year, and if he applied to a local one, maybe they wouldn't have to move, although London wasn't the cheapest place to live.

Who was he trying to kid. She was a ticking time bomb.

"How's it going?" Rebecca asked.

Kevin started, the tweezers in his hand jerking and releasing a piece of pottery. "I wish you wouldn't creep up on me like that!"

"I wasn't trying to."

"Can't you wear high heels or something?"

"Yes, because that would be so practical."

"Walk louder, then."

"Walk louder?"

Kevin waved his tweezers at her threateningly. "Back off, lady. I was concentrating. My boss is a real slave driver, you know. Always wandering in here at random to check up on me. Very quietly."

"That must be a burden."

He rolled his eyes comically. "Oh it is, believe me. Anyway, what can I do for you, She Who Must Be Obeyed?"

"I wondered if we'd had results back on those soil samples from last week."

"No, but they should be ready this afternoon, apparently."

"Great. In that case, how about an early lunch?"

"It's barely twelve Bec! I've only just started on this pot."

She stretched over, looking past him. "Huh. Looks like you haven't started at all to me, so you might as well take a break. Besides, I'm starving."

"Do I get a say? Especially as I had a snack half an hour ago and I'm not hungry at all?"

"Nope," she said, slotting her arm through his and spinning him round to face the door.

He sighed. "Let me wash my hands and get my jacket then. As you're forcing me into this, lunch is on you."

She grinned and let him go. "Fair enough." She stopped at the door. "Funny," she said casually, "I thought you'd be dying to hear how my first internet date went."

"You had a date? When?" he squawked. She could hear him scrabbling about trying to shut his computer down. "Bec, wait—"

"Saturday." She kept on walking. "See you out front."

"So what was he like? Come on!" Kevin put his knife and fork down, clasped his hands and leaned forward, with a daft grin on his face.

Rebecca chased a piece of chicken round her plate. "He was a business analyst."

"Oh dear. Name?"

"John."

"Nothing wrong with that." Kevin went back to his salad.

"No. That was about the only thing that was right with him. He doesn't like any coffee other than espresso; any other variety is a mortal sin—"

"Oh my Lord!" His fork stopped halfway to his mouth.

"He had this really weird handshake; like he didn't really want his hand to be in mine—his hand was all rigid—"

"Oo-er!"

"— but then he wouldn't let it go. And he's a hygiene obsessive." Unlike me," she laughed, scooping up a piece of lettuce that had escaped on to the table. "And he kept calling me 'my dear' like I was his niece or something, although he was looking at me in a decidedly un-uncle-ish way."

"Yuck."

"Exactly."

"How long did you put up with it for?" Kevin's eyes were dancing as he picked up his coffee.

He was enjoying this far too much, she thought. "Not long. I managed to bend down and set the alarm on my phone, thank God, because then he started calling me 'dear lady'."

He snorted with laughter and Rebecca looked at him severely. "It's not funny. He was tight, too. When I said I had to go, he wanted me to finish my coffee because he'd paid so much for it!"

Kevin's coffee stopped halfway to his mouth. "No!"

"Yes! And when I offered to pay for it, it was very much a token refusal, let me tell you. He pocketed the fiver quickly enough as I left."

"You sure know how to pick 'em." He shook his head.

"But I didn't pick him, did I! That the whole point."

"You did in a way. Scientifically he's an ideal match, remember. Perhaps it's something you said. Or rather, wrote." His eyes were full of mirth.

She glared at him. "Yes, and perhaps the dumb computer's dyslexic." She stabbed her last piece of chicken with unnecessary force.

He wiped at his eyes and tried, unsuccessfully in Rebecca's opinion, to look serious. "Poor you. Perhaps the next one will be better."

"Next one?" her eyes widened. "Don't even joke about it! You don't honestly think I'm going through that again?"

"To which I say, you're not honestly going to give up after one date? After you've paid good money for all this scientific matching stuff, too?"

"Huh! A fat lot of good that is, if it matches me up with a creep like that." She wiped her fingers on a serviette, folding it with her fingers.

"Come on, Bec, you have to give it another go."

"Er, no. I don't."

"The next one might be your ideal man. Give up now and you'll never know."

She put another fold in her serviette, ignoring him. It was alright for Kevin, he hadn't been stuck with John the snake man. He had genuinely given her the creeps, and being creeped out wasn't the way she fancied spending her weekends. Life was too short to spend your free time doing things you didn't enjoy, as she always tried to explain to Kevin when he tried to nag her into watching horror films with him.

On the other hand— well, horror films were always scary, but men weren't always snake like. Kevin wasn't, and Steve wasn't, either. She glanced towards the counter but couldn't see him. Perhaps he wasn't in today.

"I suppose you're right," she said, aware she sounded like a sulky child. "I can't presume they'll all be losers, can I. I'll give it another go."

"Hooray! Common sense prevails." Kevin grinned.

"Not with him, though. That was absolutely our first and last date."

"Absolutely. Let him go and try his 'dear lady' on some other sucker."

"I'm not sure I'd wish that on my worst enemy!"

"Not even a certain archaeologist currently digging up random bits of Italy?"

She put her head on one side. "Okay, you've got me there. If anyone deserves John the snake man, it's Marcie."

Kevin chuckled. "That's what we're calling him now, is it?"

She lifted her nose in the air. "I'd prefer that you didn't refer to him at all, thank you. Far too traumatic."

"Your wish is my command. Do you want another coffee?"

"Yes please. Mocha this time."

"Certainly dear lady."

She threw a serviette aeroplane at his head.

Chapter Seven

It was still cold but the sun was dazzling in a clear sky. I should have worn my sunglasses, thought Steve, squinting as he walked along the road to work. He wasn't complaining, though. The sunshine lifted his spirits and when the breeze dropped, he could even feel a little warmth on his face.

But when he pushed open the door of Tony's his spirits sank. Not only because Rebecca wasn't alone, but because Kevin was loading their empty salad bowls and cups on to a tray, meaning they must be about to leave. They looked round and he forced a casual, friendly smile.

"Was it something I said?"

Kevin grinned. "Not unless you're a ventriloquist." God damn him, did he have to be so friendly? And funny? Not to mention good-looking. It was unfair competition. He was allowed to have two attributes out of the three; having all of them was, as Steve's Dad would have said, just not cricket.

"Good one. You two are early."

"Yep. We were hungry."

"Excuse me! I wasn't, but she forced me to come with her, so she could warn me of the perils of internet dating." Kevin rolled his eyes and walked off towards the counter with their tray.

"Perils? Like meeting weirdoes who take you home and show you their collection of false eyes?" asked Steve, smiling.

"No, as in being matched with people you wouldn't even talk to if they were the last person on earth, let alone date," said Rebecca.

"Yes, I suppose that's a risk," said Steve cautiously, wondering why they'd been talking about internet dating. "I suppose it depends how good the agency is and how many people are on their books. If it's only ten, the chances of them finding you your ideal partner are slim, aren't they. They probably just offer the three that aren't completely incompatible."

"I hadn't thought of it like that before."

"Me neither, until now," said Steve with a half-hearted laugh. This was too much like thinking aloud. How many people did Methodical Matches have on its virtual 'books'? He hadn't given it that much thought. "But I don't know anyone who's tried it. Who's fallen foul of internet dating then?"

"Oh, just a friend," said Rebecca casually, blushing. "But it was only her first date. Perhaps she'll have better luck next time."

"Let's hope so." Steve looked at her curiously. "Right, I'd best get to the kitchen and get my gear on, my shift starts in a couple of minutes."

"See you tomorrow," she said, as Kevin reappeared at her elbow.

He smiled. "That depends if you're going to make a habit of these ultra-early lunches! Bye."

He put his jacket and apron on, thinking about what Rebecca had said. Should he check how many people were signed up to the dating agency? Perhaps he should have chosen a better-known, more established one. Say he got a succession of dates with women whom he wouldn't normally give the time of day? Or who were fine in public, but turned out to have freaky habits and hobbies when you went back to their place?

The door swung open and Tony stuck his head into the kitchen. "Steve, some on," he said, his chiding tone belied by a smile. "Let's get moving! Is filling up out here and talking of filling, the coffee machine is needing refill. Bring out pouch of beans with you, please."

"Yes, boss! Sorry." Steve knotted his apron and went to the store, but he was still on autopilot as he dragged out the big silver pouch of Colombian beans. What about bringing girlfriends home? How could he ever do that whilst he lived with Laura? He never knew when she would be at home—or what state she would be in if she was there. The more he thought about it, the more impossible it seemed.

He backed through the kitchen door and into the café, hefting the coffee beans. "That's the end of that batch," he told Tony as he refilled the coffee machine. And the end of my daft idea, he thought. Even if met the girl of his dreams through the agency, there was no way he could start a relationship with her at the moment. He must have been nuts to fill out that profile in the first place. Thank God he hadn't pasted his answers into the website and sent them off; they were still in a document on the computer. Next time he went on the PC he'd delete it.

Ron stuck his head round the door. "Rebecca, can I have a word?"

She smiled, "Sure. Don't tell me, you're about to haul me over the coals for not having the osteology report on 78C ready."

"No," he replied with a small smile, "I'd forgotten I said today for that. But now you mention it..."

She groaned. "Me and my big mouth."

"It's about the Crossrail project, so not totally unrelated. Could you come by my office in the next half hour? I've got some documents to show you."

"Let me grab a drink and I'll be there."

"Great. Mine's a black coffee. Thanks!" He walked away with a smile. Rebecca grinned. She would get him his coffee, because he was a great boss and was just as likely to get a coffee for her if she asked.

A few minutes later she was sitting opposite him, waiting for him to cut the small talk and get to the point. When he hesitated, she leaped in.

"So what do we need to talk about, Ron?"

"Ah. Yes. I was getting to that." He hesitated. "You know the plan is for you to go back on to the Crossrail project."

"Yes. I've been looking forward to it." Rebecca had been leading the team working with Crossrail's archaeologists for a while. The excavations for new tunnels, ticket halls and elevator shafts at various sites across London were giving them a fantastic opportunity to survey and dig areas and levels they'd never have had access to otherwise. She grinned. "You know I don't fare well stuck indoors for too long. I like to be out there."

"Yes." He picked up a pen and started to tap it on his desk. "But I think you might want to sit this one out."

Rebecca leaned forward. "What? Why? They've just started to uncover skeletons on the Farringdon site—why would I want out of that??"

"As you know, the Greenwich to Stratford section is being excavated by other teams."

"Under our oversight and Crossrail's."

"Yes... and you know that Swindon Archaeology's are our main partners." Ron was starting to look a bit pale.

"And Royal Surrey, yes..." She frowned. "Ron, what's going on? We've worked with all of them before—I worked with Swindon on my first dig in my teens, on the Jubilee Line Extension project. What's the big deal?"

"Stan Laurence is leaving," Ron broke in flatly.

"I know."

"They've just announced who's taking over."

"Who?"

The words were being wrung out of him. "Marcie King."

She felt her stomach plummet. "But she can't—I thought – isn't Marcie still in Italy on secondment?"

"No. She's back, the Italian team decided to end the exchange early."

"Why?"

"I'm not sure, but Stefano's gone back. Marcie takes over next week."

Her fingers gripped the arms of the chair and left sweaty indentations as she pushed them back and forth along the leather. "Shit."

"Shit indeed."

Silence fell. Then Ron muttered, "I can ask Kevin to oversee her team—"

"She'd eat Kevin for lunch and you know it."

He spread his hands. "Just making the offer. What do you suggest? Business as usual?"

"I don't know, but this isn't going to work, Ron. You know that."

"It has to work, otherwise I'll have to pull you out. Keep you here in the lab, doing all the write ups. Or move you to another project."

"Over my dead body."

"Or hers?" He gave her a grim smile. "I'm not sure which I'm most concerned about." He looked at her intently and she met the look for a while before launching herself back in the chair and throwing her hands up in resignation.

"Okay. I'll work with the woman. I don't have much choice, do I? But I want minimal contact with her."

"I'll do my best, you know that. But you'll have to meet face to face sometimes."

"And when we do, I'll make sure I meet with Mike from the Surrey team too, and I'll probably take Kevin."

Ron shook his head. "Rebecca—"

"I'm serious, Ron. I won't be in a room by myself with her. She's poison."

"Fair enough." He sighed. "That's all I had to say, really."

She got to her feet abruptly, striding to the door without a word.

"I am sorry, Rebecca. If it was up to me..."

She gave the briefest of nods in acknowledgement, shutting the door behind her. She needed to find Kevin.

He was bent over a long document spewing out of the fax machine, but looked up as she opened the door. "Great timing Becs, we've got the dendro results back from the timbers in 425, and they're really interesting because—"

He stopped because she'd leaned over, identified the end of the document and ripped across the perforations in one aggressive sweeping motion. "Leave it," she said, slapping the paper down on the bench. "I'll look later."

"Why, what are we doing?"

"Early lunch." She swept out the door towards her office.

"Again? Not another disastrous date dissection? I've only just had my coffee break..."

She was already marching away down the corridor but he caught up with her, jacket over his shoulder, "... but I suppose I could manage a hazelnut latte."

"We're not going to Tony's," she said tightly.

"Oh? Where we off to, then?"

"The pub." She stopped to grab her own jacket from the back of her office door and slammed the door behind her.

Kevin winced. "Had a bad morning?"

"No, just a bad ten minutes."

"Can I ask why?"

He opened the foyer door for her and out on the pavement she stopped a moment, taking a lungful of air and forcing her shoulders to relax.

"Don't worry. I'm going to tell you all about who's heading up the Greenwich to Stratford dig. And then you'll want to go to the pub too."

She'd delivered the news over the big, saturated fat laden burgers that they allowed themselves occasionally, and now Kevin was staring morosely into his lager. "Jeez. That will be a barrel of laughs."

"Yep. I can't wait," she said curtly. "But there's not much I can do about it. Except to avoid her as much as possible."

"I take it she—"

"Still hates me? I can't see that changing, can you? It was bliss while she was away, not worrying about when I'd bump into her next. I was hoping she'd love Italy and never come back." She swirled the Merlot in her glass and took a long drink.

"No such luck. I guess it lost its appeal."

"She's back early but Ron doesn't know why." She sighed heavily. "I feel like the woman's an albatross around my neck. If she's back for good, maybe I need to find a job somewhere else."

He sat up straight. "Tell me you're joking."

"Believe me, I'm not in a joking mood."

"Come on, Becs, that's going a bit far. If she got a job at GLAM I could understand it, but—"

"If she got a job at GLAM, Kev, you'd be without a boss." She took another big gulp of red wine and saw Kevin wince. "Probably without two bosses. I'd either kill her, or kill Ron if I saw him first, for taking her on. Whichever, I'd go to prison."

"I'm sure with our forensic experience we could commit the perfect crime." He smiled tentatively. "They'd never catch you."

Rebecca didn't smile. "Kevin, be practical," she said quietly. "More and more of these projects are being shared between different teams now. Eventually we'll finish the Crossrail project, but what then? A few months down the line there will be another project where we're asked to collaborate with another team—and you know how often that's Swindon. "Oh God," she smacked a hand down on the table, "even worse, what if there's a project in future where they oversight?"

"In fairness, I doubt if she's thrilled at the prospect of you bossing her about either."

She glared at him. "Yes, but I haven't got some misbegotten, mentally messed-up grudge against her, have I?"

"You don't like her much."

"No, I don't," Rebecca ground out, "but with good reason. It's hard to form a good working relationship with someone who's accused your father of being responsible for her father's death."

He nodded. "I know how difficult it is."

"Sorry but you don't. Kev, Marcie and I used to play together all the time. My parents weren't only David King's colleagues; they were his best friends, and his wife's. I saw Marcie's Mum all the time too, because she was always there, doing all the secretarial stuff, getting the day-to-day things sorted. We were like one big, happy family. Mum, Dad and David were like the Three Musketeers. They did everything together, and it was their joint projects that made their names internationally known."

"I know. I did do an archaeology degree, Bec, remember? I said at the time how strange it was to read about your parents in a textbook. And I know that makes it hard for you too."

"By the time you met me, I'd got a grip on myself again. But it took me that long, Kevin. Six years. I lost everything that day. Not just my parents, but my best friend too. And my second mum."

"I'm sorry."

She shrugged, her eyes glistening. "It should be water under the bridge now, but Marcie won't let it lie. That's why it might be easier to go somewhere else. Start again up north somewhere, perhaps. Or right down in the South West. Anywhere too far for the Swindon team to be involved."

"I'd miss you."

With difficulty, she found a small smile. "I'd miss you too. But you could visit. Or come with me! Leave all this behind." She waved her hand around rather unsteadily. "Make a new life in the country, with me."

"Ooh, would we make our own cheese and keep chickens?" he mocked gently.

"Definitely. Fancy it?"

He shook his head with a quickness and finality that shook her. "Not me, I'm afraid. I'm an urbanite through and through."

It was stupid but that hurt. "I see," she said, trying to keep her tone light, "you care more about the bright lights than your friend, huh?"

Kevin looked at her, his face serious. "No, I care about you far more. But you don't need me, Rebecca. You're a very independent woman, and would make new friends wherever you go, because that's what you do."

"Not close ones like you, though." She tried to laugh but it stuck in her throat and threatened to become a sob. "You're my best bud," she said huskily.

He took her hand. "Like you say, I could visit. And so could you, whenever you got fed up with your chickens and yearned for civilisation. Providing you're not moving to the Outer Hebrides or anything."

"That's a bit more rural than what I had in mind."

"Good." He put his other hand over hers. "Sorry but I love the city life, Bec. I love London. Other cities are great for a weekend, but all my friends are here, and unlike you I don't make them that easily. I'm happy in my job, have got no ambitions to rise up the ranks—although I'm not ruling out being where you are now, one day—and I think it's more than likely I'll be at GLAM until I can't climb out of a trench without a stair lift." He grinned. "And even then I might nag whoever's in charge to let me move to the graphic design department, so I can sit down all day."

"Your skills will be out of date by then," she smiled. "Everyone will be like Tom Cruise in Minority Report, moving all the info around on a big screen with a magic glove."

"Oh I'm not daft. I keep in with all those bright young things down there, just so I can stay on top of it all."

There was a pause.

"So that's your master plan, is it? I didn't know you had one."

"And I didn't know Marcie bothered you so much that you'd rather move miles away than risk working with her sometimes."

They sat where they were for a while, Kevin still holding her hand.

"Well that's that then."

"Yes," said Kevin quietly. "All done with your lunch?" He released her hand.

"Yes thanks." She was fighting to keep her tears at bay as they left, and she was winning the battle until Kevin slipped his arm through hers as they walked back to work. "Wherever you go, whatever you decide to do, I'll always be here if you need me, Becs. You know that, right?"

Her throat was too tight to answer. She nodded and laid her head on his shoulder a moment, a single tear escaping down her cheek. That was the trouble, she thought, as she wiped her cheek. She wasn't sure there was enough to hold her here anymore. Kevin would always be here. But she didn't think she would.

Chapter Eight

She'd not been able to shake the cold sensation, floating somewhere between her stomach and her chest, all day. She'd thought that pouring her worries out to Kevin and burying herself in a mountain of work would dispel it, but no such luck. She was dreading working with Marcie; more than dreading it. It filled her with a bizarre sense of foreboding that was very un-Rebecca-ish.

She wasn't convinced coffee and a cake would help, either, but it was worth a try— and the phrase 'comfort food' had originated for a reason. Rebecca hadn't fancied sitting in Kevin's flat as he either minutely dissected the situation or tried to jolly her out of her dark mood, and she knew he would have done either or both if she'd accepted his offer of Chinese at his place. So she'd said no and walked wearily to Tony's instead.

She laid her head back against the wall behind her chair and stretched out her legs under the table. In a minute she'd go and get a coffee and pick something fattening, but right now it was good to just sit. It was weird, this sense of impending doom. If she was in a fantasy film right now, some old crone—or a bloke in a cloak and a funny hat—would be waggling their finger at her and cackling (or pompously declaring, in cloak bloke's case,) 'no good will come of this, mark my words! I have Seen the Signs!' before retreating into their cave or disappearing in a swirl of magical mist. Her instincts were telling her to run in the opposite direction, but she couldn't run from this any more than she could run from the unpleasant memories that another confrontation with Marcie would stir up. She closed her eyes for a moment. Deep breaths, Rebecca.

When she opened them, Steve was standing by her table.

"What the—! Oh, hi."

"Sorry, only me. Didn't mean to make you jump, it wasn't revenge or anything. I was already on my way over to you when you closed your eyes. Felt like a bit of a berk then. I wasn't sure whether to cough loudly, or what." He grinned.

She noticed his coat and rucksack. "Going home?"

"I was. Then I spotted you over here looking, if you don't mind me saying, like the world had fallen on your head."

"Or like my kitten had died?"

"Can't use that one, that's your metaphor." He grinned. "So I thought I'd come over and check if you were okay."

"Well this all seems strangely familiar."

"Yeah, just in reverse." He smiled. "So are you?"

"Am I what?"

"Okay?"

"Oh. Yes, thanks. Well, not really, no."

He put his head on one side. "And what I'm meant to deduce form that is...?"

She sighed. "I'm not okay."

"I see. Suspected as much. You looked gloomy, and we know that's a dead giveaway," said Steve lightly. "Do you want some company for a bit? I need to be home by seven, but—"

"No, you go home. Your company will be good, but I guarantee mine will be bloody awful."

"I'll be the judge of that." He dumped his rucksack on the floor and pulled up a chair. "So what's it going to be? Do you want to 1, tell me what's wrong—in as little or as much detail as you want, 2, listen to a succession of hilarious one liners, or 3, just sit in companionable silence? With perhaps a blueberry muffin for company?" He put on the kind of overly-bright voice heard in adverts. "The blueberry muffin is available with all options!"

The icy feeling was still there, but she grinned. "Well as tempting as option 2 sounds..."

"Knew it would, knew it would. Everyone's favourite."

"Perhaps we could start with the blueberry muffin and work our way backwards."

"Okay." Steve leapt to his feet. "Large or small? With cream or without? Sharing it or pigging it all yourself?"

"Large, with, and pigging it all myself, please. Although if you're going to sit there and not eat, I'll be racked with guilt. Then I'll feel worse than I do now, and it'll be your fault."

"Suppose I'd better get myself one too then."

Ten minutes later, Rebecca sat back with a satisfied sigh, wiping her fingers and mouth on a serviette. "Well I have to confess, it's hard to keep the gloomy expression going when your stomach's full of delicious, moist blueberry muffin and cream."

"And butterscotch latte," Steve reminded her, raising his coffee cup.

"And butterscotch latte," she agreed, leaning forward to chink her cup against his.

"So," he said, settling back in his chair, "now we've got rid of the glooms, do you want to tell me what caused them in the first place?"

She hesitated. "It's about work. Well, kind of."

"Right. I don't know much about archaeology, but I could try and make some suggestions." He raised an eyebrow comically. "How about 'use a bigger spade?'"

She smiled. "Thanks, I'll bear that in mind. Actually, it is about work, and it isn't."

"Glad we've got that clear."

She looked at him sternly. "Shh! Do you want me to tell you, or not?"

"Sorry."

"And it will sound minor at first, but you'll see it's quite major, really."

"Understood. Often the way with stuff that makes us miserable, I find." He smiled. "Go on."

"To summarise the boring stuff: the team I lead will be working again with the Swindon team on another site for the Crossrail project."

"I read about that in the paper. What's the problem? Have they all got terrible B.O? Not good."

"No, although you're right, that would be gross. Their team's now being led by a Marcie King."

"And she's the problem?"

"Yes. She hates me."

"Professional jealousy?"

"Hardly, she's done at least as well as me. I suspect more people have heard of her, anyway."

"Why does she hate you, then? What's her beef?"

"Her beef, as you put it, although I never had you down for a cockney, Call Me Steve"—she grinned and he rolled his eyes—"Is that she thinks my father killed her father."

Steve stopped mid-gulp and put his cup down, giving a low whistle. "Okay, of all the things I expected you to say, that's not one of them. A more major beef than I was expecting."

"Sorry. I did warn you."

He nodded slowly. "I take it we're not talking about a cold-blooded, pre-meditated act of murder here?"

"No. Causing death by negligence, I suppose you'd call it." She sighed. "Although I suppose to her, the outcome's the same. Her father was in a car with my parents. They worked together, they were all archaeologists. Quite well-known ones. They were working on a site in Thailand with another archaeologist, Francois Villeneuve. He was a very close friend of my parents, he's kind of an honorary uncle to me, or a big brother, though I don't see him often. He lives in Paris."

"Anyway, they'd had a hugely successful day, digging up some really significant finds. Francois went straight back to the hotel where they were staying, but my parents and Marcie's father drove to a bar first to celebrate. On the way back to the hotel, there was a terrible rainstorm. The mountain road they were on was partially washed away. Their car came off the road and rolled down the mountainside. The roads were horrendous out there then—well, a lot of them still are—in the rural areas, many of them are more or less mud tracks to start with."

"I see. Were they all killed in the crash?" he asked gently.

She nodded.

"If the roads were as bad as you say, how can Marcie blame your father?"

"Because she claims he was drunk."

"And what do you think?" asked Steve gently. "Could he have been?"

She shook her head. "Never. He abhorred drunk drivers; in fact he wouldn't drive if he'd had any drink at all. He always said that other people's lives deserved his maximum concentration and his sharpest reflexes. He didn't care about what the legal limit was in whatever country he was in, because he said even a small quantity of alcohol impairs your reactions. He had a real thing about it. Dad said people shouldn't be given advice on safe limits to drink and drive; the message should be 'drink or drive—not both."

"Does Marcie know all this?"

"She must do. We basically grew up together. We spent hours around each other's houses in England, and if our parents were abroad and we were with them, normally we'd all share the same house or stay at the same hotel. We were very close."

"So why is she so convinced he was drunk?"

"Because her mother claims that my Dad phoned to tell her they were starting back to the hotel, and he sounded drunk, apparently."

"I see. And your Dad was found in the driving seat?"

"No. It was a huge drop they went over." Her voice quivered and she swallowed hard before carrying on. "They were thrown out of the car at various points, except my mother. She was partly pinned under the car at the bottom."

"So how does anyone know who was driving?"

Rebecca stared at him. "Dad nearly always drove," she said, her voice barely more than a whisper. "He could handle the roads best."

"Did the police report say who was driving?"

"I don't think there was much of an investigation, not back then. They put it down to an accident caused by the state of the roads. They were just some foreigners caught out when the road washed away, and everyone had died; it didn't matter who was driving, I suppose.

"So it's possible that your Dad could have had a few drinks, but someone else could have driven the car back?"

"I suppose so, yes." She shook her head, dazed. "I just always presumed that Marcie's mother was mistaken, or that my Dad hadn't sounded drunk at all, but that her grief made her desperate for someone to blame."

"Sorry. I didn't mean to confuse things."

"No, it's okay. You've given me something to think about. I've been making assumptions all these years that might be wrong."

"Why blame you, though? Even if your father was to blame, there's nothing you can do; it's not your fault."

"She just does."

"And it's how long ago?"

"Twelve years."

"So it should be water under the bridge. Yes, it's awful and sad, but hating you isn't going to bring her Dad back."

"She always talks about it as though it happened last week. I don't know why she's transferred the blame to me, but she's gone out of her way to make my life a misery. Yet I lost more than she did," said Rebecca bitterly. "She still had her mother."

"How old were you?"

"Sixteen."

"Poor Rebecca." His eyes were full of sympathy, "That must have been tough."

"It was. At least I had my Gran then, though. I lived with her whilst I was in sixth form, but she died before I went to Uni. I sometimes think that's where I made my mistake, because I'd never have gone into archaeology if I'd known it would bring me into contact with Marcie."

"You didn't know she'd followed in her father's footsteps, then?"

"She didn't, at first. Didn't want anything to do with archaeology. She was three years older than me, so she was already at uni when our parents died, doing physics. I lost track of her for a few years – I only heard about her through other people, because neither she nor her mother would talk to me or my Gran afterwards—and next thing I knew, she was on a team digging a site near Bristol. She'd gone to Uni in Scotland to do archaeology so I hadn't come across her on digs down here. She took the job at Swindon three years ago. I barely saw her then though and about eighteen months ago Swindon agreed to exchange her with a member of a Florence team. She went out there and Swindon got Stefano."

"Will you see a lot of her when you work on this project?"

She shrugged. "I'm not sure yet. She's in charge of their team, but I don't know how much time she'll spend at the site, or how hands-on she'll be."

"You can't ask to be assigned to something else?"

She squirmed. "I could, but..." She could feel her cheeks flush.

"It's your baby," he said wryly.

She nodded. "Pathetic, isn't it."

"No, not if it really matters to you. I can understand wanting to see something through."

"Good, because I'm not sure I completely understand it myself. I'm dreading it."

"So what are you going to do? Grit your teeth and see how it goes?"

"I think I have to. My boss, Ron, is going to do what he can to reduce the contact between us, but we're going to have to work together sometimes, and make some decisions together. It's not feasible, otherwise."

"He sounds like a good guy to have as a boss."

"He is. He's the best." She grinned. "A bit like Tony."

"You may laugh, but you have no idea. Tony really is the best," said Steve with feeling.

She searched his face for clues as to what lay behind that comment, but found none. "Well that's good," she said lightly. "Some of my friends work for monsters. It's nice to know you don't."

He smiled. "That almost sounds like you're lumping me in there as a friend."

"Definitely. It was the butterscotch latte that did it."

"And there was me thinking it was my sympathetic listening ear. Would you like another one?"

"What, another ear? Crikey, how many have you got?"

"Ha ha. You've missed your vocation there, the comedy world has no idea what it's missing," he said, rolling his eyes. "Another latte, Miss Facetious?"

She glanced at her watch. "No thanks, Steve, but I'd best be going. Thanks for listening. Sorry to waste your evening." She stood up, and Steve did too. They'd both launched themselves in the same direction and suddenly they were very close, Steve looking down at her very intently.

"That's okay, any time," he said gruffly, holding her arm for a moment. "Happy to step in if you can't talk to Kevin."

For a split second – a glorious split second, she admitted to herself – she'd thought he was going to kiss her.

"Oh, I've already bent his ear on this one today," she said ruefully, and saw Steve's eyes narrow. What had she said wrong?

"He thinks I'm just being stupid though. Thinks I should just ignore her. I don't think he realises just how dangerous Marcie can be, particularly when she's in a position to meddle with my work. Or how hurtful it can be, dredging up all those memories."

"Sometimes when you're close to things, it can be hard to see them clearly."

She wasn't sure quite what he meant by that, but a wave of tiredness was crashing over her and suddenly all she wanted to do was go home. "I'm dead on my feet, so I'm going. Thanks again for listening."

"No problem." He smiled in response but didn't meet her eyes, sweeping up their things and heading off with the tray. "See you," he said casually over his shoulder.

She stared after him. "Yes... right. Bye."

He reached the counter, put the tray down and without so much as a glance over his shoulder, got into conversation with Neil, who was cleaning the shelves.

Rebecca stood there for a moment, feeling like an idiot. When it was obvious he wasn't going to turn round, she picked up her coat and left.

Chapter Nine

The door of Tony's banged shut so hard that their table shook. Kevin frowned but stayed glued to the article he was reading in the paper. Rebecca looked up from her salad. A girl was leaning back against the door, pouting. That was the only word for it. Not sexy pouting, thought Rebecca, but proper, cross pouting. She would have been pretty, with that mass of wavy blonde hair, if it weren't for the thick, smudged black eyeliner and general grubbiness. From here the girl whiffed a bit, too. She hadn't moved, but was just turning her head, sullenly surveying everything. Rebecca nudged Kevin.

"Mmf?" he grunted around his sandwich.

"That one looks like trouble," she said quietly.

Kevin swallowed and wrinkled his nose. "Smells like it too."

"Hmm, obviously doesn't follow the 'not before lunch' rule."

"Either that or she's had a really early lunch," he muttered.

The girl pushed herself off the door and started to walk to the counter, an easy enough task as Tony arranged his tables so that there was a clear route straight to the counter, always maintaining that it was more convenient for people in a rush and takeaway customers. But the girl seemed to be finding it difficult to walk in a straight line, and lurched into their table as she passed. "Oops, sorry," she said, trying to focus on them but not quite managing it before she carried on.

"And our next model is wearing Eau de Brewery," said Kevin, raising an eyebrow as he watched her progress. "Eww."

Steve appeared from the kitchen with a fresh batch of pastries. Rebecca was close enough to see his face darken as he caught sight of the girl, and her interest was piqued. She picked up her magazine and tried to watch the action unobtrusively from behind it.

"There you are, Steve!" The ringing but slurred tones backed up the evidence provided by the smell and the haphazard walking. This girl was tanked.

"Here I am." Steve's expression was a textbook example, thought Rebecca, or what people mean when they call the look on someone's face 'stony'.

"Uh-oh. Looks like Steve's got girl trouble," murmured Kevin.

She peered over her magazine to see Kevin twisting round, staring towards the counter with undisguised interest. "Nosey!" she shot at him.

He raised his eyebrows. "Look who's talking!" he mouthed. But a minute later, every head was turned towards the counter.

"I wunnered where you were, Steve!" The girl's voice was loud and harsh. She took the final step towards the counter, leaning heavily against it then lurched forward to try and kiss Steve on the cheek.

He didn't move his feet, just quickly leant back out of the way, his eyes not leaving her face. Like Neo from the Matrix, thought Rebecca. Neat move.

"I'm at work, Laura," he said, curt but quiet. Rebecca was straining to hear him.

"I know that now, silly," Laura laughed, wobbling on the spot. She lifted a hand as though to rest it on Steve's shoulder but missed.

This time he was too slow to move and her nail raked down his cheek. He wiped his cheek with his hand, smearing the bright red beads of blood that had appeared. He was way beyond stony now, thought Rebecca. His face was like thunder; she wouldn't want to be the woman who made him look like that.

"Oh, Steve, I'm sorry, sorry..." Laura looked wildly around her and spotted serviettes further along the counter. She grabbed a huge handful, trying to reach up and wipe his cheek.

He batted her away. "That's enough. Go home."

"But, but..." Her voice got even louder and she sounded tearful. "I was only trying to help. It's your faul, your fault, Steve, I woke up and you wern there. You left without saying g'bye!" She threw her hands up in protest and wiped out two plates of takeaway flapjacks displayed on the counter cabinet. The plates hit the floor, one rolling to a halt against the counter and the other shattering, shards of china scattered amongst the flapjacks. She stared down at the mess as though she couldn't work out how it had got there. "Whoops," she said, after a moment.

"Laura, go home right now," Steve growled." "You knew I was at work, and I've told you not to bother me here." He started to walk round the counter towards her.

She backed away a little, "But you don't work on Wednesdays, Steve, "she said, pointing an unsteady finger at him. "I know you don't."

"It's Thursday."

Her forehead creased. "Thursday?"

"Yes, so I'm where I should be. Where you should be is at home in bed, sleeping it off."

"Sleepinitoff? I'm n'drunk, if thas what you're tryin t'say." She planted her hands on her hips.

The kitchen door swung open. Tony came to stand beside Steve and put his hands on the end of the counter, shoulders squared. "What is it we can for you, Laura? You have not bought anything, I think, and Steve needs to get on his work. Si?"

Rebecca stared. Oh my God. She'd never heard Tony take that tone with anyone.

Laura stared at him, and instantly became a little girl. "I haven't brought any money, Tony," she said pathetically.

"Why are you in my café, then?"

"I came to see Steve." She was half-sobbing. "He didn't say goodbye to me!"

"You have seen him. My café is for people to sit, eat my food or drink my coffee. If you are not here to do these, leave, please."

Laura went completely still for a minute, tears stopped. Rebecca found she was holding her breath. Would she just turn and walk out?

With a screech, Laura's arm lashed out, trying to claw at Tony's face. With a dexterity Rebecca would never have suspected of him, Tony grabbed both her wrists. "If you do not stop right now, I call the police." He still hadn't raised his voice. The kitchen door opened again and Neil appeared, looking questioningly at Tony. Tony gave a small shake of the head. Neil stayed where he was.

"Boy, Tony's a cool customer," whispered Kevin.

Rebecca nodded speechlessly. Her eyes had gone to Steve, and her heart went out to him. He looked frozen to the spot, jaw rigid and his face red—whether from anger, embarrassment or a mix of both, she wasn't sure.

"Get off me!" Laura shrieked, freeing one of her wrists and lashing out again.

This time Tony stopped her hand only millimetres from his face. He looked over his shoulder at Neil. "You make the call please Neil; I think police should be here, yes?"

Neil turned, but Steve suddenly came back to life. "Stop, Tony, please—"

"I'm sorry, but if she won't leave—"

"I'll get her to! I'll take her home. I'm sorry."

"Go on then," said Tony through gritted teeth, "is against my better judgement, but as it is you…"

Steve moved behind Laura. "Come on, time to go home." He brought his arms down over hers in the kind of locking manoeuvre Rebecca had seen used on violent teens when she'd done a stint of work experience in a youth custody centre. That experience had helped her opt firmly for an archaeology degree and not the psychology degree she'd been toying with.

"But I want a coffee," said Laura, quieter now, turning round in Steve's hold to face him. "Can't you buy me a coffee?"

"I haven't got any money with me, Lor." He pulled her to the side of him, against his hip, one arm firmly around her shoulders.

Her face dropped and her eyes sparked.

"I'll tell you what," said Steve quickly, "I'll make you a special coffee at home. I bet Tony will let me borrow a bottle of syrup."

"Really?"

"Really. What one would you like?"

Laura's knees sagged as she turned her head to look at the bottles on the shelf. "Oooh, I feel dizzy…"

"Okay, don't turn round, I can tell you the flavours. Hazelnut, mint or vanilla?"

"Wow, that's the short version," Rebecca murmured.

"Mmm. Mint."

Tony produced a fresh bottle from under the counter and thrust it into Steve's hand.

"Thanks." Steve sounded like a man who'd had his life saved.

"Now, you get her out of here." Tony's eyes glittered.

"Home we go." He steered Laura towards the door, eyes fixed ahead. Poor Steve, thought Rebecca. I wouldn't want to look anyone in the eye, either.

Tony watched them go, and as Steve got Laura out the door—aided by Kevin, who'd leapt to his feet to open it because everyone closer seemed paralysed—he turned on his heel, waving Neil into the kitchen before his with an impatient flick of his hand. The door banging behind him was nearly as loud as Laura's entrance a few minutes earlier.

Kevin turned to Rebecca with eyes like dinner plates. "Oo-er, missus."

"Poor Steve."

"Yeah. Poor Steve," Kevin agreed, picking up his abandoned coffee. "Eww. Cold. Never can understand how people can drink iced coffee."

"Philistine. It's gorgeous."

Neil appeared, and the heads of everyone in the shop whipped round to see what was happening now. He walked to the nearest table and squatted down on his haunches, talking quietly to the customers.

"What's going on?" Kevin hissed.

"Dunno, I can't hear. Are you done?"

"Just want to finish my muffin," said Kevin, watching Neil curiously as he moved to the next table. "At least that tastes good cold."

"Just want to be nosey, more like," Rebecca retorted. "Hurry up then, we need to get back."

"Why? There's nothing urgent on. This is better than soap."

She raised her eyebrows. "Well if I'd known you were bored... never mind, I can find plenty for you to do this afternoon. I've got a stack of site surveys on my desk that all need filing."

"No, no, not bored, just pointing out that—"

"Button it, McKenzie, and eat your muffin."

"Yes, boss." He'd just taken a comically huge bite, pretending to panic, when Neil arrived at their table and hunkered down.

He smiled. "Hi."

Rebecca chuckled. Watching as Kevin tried to look polite while swallowing his muffin practically whole in two seconds flat was making her day, and she felt the knot in her stomach relax a little. Seeing Steve so upset had been horrible.

Kevin waved a hand at Neil and shrugged apologetically.

"Idiot!" She turned to Neil. "Excuse the tame monkey, Neil, what can we do for you?"

Neil was trying hard to keep a straight face. "It's more what we can do for you, which is firstly, to apologise for the disruption."

Kevin made a choking noise and Neil thumped him on the back.

"Are you alright, dude?" He looked concerned.

Kevin nodded.

Rebecca grinned. "You look like a giant tomato."

Kevin glared at her and did a giant swallow. He turned to Neil, his face all innocence. "What disruption?"

This time, Neil allowed himself a grin. "The young lady who was – how do you say it politely over here, rather worse for wear...?"

"Oh, the one who was drunk as a skunk," said Kevin. He smiled. "That's alright, not your fault."

"Not the fault of any of the staff," said Rebecca firmly. She lowered her voice. "Will Steve be okay?"

Neil glanced round. "I hope so. It's not the first time stuff like this has happened." He looked embarrassed. "Er, forget I said that."

"She certainly looks high maintenance," said Kevin.

"And some," Neil agreed.

"I'm surprised he puts up with it."

"You have to admire him for sticking by her," said Rebecca. Her voice sounded unusually high, she thought. She felt suddenly tearful. Get a grip, woman.

"I suppose. He's a very loyal bloke, but too nice for his own good. Anyway, shouldn't be gossiping, it's Steve's business." Neil got to his feet, looking uncomfortable. "Oh, almost forgot. Secondly, Tony says today's lunch is on the house and he hopes to see you again soon."

"Ah. Flannel and flattery', as my Mum would call it," Kevin laughed.

"Yeah, well with you two it's wasted, you practically live here. There you go, anyway." He produced two vouchers out of his apron pocket, giving one to Kevin and one to

Rebecca.

Kevin looked. "Ooh, thanks!"

"Our pleasure," said Neil, carrying away their tray.

Kevin waved his voucher under Rebecca's nose. "Look, Bec, ten percent off our next bill!"

"Whoopee."

"Well don't sound so enthusiastic," said Kevin, affronted. "Ten percent off is ten percent off. Us more lowly workers can't afford to look a gift voucher in the, er..."

"Voucher code?"

"Exactly. We need every penny—Bec?"

She was on her feet, pulling on her coat. "Time we we're going."

He got to his feet. "Right," he said, sounding crushed. "Bec?"

"Yes?"

"What the matter?"

"Nothing." She picked up her bag, not meeting his eyes.

"Could have fooled me."

"I just can't believe all you care about is your discount code, Mr Me Me Me. Strangely enough, as I have a heart, I'm more concerned with the little human tragedy that's just played out here," she said tightly.

"Hey, don't make me out to be the bad guy!" Kevin protested, following her to the door. "I do care. Steve seems like a really nice bloke, but there's not a lot we can do about it, is there? None of our business."

"No, I know. Sorry. It's just... poor Steve. He must be really caring to support her like that. Most men would run a mile. She could lose him his job." They walked towards the door but she hesitated, her hand on the handle. "I wonder if I should talk to Tony?"

"What about?"

"Steve, of course. Say Tony gives him the sack?"

"Rebecca, that's up to Tony, and there's all sorts of employee rights rigmarole he'd have to go through first, you know that." Kevin reached past her and opened the door, forcing her out of it and on to the street.

"But that's the last thing Steve needs. I bet she's not holding down a job, is she, if she regularly gets in that state!"

"I'm sure Tony wouldn't do anything without giving it serious thought, Bec, he's a good guy. And he must know Steve pretty well by now, as you don't really know him from Adam. Now come on, it's nearly—"

"Actually I've had coffee with him. And lunch. And dinner, kind of." She rushed out the door, hoping he wouldn't see the blush she could feel rushing up her face.

Kevin stopped and faced her just outside.

"Really?"

"Yes. We're quite good friends, if you must know." She wasn't meeting his eyes, fiddling with something unnecessary in her bag as she started to walk. "And I know Tony's a sweetie and everything, but he's got all these old-fashioned Italian ideas—"

"Patronising alert!" Kevin tucked her arm in his as he often did, and although she was cross with him, she let him. She didn't want to make a scene.

"No, but he might think Steve should just chuck her out, or send her to the country or something—"

"Rebecca, what century are you living in?"

www.penrose-publishing.co.uk

"— and poor Steve, he doesn't deserve—"

Kevin stopped dead, bringing Rebecca to an abrupt halt by default.

"Oww." She glared and pulled her arm out of his.

"Sorry. Listen Rebecca, Tony is the guy who runs out local cafe. That's all. He's not our uncle, or a personal friend, or even a personal friend's uncle, for God's sake. You can't interfere."

"I wouldn't, normally. I just think this is different."

"And all this poor Steve... again, Steve is just a nice guy who serves me lunch. And your friend, apparently, whenever that happened, but surely only a casual one." He looked at her piercingly, and she looked away.

Too late. This time it wasn't just a blush, she felt her cheeks burn.

"Bec, you're not serious. Steve seems a lovely guy and I feel really sorry for him, but if that little scene showed you anything, it's that he's a, taken and b, in a mess with that woman, a mess that you, I, and everyone else is best staying out of. It's their business."

Rebecca's stomach was churning. Have you quite finished lecturing me like I'm a wayward teenager?" Her tone was cutting and she knew she was behaving badly, but for some reason she couldn't stop herself.

Kevin's mouth opened, closed, then opened again. "Look, Bec, I didn't mean it like that, I—"

"You'd best get back to work, you'll be late." She turned abruptly and went to the kerb, looking for a space in the traffic.

"Where are you going?" He sounded worried and unhappy as she crossed the road away from him. Rebecca Maynard, you are a bitch, she told herself. As she reached the other side, she looked across at him and gave him a small smile.

"I'm getting the bus to the Edgbaston site, I need to check how that last trench is going. They're closing up tomorrow," she called, starting to walk.

"But your stuff—"

"I've got everything with me." Truth. "I had this planned before lunch but I forgot to say, what with all the drama!" Lie.

"Okay then." Kevin started to walk slowly along his side of the road, but she was rapidly leaving him behind, speeding up as she saw the bus turn the corner at the end of the road and start coming towards her.

She waved a hand. "Bye!" The bus had stopped and she was sprinting now. There had only been two people waiting at the stop and the second had just got on. She prayed the driver had seen her.

Seconds later she jumped on the bus, paid the driver and threw herself into the first empty seat. Sometimes Kevin acted more like her bloody mother than her friend, she thought, adrenaline still racing through her veins as the bus lurched off along the street. Tears pricked her eyes as the irony of that thought struck her. She didn't want someone to act like her mother, she wanted her Mum back. Perhaps she would have understood how lonely Rebecca sometimes was, even amongst friends; and how tough it was to want someone you can't have.

Laura was gone. After the usual massive row, he'd left her to sleep it off for the afternoon and gone out to do some food shopping. When he got back, nearly everything she owned had disappeared and he presumed what she'd left behind were things she no longer wanted – many of which seemed to be gifts from him. She either taken a cab or someone had picked her up, he figured, because she couldn't have carried all that stuff away by herself.

Steve rested his head back on the sofa. He would have expected to feel either relieved, worried sick or guilty.

Strange then that instead, he just felt numb.

Chapter Ten

Laura opened the back door cautiously. By rights Steve shouldn't be here, he should be at work. But she needed to be sure. She left her boots outside on the step and padded round the house in her socks.

Ok, she was safe. He was gone and so were his work clothes. She pulled a carrier bag out of her rucksack and filled it with clothes. Then she went to the bathroom. In the cabinet was a bag she could guarantee Steve wouldn't snoop in, because it was full to the brim with tampons. She groped around at the bottom, pulled out a tampon box and removed the roll of £10 notes inside. That would do for today.

Kitchen next. She took all the multipacks from the cupboard—crisps, mini cheddars, cereal bars and a bumper bag of min rolls—and took one or two of everything. Steve rarely ate snacks himself, but she wouldn't take too many, just in case. She stashed the food in her rucksack along with a couple of juice cartons from the fridge, and then placed the bags and boxes back again with military precision. She grinned. She should apply for a job in MI5.

She was about to retrieve her boots and leave when she spotted the laptop on the dining room table. Why not check her email while she was here? It was more private than the library and cheaper than an internet café, too. She sat down and flipped the laptop open.

There weren't many messages on her webmail. She didn't dare use Outlook because then Steve would know she'd been home as soon as he got his own email. He checked it most days. She answered two messages, then looked at the third. Someone had offered her good money for a very specific set of addresses a few weeks ago; she'd put the information into a word document (with an innocuous title to prevent Steve becoming suspicious) but hesitated about sending it. Money was going to be tight now though, so she found the document, attached it to her email and hit send. Then she deleted the document, just to be on the safe side. Was there anything else she should delete?

She frowned. Steve didn't often save documents on the laptop, but this wasn't hers. 'MM Profile'. She shouldn't, but...

Her eyes scanned down the document—God, there were pages of it. Username, date of birth, age range 23-35, favourite TV shows... "Oh my God. Seriously?" she said out loud. Why had he gone to all this trouble but not sent it off?

She looked at her watch. Steve wouldn't be back for ages yet, even if he was on a short shift. She brought up the Methodical Matches website and logged in using the username Steve had thoughtfully noted. A-ha: 'profile status: incomplete'. She split the screen so she could see Steve's completed form at the same time, and started copying and pasting. She was tempted to change the odd detail to something outrageous, but decided not to. She wanted it to get some interest.

Perhaps a few dates would keep him off her back for a while.

Derek. She said it a few times, but it didn't get any better. You could quote Shakespeare's line about 'a rose by any other name would smell as sweet' as much as you liked, but there was no denying that your opinion of someone was swayed by their name. It wasn't fair, but it was a fact. Some people out there—people who knew delightful Dereks—probably thought Derek was a wonderful name, perfectly capable of conjuring up a man 'sexy, suave, great with kids and a dab hand at cooking, who independently remembers and marks their mother's birthday but is in no way tied to her apron strings'.

In Rebecca's mind, however, Dereks were the polar opposite of this ideal hero. Dereks were overly-skinny, slightly stooped contestants for 'most neglected hair' awards, sporting glasses seemingly picked for their inability to flatter the human face. In the winter they wore worn out poo-brown cords and hideously baggy, knitted-by-their-mother jumpers that had seen better days twenty years ago, swapping to knee-length beige shorts, mid-shin length socks and brown sandals in the summer. So she was almost too scared to click on the link to Derek's profile photo, because she'd had a bad day and wasn't in a rush to have her worst fears realised. She braced herself with a large glass of wine first.

Wow. Derek was a bit of a hunk. Muscles—large enough to impress but without giving him that deformed, out-of-proportion look she hated—stretched the sleeves of his t-shirt in a pleasing manner, and there was the hint of a six pack, which made perfect sense with those arms. He had sandy, spiky hair, broad shoulders and a friendly smile. Of course, perhaps eye-candy was all he was, but then he couldn't be too intellectually superior, otherwise the computer wouldn't have matched them. Would it? Whatever her qualms about the Snake Man, he had certainly been intelligent enough for her.

The message was short and sweet.

Hi Rebecca

You came through on my hot matches list this morning and I really like your picture (you have gorgeous hair!). Would you like to meet up? Regards, Dean (that's what my friends call me. I hate Derek!)

She'd always known that there would be hits and misses with internet dating. After all, the best profile matching in the world didn't mean there would be the right chemistry between people. But until her first date, it hadn't occurred to her that 'not right' might be 'downright creepy'. But Kevin was right, she had to give it another try, and Derek—or rather Dean—looked pretty fit. She hit reply.

'Are you free on Saturday? What about lunch at Frisconti's? It's on Parson Street.'

His reply pinged back almost instantly. 'Great. Just looked it up, I love Italian. 1pm?'

'1p.m. is fine, but not sure you'll find a parking space nearby.'

'Thanks for the heads-up. Look forward to seeing you Saturday.'

As she walked towards the restaurant on Saturday, she couldn't help looking at her reflection in shop windows as she passed. She hoped she'd got it right. This was the trouble with internet dating; there was so much pressure when it was a first meeting and a first date all rolled into one. She hadn't realised what how tense she would feel each time, although she'd never been keen on blind dates and never agreed to any suggested by well-meaning friends.

She preferred to meet people in a natural way, even if it was spotting them at the edge of a crowd and deciding that by the end of the evening she'd like to know them better. There was a whole language of eye contact and subtle signals that let you show you were interested, and told you they were too. But then if meeting people in a natural way had been working for her, she thought regretfully, she wouldn't have turned to the internet in the first place.

Frisconti's was just a few steps away. She took a deep breath and opened the door. Nothing ventured, nothing gained.

The conversation flowed. The wine flowed. This was going amazingly well.

Dean was excellent company and even better looking than his photo. He was confident, he was witty, and he had no qualms whatsoever about ruining the pure heritage or taste of coffee by indulging in flavoured, frothy or full milk versions. Rebecca relaxed, safe in the knowledge that if any subsequent dates involved imbibing coffee, her chocolate sprinkles were safe. Dean was a cinnamon man apparently, and when Rebecca mentioned that she baked a mean apple and cinnamon slice, he had given her a charming, cheeky smile.

"Great. I can't wait to come round and try it."

Her stomach had done a delighted little flutter at that. Out of practice she might be, but surely that was a major hint he'd like to see her again? And the suggestion that might be at her house seemed quite... intimate. Even more significantly, she realised that she was happy at the prospect of seeing him again, too.

He seemed genuinely interested in her work and impressed by what she'd achieved, and talked enthusiastically about his own work without being patronising. A definite improvement on snake-man there. Dean was level-headed. Independent. Fulfilled in his own life, but keen to share it with someone else. Well a special someone else, she amended, because it sounded like he had plenty of friends. Hooray! Not a recluse. It sounded like they all spent a lot of time at his stepfather's farm, where Dean kept his two horses.

"So your friends ride too?" she leaned forward, smiling.

"God, yes! Nearly all of them, they're horse mad. Mark's horse—he calls it Ninja, would you believe, it's black—" he rolled his eyes and she chuckled,"— has gone lame. It's going to be out of action for a while, so I've lent him Salt."

"Salt's your grey mare, you said?"

"That's right." A smile lurked round his mouth. "You do know that means she's white, don't you?"

She grinned. "Yes, I'm no horse expert but I do know that much."

"Great. I thought I should check, not everyone realises."

"You think I'm a typical townie," she teased.

He laughed. "So am I, during the week."

"And I'm guessing Pepper isn't a grey?"

"No, my big fella is a really dark bay. He almost looks black, until you see him against Ninja." He drained his wine. "You should come along next weekend and meet them."

"Who, your friends or your horses?" Rebecca laughed.

"Both!" He smiled broadly. "Man and beast alike, they'll all be there, meeting outside the pub."

"You meet outside a pub? With all the horses? That's one accommodating landlord you've found there!"

"Every fortnight. It's a tradition, that's where we meet the hounds. The landlord does well enough out of it, both before and after."

Rebecca's brain had frozen halfway through his sentence, barely registering the end of it. "Hounds?" She said faintly.

"Yes, hounds. A bit pointless going hunting without them!" he chuckled. "Horses have got fine instincts of their own, but they're no match for a fine pack of beagles when it comes to a sense of smell."

"So you go hunting?" Her voice was still calm. Miraculously.

He nodded. "The best way to give a horse real exercise, great combination of flat gallop and fences. It doesn't do me any harm either. It's the best thigh workout known to man!" he laughed, refilling both their glasses, and winked. "Or woman!"

She stared at him blankly. "And the hounds, I suppose they're chasing a, a—"

"Fox? God, of course! None of this poncey dummy scent nonsense, if you've got the horses and the hounds out there working, what the devil's the point in not ridding the countryside of some vermin? Such a disgusting waste of resources, those dummy hunts. Might as well put the dogs down, it's an insult to their intelligence and their breeding."

She swallowed, not quite believing the disastrous turn the conversation had taken. "You don't think there are better ways to control the fox population?"

"God, no. This keeps lots of people in employment, traditional employment, for one thing, and all those lame-brains who go on about it being cruel—and then sink their teeth into a nice piece of venison, or veal, come to that—they sicken me, they really do. Bloody hypocrites! They've no grip on the reality of the situation." He drank deeply.

"I think what the protesters have a grip on is the cruelty of the death," said Rebecca coldly. "The fear and desperation the foxes feel in their last moments. "That's what I've always written about when I've campaigned, anyway."

Dean paled and his glass stopped halfway to his mouth. "Campaigned? You mean—"

"That I'm an anti-hunt protester? A lame-brain?" she took her purse out of her handbag, not looking at him, and pulled out a £20 note. "God, yes." She knew that bit of mimicry was bitchy, but she couldn't help herself.

"Er, that's… that's fine. Obviously you're not a lame-brain. Everyone has to stand up for what they believe in, don't they? There's always room for more than one point of view."

"I have to disagree, I'm afraid. For me, there's only room for one point of view on this issue. The one that despises unnecessarily lingering, painful deaths for defenceless animals." She stood up, her coat over her arm. "And by the sound of it, you don't really have that much respect for anyone else's view anyway." She laid the £20 note on the table.

"Look, Rebecca, I—I mean, we were getting on so well—"

"Yes we were. Surprising, really, lame brain that I am. Not a hypocrite by the way, I don't eat venison or veal." She smiled tightly and-ever-so-politely. "Believe me when I say I'm as disappointed at how things have turned out as you are. Who would have thought that one sentence could ruin a whole evening?"

"But does this have to matter? We can agree not to talk about it." A tiny glimmer of hope sparked in his eyes.

In other circumstances, that eagerness would have been fantastically flattering for her ego, she thought. Not now. "That wouldn't change the fact that you do something that's completely against my principles. I can't ignore it." She frowned. "Unlike you. Why didn't you say you were into hunting on your profile? It would have saved both of us time. It specifically asked about things like this under 'ethics and viewpoints'."

"I know, and I did!" He looked genuinely perplexed. "That's why I was surprised by your reaction."

Rebecca shook her head. "I'm starting to think that agency couldn't organise a piss-up in a brewery."

He nodded ruefully. "They do seem to like matching polar opposites. My last date hated Italian food, and Chinese. I rarely eat anything else."

"That sounds familiar." She sighed as she pushed her chair in. "It was interesting to meet you, Dean. Sorry I wasn't what you were expecting."

"No, you were fine, I mean I... more than fine," he floundered. "But obviously we're not a good match. I hope you have better luck with your next date."

That wasn't very likely, she thought as she left. Because there wasn't going to be a next date.

Chapter Eleven

"Steve Reynolds?"

Steve, busy cleaning a sticky nozzle on the coffee machine, turned back to the counter with a smile. "Yes?" He took in the uniforms, and behind them, the craning necks and curious faces of all the customers, including Kevin and Rebecca. Not surprising. He didn't think the man and woman in front of him were here for a latte and an Eccles cake, somehow. They didn't usually get police officers in Tony's. "How can I help?"

"I'm Sergeant Duffy," said the male officer, and this is Sergeant Peebles." We've just got a few questions, if that's okay. Is it alright if we talk here? It will only take a minute."

"Of course." This would be about the robbery along the road last week he thought, watching Sergeant Peebles flip open a notebook. The police had phoned him afterwards, but finding out that he'd seen so little, they'd said they probably wouldn't have any more questions, as they had far better witnesses. Obviously they'd changed their minds.

"We're looking for Laura Reynolds. Is she still living with you, at—" he glanced down briefly at Sergeant Peebles' notepad, "—53 Dreadnought Road?"

Steve's stomach hit the floor. "Er... I'm not sure."

The sergeant raised his eyebrows. "You're not sure?"

He flushed. "Sorry, yes, I live at 53 Dreadnought Road but I think she's moved out. She's taken a lot of her belongings." back."

"I take it you parted on unfriendly terms?"

"You could say that, yes."

"And when did you last speak to her?"

"Last Tuesday."

Sergeant Peebles was scribbling away. What was she finding to write about? Steve wondered. He'd barely said anything. He took a deep breath, dropping his eyes. His knuckles were white around the cloth he still held and he made a conscious effort to relax and unclench his hands a little.

"And did you speak to her in person last Tuesday, or was it over the phone?"

"In person."

"Has she called or texted you since?"

"No. She hasn't answered my calls to her mobile either."

"Okay, and can I just verify that since she left your home you haven't seen her at all, or had any indication of her whereabouts, activities or who she has been with—via someone else who knows her, for instance?"

"That's correct. I've called a couple of people she knows, but they claim they've not seen her or heard from her either."

"We'll need the details of the people you contacted. Sergeant Peebles?"

She gave him a sympathetic smile. "Name first, then address, then phone number, if you don't mind."

"Of course." He rattled off the names of the two ex-colleagues of Laura's. "If they're telling the truth, then God knows where she's gone. It's like she's disappeared off the face of the earth."

"We're fairly sure that's not the case, sir. We think she may have been involved in criminal activity."

Steve braced his hands on the counter, hanging his head. "I daren't ask what." His voice was low.

"We can't tell you anyway, sir. Not until we've confirmed a few things," said the officer gently. "I'm sorry, I understand this isn't welcome news."

"No, it isn't."

"Well thank you for your help, sir. We need to follow up some enquiries, but we'll probably have to speak to you again. Will you be at your home address this evening?"

"Yes."

"We'll contact you there, then." He nodded and made for the door.

Sergeant Peebles lingered a moment, packing her notebook back in her pocket. "Thanks again for your time, Mr. Reynolds. Sorry to disturb you at work."

"No problem." He stared after her as she left. His stomach felt strange.

Tony approached him hesitantly. "Steve, I just—"

His stomach gave an almighty heave. He pushed past Tony and just made it to the staff toilet in time. What would his parents have said if they could see what Laura had become under his guardianship? He retched again until there was nothing left and then sank on to the toilet seat, holding his head in his hands. This was his worst nightmare come true.

Rebecca's hand hit the glass door with some force and she sailed through as it swung back on its hinges. It was the same girl behind reception. Nicola, the patronising one. Oh goody.

Nicola looked up and gave her an agonisingly wide smile, her Minnie-Mouse-pink lip-sticked lips a fluorescent slash in her tanned face.

"Good morning, how can I help?" Her brow wrinkled as she looked up at her. "Ah! Rebecca, isn't it?"

Rebecca hadn't expected that, and it threw her for a moment. "Yes, Rebecca Maynard."

"What can I do for you today, Rebecca?"

Rebecca rested the heels of her hands on the reception desk and Nicola pulled back a little, her smile slightly less certain.

"I went on my second date last night."

Nicola clapped her hands together, obviously deciding she'd read the body language wrong. "That's marvellous! So the relationship's progressing!"

There was an element of surprise in her reaction that was unnerving. How much success had Methodical Matches actually achieved? What a shame that she was about to burst Nicola's bubble.

"No, I don't mean a second date with the same person. I've had two single dates with two different men, and I don't expect to be having any more."

Nicola's face dropped like an elevator in freefall. "Oh, don't say that! Surely there are more hot matches on your list?" She began to type furiously, but Rebecca stuck out a hand.

"Stop—please. Yes, there are more hot matches, but I don't think I want to meet any of them."

"Well you can hardly expect to meet Mr Right straight away," said Nicola, half-chastising, half-wheedling. "Just give it a bit lon—"

"I didn't. Expect to meet Mr Right straight away, that is. I'm not stupid. But I also didn't expect to be matched with people who have nothing in common with me."

Nicola looked aghast. "Nothing? At all? Really?"

Rebecca squirmed. "Well okay, not nothing at all. The first man liked my favourite author but it's his guilty secret, because her stuff's so low brow, apparently. He barely has a social life, hates the food I love, calls his Mum Mother, and generally comes across as a male chauvinist Victorian relic. Oh, and he's—" a tight-arse, she was about to say, "— a penny pincher too."

"Oh." Nicola looked downcast. "What about, er, the second match?"

Rebecca counted points off on her fingers. "Good-looking. Intelligent. Good sense of humour. Loves his career. Didn't patronise me because I'm a woman. Loves Italian food, just like me."

Nicola's face brightened. "Great! But you said none of your matches are any good! This one sounds really promising!"

"You'd think so, wouldn't you? Except that he spends his weekends in Surrey with his friends and his stepfather, seeing how many defenceless foxes he can slaughter before it's time to come back to London for work on Monday morning."

"I take it you don't?"

Rebecca looked at her coldly. "No. In fact I've spent several weekends campaigning with LACS."

"LACS?"

"The League Against Cruel Sports."

"I see. I suppose that could be a problem."

"You think?"

Nicola blushed, shoulders drooping. "I don't understand. The program's meant to be set up to look at the whole person, to take notice of everything. If it doesn't find a good enough match, an alert should come through. I don't know why it keeps on doing this." She suddenly clamped her lips together.

Rebecca swooped. "Keeps on doing this? You mean it's happening to other people?"

There was a pause, and then Nicola sighed and slumped back in her chair. "Not at first. But you're the third complaint I've had today."

"Maybe someone needs to take a look at your program, then."

"Yes. We are trying our best to resolve the technical problems."

"What happens in the meantime?"

"I can refund your registration fee," said Nicola tentatively. "And extend your trial by a month? We could call this a dummy run."

"Very appropriate."

Nicola winced. "Is that what you'd like me to do?"

Rebecca tapped her fingers on the desk. "I'm just wondering if I can actually put myself through that again. I'm not sure I've got the willpower."

"Please carry on!" Nicola was welling up. "It might be third time lucky. Keep the first date brief—"

"Oh believe me, I've been trying to!"

"—And that way, if you don't get on, there's no harm done. Is there?" Nicola summoned up an encouraging smile.

She sighed. "Okay. I'll give it another try. But if my third guy is a disaster, that's it."

Nicola clapped her hands. "Wonderful! I'm so glad you've decided to stick with it! I'll confirm your refund and trial extension by email."

Rebecca nodded briefly in response and left. *Either I'm mad, desperate or too soft for my own good.*

Steve had gone to the supermarket before he came home, then straight out for a run. By the time he'd showered and changed into a comfy t-shirt and jeans, he was ravenous. He nuked a curry ready meal, switched on the laptop and opened his email, taking a mouthful of food.

"Ow!" *Was this really meant to be a Rogan Josh? It was more like Madras.* He went to the kitchen for a lager and took a huge, neutralising gulp. By the time he'd settled himself back at the table, there were 15 unread messages sitting in his inbox. He started to work his way down them, deleting all the spam and invitations to place his first bet free on the best online casino ever. It didn't leave him with that many to read.

He stopped. There were three emails form Methodical Matches. *Strange.* He guessed that at least one of them would say something along the lines of 'Hi, we notice you haven't completed your profile yet. Click here to complete it NOW, and start meeting your hot Matches!' *But what were the other two?* He clicked on the first one. And frowned.

'Congratulations on completing your profile. Now it's time for us to do the hard work! Sit back, relax and wait for your first Hot Matches email. *You should receive your first Hot Matches email within 24 hours. If you have not received it within 48 hours, please contact us.'

What? He hadn't completed his profile, and he sure as hell hadn't submitted it. It must be an error—yeah, that must be what the next email was about, it was probably an apology. The third one was more than likely to confirm he didn't have a live profile and everything was sorted.

He clicked on the second email. 'Congratulations! Your profile is live and can now be viewed by other clients who can see you in their Hot Matches list. Below are your first Hot Matches!' Underneath were two photographs. One was a dark haired woman who looked a little older than Steve. According to the caption, her name was Susan, she was 25 and she was a bank clerk. The other was a blonde name Eleanor, who looked younger but was actually 29. A teaching assistant, apparently.

Might as well go the whole hog and open the third email, he thought, shaking his head in confusion. *Perhaps it would explain what the hell was going on.*

It didn't.

'Hi Steve, I'm Susan and I saw your profile come up today on my Hot Matches. I'm really interested in meeting you. Please get in touch.'

Steve checked the time. 5.24p.m. *With any luck, there might still be someone at the office.* He punched the number into his phone.

"Good afternoon, Methodical Matchezz, Nicola speaking! How may I help you?" a voice trilled.

Jeez. What was the woman on? "Hi, I hope you can help me—"

"I hope so too!"

Steve cringed. "Er, yes... I registered on your website a while ago but haven't submitted my profile yet—"

"Do you need some help with it? We're always happy for clients to come into the office, if you're local. The questionnaire can seem long-winded, so we're recommending that you print—"

"No, that's fine. I pasted it into a blank document and filled it in there, but—"

"The online submission form timed out on you, didn't it?" she burbled. "We are trying to fix that, but if you bring the form and your completed profile up on your screen, you can cop—"

"No, that's not it," said Steve sharply. He must have made his point this time because he heard a quiet "oh."

"The problem is, I changed my mind about submitting my profile. I haven't submitted it."

Silence. Then Nicola cleared her throat. "That is of course completely your choice sir, you're not under any obligation. Do you want me to cancel your registration?"

"No, I mean yes, but... look, the problem is, you've emailed me saying you received my completed profile and it's live on the site."

"But you just said you had changed your mind about submitting it. Did you mean you changed your mind after you submitted it?"

Steve raised his eyes heavenward. She couldn't see it, but it made him feel better. "No, I don't."

"And you're sure you haven't sent it? By mistake?"

"Absolutely sure. I hadn't even started filling out the online form—as soon as it timed out first time round, I copied in into a word document, as I said. I was going to copy and paste it in."

"Until you changed your mind," she said doubtfully.

"Yes." He fought to keep the irritation from his voice. "Until I changed my mind."

"You're sure you didn't paste it into the online form and just forget? Or hit send without realising?"

Steve held the handset away from his ear and stared at it. Took a deep breath. Put it back against his ear.

"Nicola—can I call you Nicola?"

"Yes, of course," she answered, in a tone still filled with sunshine and fluffy bunnies.

Time to make rabbit pie, thought Steve. "Have you seen how long the form is?" he asked. Quiet. Calm.

"Yes, of course—"

"And do you think Nicola, that you yourself could forget copying and pasting that many pages of text into an online form?" A little louder.

She sensed the danger now, she was blustering. "No, er, of course not, I only, er, wondered if—"

"And do you think there's a chance that, having somehow mysteriously forgotten you'd spent hours copying and pasting all that text into the form, you might forget, at the same time, that afterwards you'd clicked on the submit button?"

"It doesn't seem likely, but—"

"No it doesn't. I'm not senile, Nicola, nor do I suffer from amnesia or any kind of mental illness. I also haven't had any nasty bumps on the head, before you ask."

"Well that's, that's good." He could hear her swallow, and take a deep breath. Then, just like that, the fluffy bunnies were back. Boy, she was made for this job. "Oh dear. It seems like the email has been sent in error then, doesn't it?"

"I think that seems the likeliest explanation, don't you?" said Steve, with the merest trace of sarcasm. But an odd little doubt was nagging at his mind. "Although..."

"Yes?"

"If that's the case—the email's just been sent in error—it does seem strange that I've had two more emails from you."

"Oh. When?"

"Straight after the first one. Three emails, all together. They came through this morning, around 9.30."

"Right." He could hear the frown in her voice. "And were they duplicates of the first one?"

"No, the next one said it was my first Hot Matches email, and the third one was from a lady called Susan, presumably the Susan that came up on the email before. She was asking me for a date."

"Oh, lucky you!" She chirruped. "She must be very keen, that's quick off the mark. She would only have got your details a few hours ago."

"But I haven't submitted my profile, have I! There shouldn't be any Hot Matches. I don't want to go on any dates!"

"No, no, I see." She was quiet for a moment. When she spoke again, the fluffy bunnies had seemingly bolted and he could actually envisage her as a human being. "But really, I don't see. Excuse me asking, but if you didn't want to go on dates, why did you register with a dating website?"

"It was, er, just a whim."

"It must have been a long-lasting whim, if you got all the way through the questionnaire."

Suddenly, he was on the back foot here. "Yes. Look, I did want to go, you know, on dates, meet someone. But it's just not a good time right now," he said lamely.

"It rarely is, is it?" He could hear the smile in her voice. "It's like these couples who wait for years to start a family. They always say they'll wait until they get a bigger house, or a bigger car, until they move to a better area, or they're better off, or until their Mum or Dad just gets over this illness..." she sighed. "And then one day they find they've run out of time. Or, the even crueller irony—this happened to friends of mine—they find out they couldn't have children in the first place. And they've left themselves precious little time to do anything about it."

Steve gulped, surprisingly moved by her anecdote. "I see what you mean, but—"

"It's funny, isn't it, but people usually seem to meet their partners at the most inconvenient points in their lives, and often in the most unexpected ways and places, too."

"Sometimes, yes, I guess."

Pause. He could tell she was deliberately leaving it to sink in for a minute. "Why don't you give it a try then?" she coaxed. "Just go on one date. It's not going to hurt, is it? You won't be engaged to her or anything! If there's a lot going on in your life, you can take things slowly. Although sometimes I think someone else in your life is exactly what you need when your life is, well, busy."

She was making sense, reluctant though he was to admit it. His mouth certainly thought so. "I suppose I could give it a go." Have you finally lost it?

"That's the spirit!"

Oh Lord, thought Steve, the bloody bunnies are going to trample me now. Look at them, running down the hill towards me.

"So I'll leave your profile status as live, then, shall I?"

"You might as well—hey, hold on. I mean, thanks for the pep talk – I see your point and it was very good, by the way—"

"Thanks!"

"—but we're no nearer to working out how you got hold of my completed profile. If it is mine, because I can't see for the life of me how that's possible."

"It does seem odd."

"Perhaps my details have got mixed up with someone else's, and if they have, my Hot Matches might not be all that hot, if you see what I mean."

"Good point. I'd better check."

"Please."

"What's your username?"

He cleared his throat. "Er, Stevie Blue Eyes. It's a joke." Cringe.

"Is it?" she said vaguely. He could hear her tapping the keyboard.

Steve plunged on, feeling the need to justify himself. "Yes, you know, like the Hugh Grant film—'Mickey Blue Eyes'? My mum was half-Sicilian and when that film came out, she thought it was hilarious. She started to call me Stevie Blue Eyes, you know, she did the accent and everything."

"What accent?"

He sighed. "You haven't seen Mickey Blue Eyes?"

"No, I don't think so."

"Never mind."

"Let's see... yes, the profile's under your username. Steve Reynolds, age 29, Capricorn..." She read out the whole thing, on Steve's insistence. Partly because he couldn't believe that what Nicola had in front of her really was his profile—how could it be? And partly because, once he knew that all the basic details were correct, he still needed to know that the rest were—if even a tiny part had been altered, he wanted to know. Otherwise, God knows who he might end up with. It was a hugely embarrassing experience, but by the end of it, one thing was for sure. It was his profile.

"Which still beggars the question—if you'll pardon my French—how the hell did you get my profile?"

"That's still a mystery, I'm afraid. All I can tell you from this end is that it went on the system yesterday afternoon. Perhaps it was a good Samaritan?"

"What?"

"Maybe someone else sent it in for you. Someone who thought you needed some love in your life."

"Interesting theory, but nobody else has access to my... oh, bugger. Oh, sorry."

"You've thought of someone?"

"Yes, and I'm going to kill her."

"I'm sure whoever it was only had your best interests at heart!"

Bless her and her bunnies, thought Steve. It must be good to live in Nicola world. "Hmm."

"At least that's your mystery solved. Now, if that's all then, Mr. Reynolds, I'm sorry, but I need to lock up the office."

He looked at his watch. 6.05pm. "God, I'm so sorry! I didn't mean to keep you that long."

"No problem, that's what I'm here for. Good luck with your date!"

"Thanks. Bye."

It must have been Laura, although he doubted her motives had been quite as altruistic as Nicola believed. He started setting up a separate user name on the laptop to password protect all his stuff. Why hadn't he done it before?

Of course, if Laura had discovered that document and filled in his profile, that meant that at some time yesterday, she'd been back to the house – and stayed some considerable time. He wondered what else she'd got up to while she was there. What other nasty surprises he might have in store?

Chapter Twelve

"Morning, Rebecca Maynard speaking."

"Ms. Maynard, it's Marcie King."

Ooh, subtle. Don't stoop to using my first name. Fine, if that's the way you want to play it Marcie, but I'm not calling you Ms. "Good morning, Miss. King. What can I do for you?"

"Nothing, thank you," said Marcie crisply. "I was asked to phone you in order to arrange a mutually convenient time to meet the head of the surveying team."

"Yes, Simon said he wanted a meeting this week." Rebecca hoped she sounded breezy, because that's what she was going for.

"If that is Mr. Holland, then yes." Marcie's tone would give a penguin the chills, thought Rebecca.

"Oh sorry, do you not know Simon? I thought everybody did. We go back quite a way. Very easy to work with." That was unworthy of you Rebecca.

"Yes, you seem to go back quite a way with everybody. I'm sure that's very useful."

Bitch! Rebecca seethed. "Well I always find it useful, and more pleasant, to build up good working relationships with people when I can. People skills are just as important in archaeology as technical skills, I find."

"Doubtless that's why you've had fewer papers published than many of your peers," said Marcie smoothly. "You've put your energies into other areas."

"Precisely. It's far more important to me to lead good digs and develop the skills and success of my team, rather than garner personal glory." Rebecca treated the phone to a razor-sharp sarcastic smile down the phone, wishing Marcie could see it. Marcie was obsessed with getting her name, preferably on its own, on to as many news items and publications as possible.

There was a silence. "Yes, obviously those things are important. But we seem to have deviated from the purpose of this call. Do you have time for a meeting with Simon in the next two days?" Marcie snapped. "Or are you too busy developing your team?"

Rebecca decided to let that one go. "Let me just check my schedule." She rustled some papers on her desk and hit a few random keys on her laptop, muttering about fictitious tasks under her breath. "I'm afraid I can't do the next two days, not on this short notice."

"Are you sure? I can't do the end of the week. I have to go to Luxembourg for a few days."

"Now that is unfortunate," said Rebecca, exulting inside. "I'll ring Simon, and ask if it's okay with him if he sees us separately. He can tell me what you two discussed when I meet up with him, and then between us we can make the final plans."

"I thought we were all to be involved in the final planning," said Marcie, a note of panic creeping in under the anger. "It's hardly appropriate to have two separate meetings."

"Well as that's impossible, we will just have to work around it," said Rebecca brightly.

www.penrose-publishing.co.uk

"I'm sure it won't be a problem. We're all adults."

Silence again.

"Very well. I'll ring Mr. Holland now, and see it that meets with his approval."

"Great. Thanks, Marcie. Give Simon my love, will you?"

There was no proper reply, just a barely growled "goodbye," and the resounding thump of the phone being slapped down.

Rebecca didn't feel great about herself when she put the phone down. Granted, it was unusual for her to start the sly digs first; Marcie normally had her, metaphorically, by the throat in the first minute of any conversation. And granted, Marcie usually said things far worse than anything Rebecca would ever say, many of them not-so-thinly-veiled threats. She made no secret of her hatred for Rebecca, only pretending a borderline civility towards her when absolutely necessary.

But two wrongs didn't make a right, and Rebecca hadn't meant to inflame the situation. When she heard Marcie's voice, though, and knew this was the start of what she'd been dreading for days, the compulsion to lash out before she was attacked was overwhelming.

How was she going to work with her? If this was what a brief phone call was like, how the hell would they get on once they were both on the same dig site?

She found out soon enough. Over the next fortnight Marcie took every opportunity to contradict her and twist everything she said, especially when relaying it to someone else. She stirred up trouble wherever she could and Rebecca's stress levels went up on a daily basis.

Kevin thought she should let Marcie have more control and defer more to her opinion.

"Working for you makes her feel belittled and undermined. Don't forget she's used to leading projects herself. It can't be easy for her, having to follow orders from someone she hates."

"Oh, thanks!"

"You know what I mean. Go on, try it. Give her some responsibility. What have you got to lose? Either things will improve, or you'll have given her enough rope to hang herself."

Rebecca took his advice. Later on that week she told Marcie that she wouldn't be around the next day. "Two new trenches need to be placed, marked out and started tomorrow, but I know I can leave that in your capable hands."

"Yes of course."

"I should be around the day after to give some practical help, so you can tell me what you'd like me to do then."

"That's a good idea, since it's a situation we'll have to get used to."

Rebecca frowned. "Pardon?"

"There are some changes afoot at GLAM," said Marcie. "They'll affect the leadership and the middle management. I'm sure you'll hear about them shortly, but it's on a need to know basis. But based on what I know, the boot will be on the other foot very soon. Learning to follow my instructions will come in very useful to you."

Rebecca walked away without answering, and tried to put it out of her head. Marcie must be lying, it was just another ploy to put Rebecca he back foot. If there was some kind of leadership vacancy coming up at GLAM, and Marcie was in line for it, she would have heard.

Wouldn't she?

Steve slowed as he got to the restaurant. He'd never been here before. Was the tie too much? He was early, so he could always take it off if he got inside and everyone else was in jeans and t-shirts.

He scanned the restaurant as he went in and saw a few men without ties, but no jeans in sight. He'd got it right then, which was lucky because a woman with long dark hair was casually raising a hand. Susan was already here. He headed towards her but a waiter intercepted him.

"Have you booked a table?"

"No, I, er..." he felt flustered with Susan's eyes on him. "I'm joining the young lady over there."

"I see. Shall I bring the wine list over?"

"Could you give us a minute?"

The waiter's eyes narrowed. "We are quite busy this evening, sir. Do you mean literally a minute, or did you want me to wait longer? You only have the table until 9.15."

"A few minutes will be fine," said Steve abruptly. The prices here certainly didn't include service with a smile, he thought.

Susan was looking away as he came up to the table. Probably expecting me to get caught up with the waiter, Steve thought. She'd chosen a table in a little alcove with orange leather bench seats.

Steve smiled. "Susan?"

She glanced up, with just the hint of a smile. Maybe she was shy. "Hi."

Steve sat down and slid around the curved seat until he was a little closer, but not too close. The walls of the alcove were high and he felt smothered. This wasn't the table he'd have chosen—you couldn't see much of the restaurant and it felt a little too intimate for a blind date.

"Have you ordered a drink?"

"No, not been here long. Thought I'd wait for you." Her eyes were fixed on a point over his shoulder.

Steve turned but could see nothing. When he looked back, she was looking at her mobile.

"Right. Shall I order us a drink from the bar?"

She shrugged, not lifting her eyes. "If you want, but the waiter will bring the wine list."

Steve was wishing he'd let that waiter follow him with the wine list after all. At least they'd have something to talk about. His tongue was paralysed and his brain wasn't far behind. Ask her about herself then, moron. Let her do the talking.

"So which bank do you work for?"

"I don't, now."

"Oh. Should I say 'sorry to hear that', or 'congratulations'?"

She shrugged. "I wasn't fired." She put her phone away in her bag.

"Ah. You decided to leave?"

She nodded.

"Right. I suppose it's congratulations, then." He smiled. "Where's your new job?"

She shrugged again. "Haven't got one."

"Oh, so you're looking for something?"

"Not really."

Steve's nails dug into his palms. This is real blood from a stone stuff, he thought grimly. I'm all for using body language but speaking is good too. Preferably with the odd full sentence thrown in.

"Are you planning to travel? Or perhaps work for yourself?"

"Dunno." She shrugged, gazing past him.

Steve twitched. If she shrugs once more I'll stick her shoulders to the chair with duct tape. That would probably snap her in half though, her arms were stick thin. She hadn't looked that skinny in her picture and all the black clothing didn't help. He groped round for an appropriate response.

"Oh. I'm sure you'll find something to keep you busy."

She nodded and blew a huge bubblegum bubble.

Steve stared at her in horror, which wasn't a problem because she was looking anywhere but at him. He wished they had agreed on lunch at a café. It could have been over and done within an hour.

She shifted on her seat. "I'm hungry."

"I'll get a menu," said Steve hurriedly, raising his hand and trying to catch the eye of the waiter who'd just emerged from the kitchen. How quickly would she eat? He wondered if this potentially three course nightmare could modified into just a main meal, preferably from the 'lighter selection', if this restaurant had such a thing. If he said he wasn't hungry and didn't know if he could manage a starter, would she follow suit out of politeness? It had to be worth a shot.

The waiter slid up to the table. Oh great. It was the one who had accosted him. "Is sir ready for the wine list now? Or appetisers? Or both?"

Oh God! There were appetisers! "The wine list, please, I don't think we want app—"

"Both please," said Susan, with alacrity, coming out of her stupor briefly to smile. Even as the waiter turned, she sank back against the seat and got her phone out again.

Steve cleared his throat and tried again.

"So Susan, what kind of books do you like to read?"

"Don't read, usually." Her eyes were fixed on her phone screen. She appeared to be playing a game.

"What, not at all?" He tried to turn the shocked tone into a teasing one, mid-sentence.

"Read a Jodie Forrest novel last month. Crap though." She blew another bubble.

Steve put his head in his hands. It was going to be a long night.

Why was the alarm going off? He hadn't set it because after last night, he needed a lie-in. Susan had been a nightmare, only showing signs of life when the food appeared—including all the side dishes she'd ordered with each of the three courses that followed the appetisers.

She'd eaten every mouthful of food and hadn't spoken to Steve other than to answer his increasingly sparse questions with monosyllables, grunts and shrugs. She hadn't offered to go halves on the horrendous bill, and when he'd commented how expensive it was and looked at her meaningfully, she'd revealed she only had enough money for the cab fare home.

He reached out a hand towards his alarm clock, but then his sleep-fogged brain worked out the ringing was from the phone. He struggled upright.

"Hello?"

"Hi, bruv." Laura's voice sounded high and strained.

"Laura? I've been worried sick, why didn't you call?"

"Sorry. Don't worry, I'm safe."

"Good. Where are you? I've been looking everywhere."

"I know. I heard."

Steve gritted his teeth. So some of her friends he'd contacted had known exactly where she was. Now she was safe, he felt the anger kick in.

"The police have been looking for you too. But not as a missing person," he said coldly.

There was a short silence. "I know. They found me."

"They—Laura, what's happening?"

"They've arrested me, Steve," she said, her voice quivering. "I don't think it will b-be just a s-slap on the wrist." She disintegrated into sobs.

"What have they arrested you for?"

"Possession." Silence. "And mugging," she finished, barely loud enough for Steve to catch.

He sat bolt upright. "Mugging? You MUGGED someone? Bloody hell, Laura!"

"I know it was stupid—"

"STUPID? That's all? Why, because you got caught?" Steve was on his feet, pacing, his unoccupied hand clenched by his side.

"No, I know it was wrong, too. I wasn't thinking straight—"

"Oh and I wonder why THAT was!"

"I was with this guy, but he ran—"

"I'm coming down there." He grabbed his jeans and started to pull them on, hunching his shoulder to hold the phone against his ear.

"No! Steve, please don't—"

"Course I bloody well am, Laura. I'm legally in charge of you—"

"You're not any more. I'm nineteen, remember?" He could tell she was gulping back tears.

"I need to know you're alright."

"I am. Don't come today. Please! B-but can you come tomorrow? I really want you there."

"What's happening tomorrow?"

"I'm in court." he voice was flat now, although she'd run out of tears. "To see if they'll grant me bail."

Steve drew in a slow breath. He hadn't thought that far.

"Bail?" His voice dropped as anger gave way to a grim disbelief. He shook his head as though that would make this nightmare go away. "Jesus Christ, Laura…"

"Hold on." He could hear her speak to someone else, then she was back. "I have to go. The officer wants to talk to you about tomorrow."

"Right… I'll see you tomorrow. Take care of yourself. You know where I am if you need me."

"Bye."

Even after he'd been given the facts, but it all seemed unreal, a blur, as though it was someone else discussing Laura and her court appearance with the police officer in that calm, matter-of-fact voice. Afterwards he walked downstairs, still bare-chested, and poured himself a whisky. Good job Laura isn't here, he thought with some irony. A fine example I'm setting at ten in the morning.

Life seemed to be running in slow motion. He drained the glass and took it to the kitchen to rinse out, then remembered there was something more urgent to do. He grabbed the handset mounted by the kitchen door. Punched in a familiar number.

Waited, rigid, until a voice answered.

"Tony, it's Steve. Sorry, but I won't be in tomorrow." He knew he sounded curt and unapologetic. But his throat was tight and his mouth felt dry, even after the whisky. It was an effort to form a sentence, use the niceties.

He steeled himself to answer the inevitable questions, walking back into the lounge with his glass. It would have been a waste to rinse it, because it was easier to answer Tony with a little help. He poured his second whisky of the morning.

Chapter Thirteen

"Hi Tony."

He nodded. "Rebecca. What would you like?"

"Butterscotch latte, please."

He gave a small smile. "You like the butterscotch, eh? Is very popular. Steve made good decision to buy it." He busied himself at the coffee machine.

Rebecca fidgeted. "Talking of Steve, where is he today then? Don't tell me you've let him have a day off." She hoped she sounded casual.

"Yes. He had day off."

"Oh? Is he going somewhere nice?"

"I couldn't say. What he does when he is not here, it is his business," replied Tony curtly.

Rebecca flushed. "I didn't mean to pry. I thought you two were friends." She slapped some coins down on the counter and grabbed her tray, spilling some of her coffee.

"Rebecca!"

She turned.

"Sorry. I am being rude. It's just, I worry about him." He said quietly.

"Why?" She leaned against the counter again.

"Because he risk everything for that ungrateful bitch!" he snapped suddenly, throwing his hands up in the air.

Rebecca flinched.

"Sorry. But I see him, wasting his life, he's getting her out of trouble again and again. He is always there for her, but who is there for him, eh? Laura, she will not change. He's given her more last chances than she deserve."

"Why doesn't he leave her?"

He shrugged. "Because still, he feels responsible for her. A hard habit to break, I suppose, after all the years."

Rebecca frowned. "All the years? She only looks twenty."

"She is nineteen."

"Well he can't have been with her that long—what were they, childhood sweethearts? How old was she when they married?"

"What?" Tony started at her. "No, I talk about Laura. His sister. Steve is not married! If he is, is big secret he keeps from me."

"His sister," she said faintly. Cogs whirred in her brain. "So how come he's been responsible for her for years? What about his parents?"

"Very sad story." Steve shook his head. "Both are dead. Steve, he is only young when his father die and make them both orphans, and the government want Laura to be—" he frowned "fostered? That is right? But Steve fights and he signs papers, becomes – how you say – legal guardian?" He sighed. "Is big responsibility."

Rebecca was about to ask more, but a family came up beside her to order coffees and milkshakes. She took her coffee over to her usual table and stirred it for a long time, lost in thought.

Rebecca had read real-life internet dating stories and knew, not surprisingly, that most people who had found their perfect partner had lots of dates before they struck lucky. So why was she on the verge of giving up after two? And why was the prospect of a third date, with yet another man, too depressing for words?

She suspected some of her feelings were to do with discovering that Steve was single. Even so, Laura was still a big part of his life; Kevin's warning about getting involved in what was obviously a messy situation was still valid, and she's been adamant that she wasn't getting herself involved with men with complicated lives. She wanted to keep things simple. If only Steve wasn't so darn attractive. Or so funny. Or such a good listener. If only he didn't have that devastating smile that made her... well never mind. Argh!

Anyway, she could never decide if he was attracted to her or not. The signals were too confusing. At the moment, it would be wise to keep her distance, and wise to make use of the dating website. But her first two experiences hadn't filled her with confidence.

Still, in for a penny, in for a pound, she told herself firmly. Okay, no.2 hadn't been suitable, but at least he hadn't been creepy. Perhaps this time she should look at her hot matches and do the picking herself. Third time lucky.

You have 3 new Hot Matches!' said yesterday's email. Underneath were three sample pictures of suspiciously good-looking people, with a big blue question mark on them; Rebecca doubted any of them had ever been Methodical Matches clients.

She clicked the link and logged in. Stewart, Peter and Malcolm appeared. She didn't like the look of Malcolm; instant reject. Stewart and Peter were both reasonably good-looking and neither looked creepy. So which should she tackle first? She giggled. That sounded like she was bracing herself to climb a mountain, not deciding who to date. Wasn't this meant to be fun?

She clicked on Stewart. He was a 39 year old accountant who ran marathons, apparently. Peter was a fund-raising co-ordinator who belonged to a local history group and he was 34. There was nothing wrong with either of them, but she had to pick one—and Stewart, although undoubtedly fit in both senses of the word, was right at the upper age limit she'd set. If she met someone, liked them, and then found out they were 10 years older, no problem; but a large age gap wouldn't be her first choice. Peter was interested in history, so that would be a good starting point for a conversation; and if he was a fundraising co-ordinator, he must be socially aware and caring. Mustn't he?

"Don't be so naive," she muttered to herself. Still, there was only one way to find out. She clicked on 'Send a message to Peter.' What should she write? What had John and Derek's messages said? After dithering for a bit, she finally wrote: "Hi Peter, I noticed you on my Hot Matches list. Would you like to meet for a coffee?" Short and simple. That would do.

She spent another hour on the computer, surfing archaeology websites and playing a word game, then checked her inbox. Nothing yet, but hey, Peter had a life to live—hopefully. She didn't want to date someone who spent all their life on their computer. After vacuuming the whole flat, she relaxed in a deep bubble bath and then lounged in front of the TV in her PJs with a glass of wine. Not the most glamorous Friday night, she thought, but now she felt virtuous and relaxed. So relaxed that she fell asleep, waking after midnight in front of what looked like a very old horror film, and dragging herself groggily to bed.

She didn't get an answer from Peter until early Sunday morning. "Yes, meeting for coffee would be good. When are you free?"

"Not until next weekend," she typed. Then, after some thought, she added, "I am free today if it's not too short notice?"

"Sorry, I have church at 10.30. What about next Saturday?"

Church? Okay... how had that happened? She had said she had no religious affiliation, but on the other hand, she hadn't precluded dating someone who had. There was a tick box for that and she'd left it blank. Perhaps the computer, in its wisdom, had decided religious differences weren't an issue. That was fine, providing Peter didn't object to her lack of faith or try to convert her. It made her a little uncomfortable though.

"Next Saturday's fine. 10.30? Where would you like to go?!"

"Do you know Vincenzo's, near the Meredith & Partners on Parson Street? They do coffees, soft drinks and smoothies as well. I was going to suggest a wine bar instead, but I don't want you to think I'm a raging alcoholic!"

Wow. Good taste and a sense of humour. Vincenzo's was lovely, if a bit out of her usual area. The atmosphere was sophisticated but friendly. Not so upper crust that you couldn't pop in at the weekend in smart jeans, but not so lowly as to allow grinning idiots in Hawaiian shorts or girls in fluorescent boob tubes, either.

"Yes, I've been there a couple of times before. Look forward to seeing you there."

So that was it. Date no.3. And nearly a whole week to wait and worry about it.

She needn't have worried. They had a great time. As she suspected, Peter did have a good sense of humour. He liked some of the same music, he tried three different coffees without having a panic attack, and he was enthusiastic but not obsessed with studying the origin of place names. He knew a lot about it – far more than she did – and he talked about it in an entertaining and witty way. Rebecca was fascinated and they talked for hours. They mutually agreed, without a second thought, to extend their date into lunch and walked to a nearby Indian restaurant that did a lunchtime buffet.

When they said goodbye, Rebecca was left with an invitation to accompany Peter in a month's time to a talk on how historic industries influenced place names and surnames, and the warm, cosy certainty that she'd made a good friend.

And that was all she'd made, because Peter, bless him, hadn't taken long to tell her in his light-hearted but direct way that he thought she was a lovely, interesting person, and would be delighted to be her friend, but his faith was a fundamental part of his life. He only wanted to date people whom he could share that with, which was completely fine with Rebecca and was also, surprise surprise, what he had stated on his Methodical Matches profile.

At least it wasn't a total loss, she thought, as she made her way home. The only thing that was a total loss here was the dating agency. That was one friendship that was definitely over.

Rebecca glared and Nicola shrivelled behind her stainless steel and glass desk. She was probably wishing she was behind one of those bank style reception desks, thought Rebecca, the tall ones where the receptionist was only visible through a small gap. And that was quite a wise thing to wish, because Rebecca, who liked to think of herself as relatively calm and reasonable, was sorely tempted to reach over and wring the bimbo's toasted-on-a-tanning-bed neck.

"It would have been better," she continued, "if I'd wandered out into the street blindfolded, spun around a few times, then grabbed the next three people I laid my hands on. They would have probably have been a better matches. Even if one of them was a dog!" She threw up her hands dramatically. Even if one of them was a dog? You're overdoing it, girl that just sounded daft.

"How you can have the nerve to call your company—and let's be honest, it is your company, isn't it, Nicola? There are no other staff, you're the be all and end all—Methodical Matches, is beyond me. It's about as methodical as a lobotomised hamster on acid."

To Nicola's credit, she attempted to talk to her. "So what I'm hearing is, that you've had three dates but not found Mr. Right?" she said, the quiver in her voice belying the desperate cheerfulness of its tone.

"I'm not complaining because I haven't found Mr. Right within three dates. That would be naive in the extreme. But what I didn't expect was three men that I didn't want to spend two hours with, let alone want to see again!

"So number three wasn't any better?"

"No. Nice enough man, but he's a born again Christian who, surprise, surprise, is looking for another Christian to spend his life with. It seems a reasonable enough request, particularly as he made it very clear in his profile."

"I appreciate there have been problems with our computer-aided matching—"

"If this is a result of using science, I think I'll take the opposite approach and just pick someone from the phonebook."

"We are trying our best to resolve the technical problems."

"That's what you said last time. And please don't keep saying 'we' and 'our'. You're not fooling anybody.

Nicola had gone very pale under the tan, but her expression didn't change. She really could be a Barbie doll, thought Rebecca.

"We want our customers to be satisfied with our service, so I can offer you another three months membership free of charge."

"Why on earth would I want to prolong my membership?"

"Naturally, it's up to you if you wish to deactivate your profile," said Nicola. "But your membership will still be valid until the new expiry date, if you change your mind. As I say, we are working hard to make improvements."

"Glad to hear it. But yes, I'd like to deactivate my profile, please."

Nicola tapped away on her laptop for a minute or so.

"There. That's all done for you."

"Thank you." Rebecca marched out. What did computers know about her perfect partner? If she ended up being a batty old spinster, so be it. She was never trying internet dating again.

Chapter Fourteen

"Another busman's holiday?" Steve looked up from his book and instantly wished he'd put a decent shirt on before he came out. Rebecca was smiling down at him and looked, as usual, gorgeous.

"Yeah, I know." He smiled. Great. Now she would think he was really sad. "See? I really can't stay away from the place."

"You must really love it, to choose to spend your Friday night here."

"Says the girl who's at a modest café on Friday night." He wondered where Kevin was but didn't want to ask.

"Fair cop. Although I could be here to meet Tom Cruise, for all you know."

"No. I know you're impressed with his bottle-juggling skills, but he's too short for you."

"True. Cute, though." She fished in her handbag for her purse. "Anyway I'm dying of thirst, and Tom doesn't seem to have made it, so I'm off to drown my sorrows by myself."

"If you fancy some company, I can draw up another chair," he said, hoping he sounded far more suave and sophisticated than he felt. He held his book up. "This is your only competition."

She looked at the cover, then shook her head. "I was going to say pull me up a chair, but I'm not sure I can compete with that."

"Ooh, sarcasm." Good move. Your status as a complete loser, in her eyes, is assured. Young single man alone, reading a book, once again spending his Friday night at the café where he works.

"Nope." She shook her head emphatically. "Not sarcasm. I love Jodie Forrest. Got them all. Grab me a chair. Do you want anything?"

Just you, he thought, but unfortunately you're not on the menu. "No thanks, I'm fine."

"Ok."

Rebecca wasn't at the counter long—it was quiet this evening—but it was long enough for him to get nervous. Why had he taken it into his head to ask her to join him? She must know all about Laura by now, which was enough to put any woman off, and nothing changed the fact that she was attached. Normally he would have had the sense –and the decency – to back off long before now.

He looked over at her, in slim fitting black jeans, neat black boots with a small heel and a bright, checked shirt, seeing her smile at Tony and hearing her laugh ring out. He would give a lot to be the person who got to hear that laugh every day. She was nearly finished at the counter so he quickly pretended to be reading his book again, although in reality he was aware of every step she took towards him, watching her from the corner of his eye.

"Mind your book!"

Steve hastily shut it, sliding it into the pocket of his jacket that hung on his chair. Rebecca plonked the tray down without ceremony, and started to transfer everything to the table.

He looked at her latte. "Don't tell me. Butterscotch."

"Oh dear, oh dear. Very poor show. You'll be getting the sack."

He bent forward and sniffed. "Ah. Hazelnut. Didn't know you liked that, I thought that was normally Kevin's—" shut up, Steve! Shut up, shut up, SHUT UP! "...choice," he trailed off.

Rebecca didn't seem to notice, busy unloading the tray. "It is, but I fancied something different. Sometimes butterscotch seems wrong for this time of day, unless I'm really cold – or really fed up! Too sweet, somehow. Don't tell me, I know. I'm weird."

"No, I know what you mean. I never have mocha in the morning. I always wait for lunchtime. Mornings are for cappuccinos."

"Exactly." She took the empty tray and put it on the rack nearby.

Steve looked at the items she'd spread out on the table. "Hungry?" he asked, quirking an eyebrow in amusement.

She pretended to glare and thrust a Southern Fried Chicken Wrap with Salad at him. "This is dinner, pal. I'm ravenous." She ripped open the end of the packet.

"I'll let you off then."

"And these—" she waved her hand at two Apricot Danish pastries—are not both for me. One of them's for you."

"Thanks. You shouldn't have, I've already eaten—"

"No problem." She took a big bite of wrap and swallowed it with relish. "It's not kind of me really, it's selfish. I couldn't stuff my face while you just sit here. Think of the guilt! And I know they're your favourite."

"How?"

"A little bird told me."

"Was this little bird about five foot six, measuring nearly the same round the waist, by any chance?"

"Could be. I didn't measure his waist," she said, her eyes twinkling as she picked up the second half of her wrap. "But I think he said his name was Tony."

"There you go then. Proves what I've always said."

"What have you always said?"

"You can't trust birds to keep your secrets."

She giggled. Pushing her plate to one side, she picked up her coffee and took a long drink, sighing in appreciation. "I so need this."

"Dangerous phrase. Saying 'need' smacks of addiction, you know," Steve said solemnly, then cringed. Funny how innocent jokes could be so unfunny in the right circumstances.

But soon he began to relax for the first time in days as Rebecca chatted about her day. She was such good company. So easy to be with. He could happily sit here all weekend with her, given the chance. But he didn't think that was a chance he'd ever get.

"Are you not going to eat your pastry? Please don't tell me you're on a diet," she said, her tone leaving him in no doubt of how she felt about that.

"No, why, do you think I need to be?" he stared at her, mock-affronted.

"Good Lord no. You're not fat! But then you're not too skinny, either. You're just right," she said, laughing. Then she seemed to realise what she'd said and blushed to the roots of her hair.

There was an awkward silence which Steve tried to break quickly, but failed to, his throat suddenly dry. If he didn't know better he would think she was interested in him.

"Good," he managed to croak eventually, "because I was only waiting for you to finish your main course. Just good manners, don't you know."

"Ah, your mother taught you well."

"I'm afraid she can't claim all the credit for that," he said quietly. She died when I was 9."

Rebecca put her coffee down. "Wow. I really am an idiot," she said. "That was a completely insensitive thing to say."

He smiled awkwardly. "What, because I have Laura to advertise my complete ineptitude at being a surrogate parent?"

"Nobody in their right mind would put the blame for that on you," she said, looking stricken. "I can't imagine how tough it must have been, bringing her up alone, especially when you were so young yourself."

"It was. Very tough. Doesn't change the fact that I didn't do a very good job though." He couldn't look at her, and his throat was so tight that for a minute he couldn't say anything.

"Lots of children have two sensible, mature parents who try their best, yet they still go off the rails." Rebecca sat there, looking at a loss for what to say next.

Well done Steve, this is going swimmingly. Now she feels guilty and uncomfortable and you sound bitter and twisted. He blinked hard, cleared his throat and raised a smile. "Sorry. Boy, I bet you're glad you accepted my invitation now, aren't you. I've cheered up your evening no end."

"No, it's fine, it's my fault. It was a thoughtless thing to say."

"It was a perfectly normal, off-the-cuff comment," said Steve. "Now please start on that pastry and then I can start on mine. It's calling to me."

"Okay. Sorry." She picked up her Danish and dutifully took a big bite.

"I think we need to ban that word," said Steve, picking up his too, "or we're going to spend all our time apologising."

She nodded, mouth full, and they at the rest of their pastries in a companionable silence. Rebecca wiped her hands on a serviette.

"Would it be awful of me to ask what happened to your father?"

"No. But I'd rather not go into details, if that's alright. He died ten years after my mother."

"So you were 19?"

He nodded. "I hadn't been at university very long."

"Which one?"

"Southampton. I took Architectural Technology."

"Ouch. Try saying that when you're drunk."

He smiled. "I did. Several times."

"Did you get your degree?"

He shook his head. "No, otherwise I wouldn't be working here. I'd already been working at MacDonald's quite a while to help me get through uni."

"Oh yeah." Rebecca nodded emphatically. "Been there, done that."

"So has nearly everyone I know!" He fiddled with the pastry crumbs on his plate. "After Dad died and everything was sorted, I begged all the hours I could and dropped out of uni. A few months later they gave me a full time job. I worked my way up and became a manager eventually."

"So that you could support Laura?"

He nodded. "Yes. The mortgage was paid when Dad died, but there wasn't any money for anything else. He only had enough life insurance to pay for funeral expenses, and he had a few debts. He'd been ill for a long time."

"It must have been hard, giving up your degree."

"It was. I was really enjoying the course."

"So how did you end up here?"

"I'd managed to build up some money and I wanted to go back to studying—either distance learning, so I could keep an eye on Laura and work, too, or else doing architecture at UCL. Stay closer to home. I wanted something closer to home, with hours that were a bit more regular, too, because Laura was starting to..." He hesitated.

"Go off the rails?" she said gently.

"Yes."

"And you like it here?"

"Actually I love it. Tony's been so good to me. It's a good place to work, and-," be bold, Steve, "—you get to meet some really nice people."

She met his gaze. "I hope that includes me."

"Definitely." Steve's heart seemed to be thudding very loudly in his chest. He let his eyes linger on hers for a moment. It was no good. He had to broach the subject.

"So where's Kevin tonight?"

She grinned. "D & D, would you believe?"

"D&D?" He frowned. "Am I meant to know what that is?"

"Dungeons and Dragons."

"Ah. Got it. He's into that, then, is he?"

"Madly. He loves his RPG. D&D every Friday. Every Friday."

"I take it you don't share his enthusiasm."

She shuddered. "Wild horses wouldn't drag me there. I can't think of anything worse."

"You don't have shared hobbies, then?"

"Oh we do. We like a lot of the same music, so we nearly always go to gigs together. He hates Robbie Williams though, so I have to drag my friend Anna out instead," she laughed. "Not that she minds. She takes a supply of lacy knickers with her."

Steve's eyebrows shot up, momentarily distracted from worrying about her relationship with Kevin. "Really?"

"Really. Five pairs, last time, in her jacket pocket."

"How old is she?"

"38."

"Blimey." Steve whistled. "It must be true what they say about women in their late thirties."

"I wouldn't know," she said with a wicked grin. "When I get there, I'll let you know."

I'd rather be around to find out for myself, thought Steve, starting to feel rather hot under the collar. That cheeky smile of hers was killing him. This conversation wasn't helping him keep a friendly distance. He found her presence more disturbing than ever—in the most pleasurable way but dangerous way.

"So have you got any plans for the weekend?" he asked, trying to steer the conversation into safer waters.

"Shopping tomorrow morning—Kev and I have got an engagement party to go to tomorrow evening, so we'll be combing the streets of London for a decent gift."

Gloom settled over Steve. Whatever signals he thought he was getting, they must be wishful thinking. Shopping together sounded a very couple thing to do.

"Who's getting engaged? A friend?" he asked, trying to keep the disappointment out of his voice. Bang went his plan to hint at a possible lunch date, to see how she reacted.

"Anna."

"Anna? Anna throws-lots-of-knockers-at-Robbie Anna?"

"Yep, that's the one."

"Does her boyfriend know? Or doesn't he care?"

"She hasn't got a boyfriend." Rebecca's eyes danced with mischief.

"What?"

"She's getting engaged to her girlfriend."

"I... see," said Steve slowly. "Actually, no I don't. The knicker-throwing...?"

"To put it in the vernacular," said Rebecca, laughing, "she bats for both sides. But mainly, very mainly, for her own. Robbie's a bit of an exception, really. Him and Daniel Craig, for some reason."

"So she just doesn't date real men?"

"Well she's dated a couple, but—"

Steve put a hand up. "Sorry, I don't know why I asked that. It's really none of my business."

"That's alright. She wouldn't mind! She's always been very open about her sexuality. I find most people are, these days. They make a lovely couple—they're so happy together." She got out her phone, swiped the screen a couple of times with her thumb and then turned it towards him.

Steve looked at the picture. Both women were beautiful; pictured hand in hand on a beach, tanned and relaxed in long, bright summer dresses, wearing big smiles. Rebecca leaned close to him and Steve caught the scent of her perfume. He tried hard to focus as she pointed to the woman on the left, with long, wavy blonde hair.

"That's Anna. The dark-haired one is Jessica."

"They're stunners."

"Aren't they. Sickening." She twisted to put her phone away, and Steve felt emboldened by her turned back.

"You've no need to be envious, have you. You're hardly a wallflower yourself." Oh God. He could feel himself going red.

She turned round quickly. "You're going to make me blush."

Not nearly so much as I am, he thought, trying to look casual as he tidied up his sugar sachets and avoided her eyes.

"Thanks."

"My pleasure," he said quietly.

There was a pause. "So what are your plans for tomorrow?"

He sighed. "I'll be visiting Laura."

"She's not back living with you then?"

"Hopefully she will be. She's in a secure drug rehab unit at the moment."

"Oh." Rebecca squirmed. "God, I'm sorry. I didn't know. I seem to be making a great job of putting my foot in it this evening."

"Don't worry, you weren't to know." He smiled at her. This bit's the easy bit in a way.

It's what happens next that I'm dreading."

"What's that?"

"When she comes out, her bail conditions mean she has to spend two weeks under the supervision of a named person, whom the court approves, at all times. I can cover most of it if I use my annual leave, but Tony has to go into hospital for some tests. With Neil gone, that leaves me and Rinaldo." He shrugged.

"Can't you ask someone else to supervise her?"

"The police can authorise someone else—it doesn't have to be just me—but who else can I ask? Anyone else has to have a valid CRB check. I haven't exactly got a huge social circle, and everyone I know works. It's a huge ask, even if you're really close to someone. They'd have to come to a meeting before she gets out, have their ID checked..." He shook his head. "And she seems a lot better, but I can't guarantee she won't flip out."

"Poor you." Her eyes were full of sympathy. "That must be really worrying. Have you spoken to Tony about it?"

He shook his head. "Not in any detail, not yet. I was hoping I could figure something out."

"Let's hope something turns up."

"Yes, let's. Anyway," he said, trying to muster a smile and turn the conversation, "I think I can guarantee your Saturday will be fun. Don't do anything too wild."

"Well I hope yours isn't too bad, I really do," she said putting her hand on his for a moment. "I won't be having too wild a time. We're going for dinner at Kevin's parents on Sunday, and that makes it my job to keep us both sober. Relatively sober, anyway."

Dinner with Kevin's parents? This was the end of any doubts he had. They were obviously a couple, and she was just one of those open, friendly women to whom a little low-level flirting comes naturally, as part and parcel of their character. Rebecca probably wasn't even aware of the effect she was having. Thank God he hadn't read anything into it.

Yeah right, Steve. You read quite a lot into it. You'd have liked to read the whole damn book, given half a chance.

"Sounds like fun," he said dully.

"Well Kevin's Dad cooks a mean roast and his mum is the queen of puddings. Rumour is she's making a very alcoholic zabaglione, so chances are we might end up more sloshed on Sunday than Saturday!" She grinned. "And talking of Saturday, now that I've refuelled I'd better go, otherwise I'll never face shopping tomorrow. Shopping with Kev is a nightmare. I need to brace myself." She stood up and pulled her jacket on.

"Enjoy your party." Steve tried to summon a bright smile. "And your Sunday dinner."

"I'm sure I will. Saturday should be good, and Kev's parents are lovely." She buttoned her jacket. "They've been like surrogate parents to me, really."

"That's nice." His chest felt tight. What was up with him? He felt jealous of Kevin but envious of Rebecca, too, he realised, with her 'lovely, surrogate parents'. Her weekend sounded idyllic. He wanted Rebecca, and part of him wanted to be Rebecca, and live her life.

"I'm very lucky." She swung her bag on to her shoulder. "I doubt if I'll see you this week. I think we're going to be on site right the way through."

"So you'll be drinking coffee somewhere else, will you? Traitor."

"I'm afraid so." She rested a hand briefly on his shoulder. "I'm sorry about Laura. I really hope she gets better soon. And that your weekend's not too grim."

"Thanks." he didn't know what else to say. "See you."

"Bye."

He sat there for a long time after she left, staring at nothing much at all. After a while he became aware that Tony was standing beside him.

"You want a wrap, Steve?" asked Tony gently. "We've got two left. Or another coffee, if you want? On the house. I'll have to send you home soon though, my friend. Maria's waiting."

Steve looked down at his watch. How had that happened? It was nearly 9. Looking round, he realised the only other customers left, a couple who were sitting near the door, were getting to their feet and putting their coats on. He stood up, shaking his head. "No thanks, Tony. I think I need something stronger."

He went to walk away, but Tony put a hand on his arm.

"Look after yourself, eh? And don't do anything silly. You're a good boy, Steve, but I worry for you. You've got to have some faith, si? Things will turn out okay in the end."

"I'm sure it will, if the end ever gets here," he said bitterly. His eyes stung and he didn't trust himself to turn round. Instead he headed straight for the door, only giving the briefest of nods and well aware that he'd left Tony staring after him, looking worried sick. He knew Tony deserved better, and as he strode towards the pub he was filled with guilt.

How could he feel any worse? arm. "And by the sound of it, you don't really have that much respect for anyone else's view anyway." She laid the £20 note on the table.

"Look, Rebecca, I—I mean, we were getting on so well—"

"Yes we were. Surprising, really, lame brain that I am. Not a hypocrite by the way, I don't eat venison or veal." She smiled tightly and-ever-so-politely. "Believe me when I say I'm as disappointed at how things have turned out as you are. Who would have thought that one sentence could ruin a whole evening?"

"But does this have to matter? We can agree not to talk about it." A tiny glimmer of hope sparked in his eyes.

In other circumstances, that eagerness would have been fantastically flattering for her ego, she thought. Not now. "That wouldn't change the fact that you do something that's completely against my principles. I can't ignore it." She frowned. "Unlike you. Why didn't you say you were into hunting on your profile? It would have saved both of us time. It specifically asked about things like this under 'ethics and viewpoints'."

"I know, and I did!" He looked genuinely perplexed. "That's why I was surprised by your reaction."

Rebecca shook her head. "I'm starting to think that agency couldn't organise a piss-up in a brewery."

He nodded ruefully. "They do seem to like matching polar opposites. My last date hated Italian food, and Chinese. I rarely eat anything else."

"That sounds familiar." She sighed as she pushed her chair in. "It was interesting to meet you, Dean. Sorry I wasn't what you were expecting."

"No, you were fine, I mean I... more than fine," he floundered. "But obviously we're not a good match. I hope you have better luck with your next date."

That wasn't very likely, she thought as she left. Because there wasn't going to be a next date.

Chapter Fifteen

Rebecca leaned on the counter. "Hi."

"Hi." Steve smiled, but there was a weariness about it that meant although it reached his eyes, it didn't make them shine the way they usually did.

Poor Steve. Rebecca saw the shadows under his eyes and that tell-tale stretched look she'd seen on herself in the mirror a few times, when sleep was coming rarely and not giving you any proper rest when it did. She knew how it felt to have grief and worry gnawing away at you.

"Have you got time for lunch?" she asked gently. "I can come back if now's not good."

"Thanks, but I don't think I'm very good company at the moment."

"I wasn't asking if you were good company. I was asking you to have lunch with me." Why did he put these barriers up? She couldn't understand it. She didn't think she'd made a very good job of keeping her distance; whenever he looked sad she felt compelled to touch his arm, or his shoulder. Surely he knew how she felt?

"I'm sure you'd have a much better time with Kevin. I'll probably only take a short break anyway, we're pretty busy today."

"Well, I'm not going to beg, because a lady never does that," she said lightly. "But I am disappointed." A lot more disappointed than you know.

He looked up sharply. "Disappointed? What do you mean?"

"Because I thought we were more than just café supremo and customer lady." She flashed him a small smile. "I thought we were friends. And friends are there for you even when life's not all butterscotch lattes and chocolate sprinkles."

He smiled, and some of the tension left his face. "And Cajun chicken wraps?"

"Life's definitely not always those. Particularly if you've got clothes you don't want dry-cleaned." She smiled. "You never did talk to Tony about that excess sauce, did you?"

He shook his head. "If you really want to have lunch, then I'll go and ask Tony if I can go now. I might as well, to be honest. I've been cleaning the same bit of the counter for the last ten minutes."

"Mind not on the job?" she asked wryly.

"You could say that."

Steve went to the kitchen door and had a brief muffled conversation.

Rebecca leaned on the counter waiting and pondering. Perhaps he just didn't fancy her. After all, now she knew he'd been unattached all this time, it did raise the question—if he did like her, why hadn't he done something about it before now?

Rebecca could hear Tony rumbling in reply, with the occasional discernible, 'si, si'. A few moments later, Steve came back to the counter and pulled his apron off, closely followed by Tony.

"Rebecca, what would you like today? Something special, eh, that I make just for you? Or perhaps you try my new Caribbean Chicken wrap, and tell me what you think?"

"Thanks for the offer, Tony," she smiled, "But I was wondering if Steve would like me to take him away from all this, and go somewhere else for lunch. Just for a change." She looked at Steve questioningly.

Tony clutched at his chest. "Somewhere else?" he said dramatically. "I cannot believe what I am hearing. Is not good for Tony's heart!" Then he grinned. "She is a wise woman, this one, eh Steve? A very good idea. A change of scenery!"

Steve looked dazed. "Right, that would be great." Then he looked quickly at Tony. "When I say great, I mean different. Obviously the food won't be as good as yours, and the coffee—"

Tony shut him up by flicking him with the cloth he'd left on the side, and pushing him away from the counter. "Go, go, foolish boy! Enough! Take as long as you like."

Laughing, Rebecca and Steve scuttled out.

"So where are we going?" He asked. He hadn't been in the mood for this at all, but now they were out here on the pavement he was glad she'd persuaded him.

"Where would you like to go?" She smiled into his eyes and he felt the familiar lurch inside him.

"You choose."

"Alfresco, or is that a bit optimistic?"

He squinted upwards to where a weak sun was managing to shine hazily through a thin layer of cloud. "Alfresco. I don't think it's going to rain. I'm not sitting on grass though, everything's still wet."

She punched him gently on the arm. "I invited you out for lunch, not a picnic. What do you take me for?" She smiled. "I know just the place. It's a ten minute walk though."

"That's okay."

They walked in companionable silence for a while, only exchanging the odd remark until they came to the canal. Rebecca turned on to the bridge and Steve raised his eyebrows.

"Where are you taking me, woman?"

"It will be worth it, you'll see. I know it doesn't look very promising at the moment." He smiled. "I'm glad you said it first."

"You don't have a favourite café, then? Other than Tony's?"

He shrugged. "I've not really explored the cafés around here, to be honest."

"How come?"

"I haven't lived here that long."

"So where you're living now—it's not your father's house?"

He nodded. "No. He wanted to downsize, release some money from our old house, but it wasn't practical. He was too ill to handle it. If I'd have realised how ill he was, I would never have gone to uni, but he hid it from me too well."

"He didn't want to stop you living your life," she said gently.

"No, he didn't." He paused. "Anyway, in the end it was Laura and I who downsized eight months ago, because the old house was high maintenance. And," he said, "Laura wasn't earning any money. I didn't want to, but..." he shrugged. "Needs must. Our new place is tiny."

"At least your Dad knew he was leaving you a home."

"Yes. Although I'd rather have kept my Dad. Sod the house."

"I can understand that. Losing a parent is awful."

He touched her arm. "I'm sorry. It must have been a lot worse for you."

She shook her head. "Don't worry. The fact I've lost my parents too doesn't change the fact you've lost yours, or negate your feelings. It just means we both know how painful it is. That's what I wanted to talk to you about... whoops!" She grabbed his elbow and he stopped. "What?"

She grinned. "That's what I get for talking too much. We need to go down there."

"Down there? But that just leads to the canal."

"Yep. Lead on cowboy," she said, attempting a Wild West accent.

"That was terrible," he said, looking around, puzzled, as they started down a paved slope.

"I know, sorry! I love cowboy films."

"Me too. I watch them for the horses." He kept his face straight. "What about you?"

"Oh absolutely. Horses, every time." She said innocently.

The sun came out as they reached the canal, making the water sparkle.

"Perfect," she breathed. "Now that's good timing."

He stopped. "Right, we're at the canal. Are you taking me on a boat? I know Tony said to take as long as I want, but—"

"Shh! We turn along here." She tugged him along the towpath for a short distance then brought him to a stop. "Ta-da!"

"Neat." Steve shook his head and stared in amazement. "I had no idea this was here." At the ground level of a large industrial building, a long, skinny café squeezed itself along the side of the towpath. Several brightly coloured tables stood outside, some protected under large red canopies.

"Ah." She tapped the side of her nose. "London's best-kept not-so-secret secret. The Towpath café." They took a seat at a small, square table, painted postbox red.

"Do you come here often?"

She giggled and Steve buried his head in his hands. "Oh God," he said, his voice muffled. "I can't believe I just said that. That wasn't me trotting out the most cheesy chat-up line known to man, honest. It was a genuine question."

"It's shut in the winter, more's the pity," she answered, still laughing. "But I come fairly often once it opens. Usually on the weekends when I've got more time, but sometimes I come here for a change in the week, if I've got time. Or if I'm working on a site nearby. They do a great breakfast."

"Just you? Doesn't Kevin come too?" What strange compulsion made him ask that, when he didn't want to know? Just the thought of them together in the sunshine, enjoying a long, lazy lunch, provoked a hot surge of jealousy in his chest. The last thing he wanted to do was picture the pair of them here, but his stupid brain seemed to have other ideas.

"No. This is a me thing. A place I like to come by myself."

It was ridiculous that he felt a ridiculous wave of relief wash over him when she said that. In that case, I'm honoured m'lady," he said, touching an imaginary hat to her.

She smiled back at him in a way that stirred up all the feelings he'd been trying to put to rest. "So you should be," she said. "I've never brought anyone else here."

"Really? Nobody?" His throat felt tight.

"Yep."

She looked at him intently and Steve felt that the atmosphere between them was more intimate than ever. His brain went blank, and he tried to look at anything but her. "It's a great location, right by the water," he said, voice hoarse.

She leaned back in her chair. "Yes, it is." Her voice seemed a little flat. "In the summer, it gets heaving. People bring picnic blankets and put them on the towpath."

"Sounds great."

"Yes, although there's always a few people who put their rugs too close to the canal edge so that nobody can get past. Nutters! Sometimes it's so hot here in the summer, though, that people sit in that alcove back there." She pointed awkwardly back over her shoulder. "It gets crammed in there when it rains, too, although it's too shallow to keep you properly dry."

"I can see that." he smiled. "Now as you're a regular, what do you recommend?"

"Well as a frequent visitor, more than a regular, I can tell you that the menu changes frequently – they try and keep it seasonal, and buy local – and that nearly everything here is homemade. Oh, and gorgeous. I can particularly recommend the ginger beer, sir, if you're feeling brave."

"Brave?"

"It'll put a fire in your belly. It's fierce." She sounded like a pirate and Steve laughed.

"What is it with you and accents today?"

"No idea. The canal air's obviously gone to my head."

"What about food?"

"There's the menu..." she craned her neck to look past him and Steve realised there was a blackboard on the wall.

"Ooh, I can definitely recommend the salmon terrine and salad. Well, if you like fish, I can." she eyed him doubtfully.

"I love fish." He twisted round in his chair. "Hmm. Decisions, decisions. They've got kedgeree, too. I love kedgeree."

"Theirs is great."

"I'll have that then."

"Sorted!" She grinned. "You can always have the terrine next time, if it's on." She bounced out of her chair and went to the counter.

Next time? There was going to be a next time? That sounded marvellous, but Steve didn't know if he could stand anymore. It was wonderful to spend time with her like this, but it was torture as well. He wasn't sure he could cope with a close friendship. His heart was too involved already, and it was proving it right now, thudding in his chest as he looked at her. He hadn't seen her in a skirt or dress before, but she was wearing a dress today, white with tiny blue flowers embroidered all over it. The material was blowing against her legs in the breeze and he saw her pull her denim jacket more tightly round her and smooth down her hair.

He took a deep breath, releasing the tension that had built in his stomach as he looked at her. He made himself lean back in the chair and relax, taking the opportunity to have a good look round, preferably not at Rebecca; far too dangerous, because she was just too beautiful.

It really was a unique little place, nestled into the industrial buildings as though it had burrowed in, hoping to go unnoticed. There was a floating pontoon tethered nearby with a few tables on it, too. He had a great view along the canal, and Steve couldn't help smiling at the little fleet of ducklings who came paddling by placidly following their mother, unperturbed by all the attention they got from their ready-made audience.

"Cute, aren't they."

Steve started.

"Sorry. Me and my ninja feet! Kevin's always complaining about them." She put the drinks on the table, leaning close. Steve swallowed and looked away as she sat down.

"Yes, they're very, very cute. I bet they don't go short of food."

"You bet correctly." She smiled, and took a drink.

He peered at her glass, suspicious. "Hold on, yours doesn't look like mine."

"That's because mine's not ginger beer. I went for watermelon juice."

"Watermelon juice? Couldn't handle the ginger beer, huh? Wimp!"

"Of course I can. I've had one of your butterscotch lattes when you've way overdone the syrup, and if I can handle that..."

Steve's splutter was as much a result of her cheekiness as it was the huge gulp of ginger beer he'd taken in a burst of bravado.

Rebecca giggled. "It's traditional to drink ginger beer, you know, not inhale it."

Steve coughed. "You'll never have to suffer my butterscotch latte again, I assure you," he said darkly. "You're barred."

She stuck out her tongue, and he reciprocated.

"Behave yourself. The food will be here in a minute."

"Good, I'm starving."

"It's all this fresh air."

"It's all this walking you've made me do!" He pretended to glare.

She put her hands on her hips, unconsciously drawing attention to her figure, which was curvy in all the right places, thought Steve. "Well, that's gratitude for you!" she laughed. "In that case, I bar you from here!"

"Good. We're quits." On an impulse he instantly regretted, he held out his hand for her to shake. The feeling of her strong, warm hand in his did nothing to slow his heart rate. Even worse, she seemed in no rush to take away her hand. Steve was only saved by the arrival of the food.

He busied himself with the kedgeree, which was just as delicious as Rebecca had promised. After a while he thought his face was probably a more normal colour, and he risked a look at her. She looked like she was enjoying her lunch, which seemed to be a tart of some kind with a salad.

"Good?" He nodded at her plate.

"Gorgeous."

"Is it goat's cheese?"

She nodded, mouth full, then swallowed. "Uh-huh. With sweet red onion relish and sundried tomatoes. What's not to love?"

"I'm almost envious, but this kedgeree's delicious."

"Told you." Her eyes twinkled at him.

Steve held her gaze for a long moment, until she suddenly put down her knife and fork and sat back.

"Full up already?"

She shook her head. "No. I want to talk to you about something, and I want to do it now in case you come over all virtuous in a minute and tell me we have to leave our lunch and get back."

"I wasn't planning to, but go on." Steve felt uneasy. She looked quite solemn. He put his own knife and fork down and sat back, sipping his ginger beer.

"It's about Laura. The whole situation's been worrying me since you told me about it."

Worrying her? Why? And what was worrying her, specifically? It was too much to hope for that this was where she revealed she was crazy about him, and would leave Kevin for him in a flash if it weren't for how complicated his life was. He wouldn't blame her. Laura was a major complication. Thinking about her now, Steve's heart began to thud again for totally different reasons. He felt sweat break out at his hairline and his mouth was bone dry.

"Go on," he said croakily, raising the ginger beer to his lips. A drink would help.

"I'd like to help her. Help you with her, I mean. When she comes home."

He stared. What did she mean? "What? How?"

"Those two days you can't cover. I checked with Tony when they are." She sounded calm but her cheeks were flushed. "I can have Laura with me on those days, and a few others too if you like."

"But..." Steve held out his hands, not sure how to say all the things clamouring in his head. He was finding it hard to take in. Rebecca's voice sounded strangely tinny.

"Don't worry, I'm CRB checked and everything," she said, obviously misunderstanding his hesitation. "I have been for years. I'm involved with The Young Archaeologist's Club YAC, for a start. That's how I met Tony Robinson."

"Who?" Was this ginger beer alcoholic? Everything seemed to be moving.

"You know, Tony Robinson, he's the guy who played Baldrick—"

"But Laura's nothing to do with you," be blurted. There was a buzzing in his ears. A sudden certainty he was going to cry, here, outside a busy café with lots of strangers trooping past on the towpath. His chest felt tight. He couldn't breathe. Rebecca closed her hand over his, very firmly.

"Steve, listen. It's going to be okay."

He curled his fingers tightly round hers, although he couldn't see them anymore, just swirls of purple.

"Take a minute. Close your eyes, just for a moment. Breathe slowly, in through your nose, out through your mouth." Her voice was very calm and she was rubbing her thumb soothingly, slowly across the back of his hand. "Think about what how cool the air feels. Think about what you can smell. Hot cheese. Apple crumble. Your ginger beer." He felt his other hand lifted towards his face. "Smell that?"

He nodded.

"Now take a slow, deep breath in and try opening your eyes."

He opened them and saw the coloured squiggles receding to the corner of his vision and then disappearing altogether. To reveal Rebecca's face only inches from his.

"Feeling better?" He nodded. He could feel his chest ease and his heartbeat slowing.

"Good," she said, bending forward. For a split second he thought she was going to kiss him on the lips, but instead she kissed him lightly on the cheek. He was sure she'd thought about it though. It had been in her eyes – hadn't it?—and she was still holding his hand.

"I know Laura's nothing to do with me," she said quietly, "but we have a lot in common. We've both lost our parents, and I'd love to help her if I can." She smiled. "I'm actually pretty good with young people, you know."

He nodded. "I can imagine that." He blinked, hard.

"And even though she's nothing to do with me, she's a lot to do with you, and I want to help you, too. Will you let me?"

He nodded. Rebecca put her hand up and wiped away an escaping tear with her thumb. And then, as though nothing had happened, she went back to her lunch.

After a minute, Steve followed suit and by the time he'd finished, he thought he could trust his voice again.

"Rebecca, are you sure you're happy to have Laura at your house?"

"Yes. I've got lots of work to do from home, so it won't even slow me down."

"And nobody else will mind?"

"Like who?"

Steve shrugged. "I'll be in the café until late on those two nights, and if anyone else will be in your house with Laura for any length of time, they would have to have a CRB check too." And here's where she mentions Kevin, he thought.

"Lucky I live by myself, then." She raised an eyebrow. "I can check the calendar, but I don't think I've planned any wild parties."

So Kevin didn't live with her.

"You're really sure about this?"

She nodded.

"I'm afraid you'll have to come to a meeting next Thursday morning, with a social worker and a police officer. Will that be okay?"

"That's fine."

"And probably another one with Laura there, too."

"Not a problem.

He shook his head. "I don't know how to thank you. I can't believe you're doing this."

"Well believe it, buddy. What are friends for?" She smiled and reclaimed her hand. "Anyway, it keeps me out of Marcie's way. She's throwing her weight about on site at the moment, so Kevin can have that joy for a couple of days." She crossed her arms. "As for thanks, well, next time lunch is on you. Talking of which, if want pudding, make it snappy. Your boss might have told you to take as long as you want, but mine's expecting me at a meeting in forty minutes."

Chapter Sixteen

"Sorry. I'm sure the last thing you want to do on your day off is babysit a waste of space," said Laura, with a tight smile. She took off her boots and followed Rebecca into the kitchen.

"You're way too old to need babysitting, and it's not my day off, I'm working from home. Coffee?" Rebecca smiled and turned the kettle on.

"Yes please. It's the strongest thing I'm allowed to have." She gave a harsh little laugh which Rebecca ignored.

"I've got cappuccino sachets." She flicked through the packets. "Cappuccino, mocha, caramel?"

"Caramel sounds good, thanks."

"Good choice. Think I'll join you." Rebecca made the coffees and grabbed a pack of biscuits. "Hope you like Gingernuts, they're all I've got at the moment."

"I love them. Thanks."

"Me too, and they go great with caramel latte. Dip 'em and see."

Laura sniffed the coffee appreciatively. "It smells really good."

"I know. Don't tell your brother, but I think they're nearly as good as the real thing. Plus I can buy a box of sachets for the price of one cup at Tony's," Rebecca grinned. "Sometimes the thrifty ex-student in me rears her ugly head."

"Where did you go to uni?"

"Bristol."

"Was it good?"

"Fantastic. I had a blast. Hard work, though, and a lot of summer holidays spent volunteering on digs instead of getting holiday jobs and earning. But yeah, I loved it."

Laura smiled, and silence fell for a while.

Rebecca shook the biscuit packet at Laura.

"I shouldn't."

"Why? There's nothing of you! Go on."

"Okay then, thanks. You're right, they do go well with this coffee."

"Did you ever think about going to uni, Laura?"

She shrugged. "I suppose it's what I thought I was working towards when I started sixth form. But I soon screwed that up."

"What did you want to study?"

"I was doing A levels in Art, History, Graphic Design and IT, just because they were the things I enjoyed really."

Rebecca smiled. "That's the best reason for doing subjects—well, that and obviously choosing subjects that'll get you on the uni course you want. I had some friends whose parents dictated their A level choices because they wanted them to do degrees that would make them 'successful'." She grimaced.

www.penrose-publishing.co.uk

"That's one problem I didn't have." Laura gave a small, crooked smile. "Steve got on my case a bit about studying, but he never tried to dictate what I should study."

"He's not all bad, then." She smiled.

"No. He's not bad, full stop. I'm lucky. I know that, deep down, even if I don't show it." She looked down.

Rebecca steered the conversation back to safer waters.

"So what did you see yourself doing at uni?"

"I didn't get that far. I always thought I'd love to have a job where I could combine the subjects I loved, but they don't exactly go together."

"You'd be surprised," said Rebecca thoughtfully.

"I love IT and history, but how would I combine them—unless someone pays me to make a giant database, and that sounds really boring! But I loved art and graphic design too and I was pretty good at it." She shook her head. "I know I'll never get a job that combines all those. Steve says that's my problem, wanting everything to suit me."

"Hmm." Rebecca got to her feet. "I'm just going to go and grab something, but help yourself to more biscuits, I won't be a minute. Make yourself another coffee if you like—if you want a frothy one, the sachets are in the cupboard above the kettle."

"Thanks." Laura smiled. "Not sure I should though. I bet those coffees are mega fattening."

"But compared to an all-milk latte, they're positively healthy!" Rebecca went into the tiny second bedroom that served as her study and picked up her laptop and field report from her desk, then pulled a book off the shelf. When she came back, Laura had disappeared and she could hear the sound of the kettle. She fired up her laptop and flicked through the report until she found the page she wanted. She paper-clipped the page in place.

"Can I get you another coffee, Rebecca?" Laura called shyly.

"Go on then. Mocha, please." She started up CorelDraw. By the time Laura reappeared, Rebecca had moved the long coffee table parallel to the settee and laid out the laptop, report and book.

"Oh!"

Rebecca looked up. "Thanks. Pop the coffees on the mantelpiece a minute." She smiled encouragingly. "I think you might find this interesting."

Laura sat down beside her and frowned at the laptop, which was showing a blank screen framed on all sides by toolbars. "What am I looking at?"

"Nothing, yet." Rebecca picked up the field report. "This is a photograph of a pottery sherd I found last year."

"Right." Laura glanced at her. "That's... great," she said, trying to sound enthusiastic. "Sherd? I thought it was shard."

"Similar word, but sherds are pottery pieces."

"Okay."

"Because of other material we found at the same level in the trench, we knew it dated to the tenth century. Pottery was limited at the time, and because of the colour and chemical composition of the glaze, we could tell this was a piece of Stamford ware. So pots already discovered, from the same era and area, could give us an idea of how it looked originally." She pointed to the book. "This pitcher was found in Oxford." Laura looked at an image of a bright yellow pot with a strange flaring spout near the neck. "It's in the British Museum."

"Cool. The piece you found looked tiny, though. How would you know what the whole pot looked like?"

"A-ha." Rebecca grinned. Great, Laura was looking interested. She turned to the paper-clipped page in the report. "These are photos of more sherds we found nearby—can you see the way this one's curved?—and we also had some idea of what they were used for, because of their location and evidence of nearby activities." She leant over in front of Laura and pressed a key on the laptop. "So we think it looked like this." A short animation started, showing all the sherds separately at first, large in the foreground, until they zoomed backwards into position, with the rest of the pot appearing around them.

"Wow, that's so cool." Laura leant forward. "I can't believe you reconstructed that huge pot just from those pieces, they were tiny!"

Rebecca sat back, smiling. "Our graphics and design team do this kind of stuff all the time. Pots, buildings, skeletons; even whole villages."

Laura's eyes were wide. "Whole villages? That's amazing."

"Uh-huh. And they do it using their art, history and graphic design talents," she said lightly, "normally with software like this, using their I.T skills." Laura nodded slowly. "So what you're saying is..."

"What I'm saying is, this is a job you could do. That combines all the things you love."

Laura looked wistful. "I wish someone had told me about this at school. I didn't have a clue what I wanted to do. It all seemed a bit pointless, in the end."

"Well you know now," said Rebecca lightly. She nodded at the laptop. "This programme's called CorelDraw. I'm by no means as expert as my graphics colleagues," she laughed, "but would you like a quick tutorial?"

"Really? Yes please!"

Rebecca gave her a rudimentary tutorial and then let her have a try herself. She was impressed with how quickly Laura picked up the basics. Later, sitting at Rebecca's tiny dining table and tucking into the chicken and mango salad Rebecca had prepared, all she talked about was archaeological reconstruction. She bombarded her with questions until Rebecca threw up her hands, laughing.

"Laura, stop! I feel like you're turning my brain inside out!"

Laura went pink. "Sorry. It's just really interesting. I never knew this stuff could be so, well, cool."

Rebecca smiled. "Glad to have been of service."

"I suppose I'd need a degree to do this for a job."

"Afraid so. Archaeology's a great degree though, even if you change your mind about what you want to do, because it teaches such a wide skill set."

"Would it teach me how to do all the IT stuff too?"

"Courses vary. They'll all touch on it, but it's best to go on separate courses for the different programs as well. Preferably ones that give you a piece of paper at the end."

Laura nodded. "I don't think I'd mind that. Three years seems a long time, but if I could do something I loved at the end of it..."

"Competition can be fierce for some jobs, but the important thing is field experience."

"Cool."

Rebecca hesitated, about to make a suggestion, but thought better of it. Let's see how today goes first, shall we, she thought.

"Well I've got work to get on with—I'm going to need my laptop, I'm afraid! But there are lots of archaeology books in the hall or study. See what takes your fancy. They're not all really highbrow, some at the bottom of the hall bookcase are ones I've written for the public."

"Ones you've written?" Laura stared.

"Yep. It's no big deal, most project leaders have stuff published," she said quickly, embarrassed. She hadn't meant to big herself up. "There's palaeontology stuff, too, if you're interested."

"Thanks."

Rebecca was quickly embroiled in her work. It was lucky that she had so much report-writing to do, and work on the new GLAM publications; otherwise she couldn't have taken time away from the Museum. When she went to check on Laura later, she was on the sofa, legs curled beneath her, with what looked like the Jubilee Line Excavation reports open on her lap and a large pile of pamphlets and books beside her.

Rebecca tiptoed away, smiling. She might just have done her good deed for the decade.

Laura spent the next morning checking out websites that Rebecca recommended to her, and looking through more files and books. She even asked Rebecca if she could spare some paper so that she could take notes. Rebecca went one better and given her a shiny new notebook and a pen emblazoned with the GLAM logos.

"They cost a fortune in the gift shop." She winked. Perks of the job."

The morning shot past. Rebecca had been making notes and planning out pages for a joint publication with Crossrail.

"How's your morning been?" Laura asked her politely as Rebecca stood in the kitchen, heating soup.

"Fine thanks, I think I've got it all clear in my head. I'll need my laptop again, though."

"Of course! Sorry, I didn't mean to hog it."

"No, I didn't need it this morning, honest. I'd soon have said if I did!"

She filled two bowls and they carried them to the dining table, where they fell silent for a while, enjoying the soup and crusty rolls.

"Laura, how would you like to come to work with me next week and see this stuff being done for real?"

Laura stopped eating, eyes like saucers. "Would I be allowed?"

"Wouldn't have offered if you weren't," Rebecca grinned. "I can pull a few strings. We'd have to fill in some paperwork"

Laura looked uncomfortable.

She's wondering whether it's because of her criminal record, thought Rebecca. She smiled at her. "Don't worry, we get all our work experience and volunteer people to do it, just to say you've read all the health and safety procedures, things like that."

"Oh. Okay."

"If you want you can stay with me at first, though we'll have to find you something to do when I'm in meetings. Then you can spend time with the graphics team—Kev's got a heap of work to talk through with the graphics team, so he could look after you.. He's a sweetie. Would that be okay?"

"Ok? Are you kidding?" Laura's eyes were glistening. "It would be great."

"Good! That's settled, then." Rebecca got up.

"Rebecca, why are you doing this for me?"

"Because you're interested in this stuff, and it will give you an idea of what the job's like."

"But..." Laura looked down, blushing. "I'm hardly reliable, am I," she said, sounding bitter. "How do you know I won't let you down?"

"You won't."

"But why are you going to so much trouble for me? Someone you barely know? Is it for Steve?"

"No. Steve's a great guy, Laura, but you're a person in your own right. Plus..." The lump in her throat seemed to come from nowhere. She swallowed.

"Plus what?" It was almost a whisper.

"Plus I know how it feels to lose your parents when you're young," said Rebecca. Her voice shook a little and she blinked away tears. She tried to make her voice light-hearted as she looked at Laura. "Us orphans needs to stick together."

"Thanks!"

Rebecca started a little as Laura gave her a quick spontaneous hug, and catching the look on Laura's face afterwards she wasn't sure which of them had been most surprised by it.

Chapter Seventeen

"I wanted you to be the first to hear my news," said Ron, shutting his office door. "Biscuit?" He proffered a pack of smeary chocolate digestives.

"No thanks," said Rebecca, settling herself into a chair.

He looked at the biscuits and winced. "I don't blame you. I should have left them in the fridge." He sat down and rested his elbows on the desk, steepling his fingers. "Firstly, I'm leaving."

"Leaving?" She sat forward. "Why?"

"Not because I'm unhappy here," he smiled. "But I've had an offer I can't refuse."

"A new job?"

"New everything. Joint director of a new international archaeology team, based in Milan, whose focus will be on urban archaeology."

"Wow."

"Wow indeed."

"We'll miss you round here."

"I suppose that's good. It must mean I've done something right."

She hardly heard him. A cold, uneasy feeling settled in her stomach. Had Marcie known about this? This must have been what she'd meant. Was she really going to take over Ron's post?

Ron cleared his throat. "Anyway, with my leaving, the powers that be have decided it's a good time for restructuring.

"Sounds scary." She tried to smile.

He grinned. "Not at all. For once, I think the powers that be are talking sense. My role will disappear."

She looked at him incredulously. "There's going to be nobody in overall charge? Seriously?"

He shook his head. "No, that's not it. Much as that might appeal to those whom I have to nag when their reports are late."

"Can't think who that would be. Mine are always on time," she said innocently.

"Just."

She waggled her head in a non-committal way.

"There will be two posts—a Director of Fieldwork, who will oversee surveys, digs, liaison with other agencies, site management etcetera, and a Director of Analysis; any follow-up work that gets done here, including graphics and design, and our publications, archives. Exhibitions and fun days will be a joint enterprise."

"Okay." She nodded. "I can see that might work, although they'll have to be people who work well together."

"Ultimately they'll report to the head of GLAM."

"Oh," said Rebecca archly, "That'll be fun for them."

He leaned forward. "Do you think it would be fun for you?"

"No, I think it will be hell for me if my boss is Marcie, frankly, which I suspect you're about to tell me is the case."

"What?" His eyebrows shot upwards.

"Marcie hinted she might have a position of authority over me, very soon. I guess this is it."

"Believe me, that would never happen," he said grimly. "Particularly with some of the things I've been hearing."

She frowned. "Like what?"

"I can't go into details. Let's just say that those in charge of her have noticed some... erratic behaviour. She certainly won't be assuming a more senior position any time soon. Not anywhere."

"I thought she was just that way around me. Is that why the exchange ended early?"

"I can't say." He looked uncomfortable.

"That's a yes."

He let that go. "Anyway, when I asked if it would be fun for you, I meant the Director of Fieldwork post. I thought you might apply."

She stared at him. "You're joking."

He shook his head, smiling.

"You're not joking." She fell back in her chair. "I don't think so."

"Why not? I thought that would appeal more than heading up analysis."

"Oh it does. Of the two, that's the one I'd go for, but there's no way I'm ready for a role like that."

"Hmm. You might be interested to know you're in a minority with that opinion. Everyone upstairs seems to think you're not only ready, you're the ideal candidate."

"They're mad then."

"Come on Rebecca. You've been basically doing the job, on and off, for this past year."

"But you've inspected the sites first—"

"Something you're more than capable of doing."

"Liaised with the other agencies—"

"As have you, very successfully, after the initial meet."

She waved a finger. "Decided trench positions, test pits—"

"After asking your opinion," he amended.

"I'm flattered by your confidence in me, but I'm not sure I share it." Her? In charge of all those other people?

He sighed. "Will you at least promise me you'll give it some thought?"

She nodded. "I will. You have to admit it's a lot to get my head around."

"Hmm. If you think that's a lot to get your head around, perhaps I shouldn't tell you about my other proposition."

"Don't tell me, NASA wants an archaeologist on the next shuttle flight," joked Rebecca weakly.

"No. If they did, I'd fight you for it."

"Sounds fair."

"The team I'm joining need two more archaeologists, capable and experienced in urban archaeology. I know I shouldn't be discussing this with you—it smacks of poaching, I suppose—"

"Why? Which member of my team are you hoping to entice away?"

"You."

She shook her head slowly. "Wow. Again."

"I know it's a big deal; it would mean moving to Milan. But you're made for the job. I've already told Francois you're the ideal candidate."

"Francois Villeneuve?"

"Sorry, I should have mentioned that. He's the other joint director. He'll probably ring you soon himself."

"I should hope so." She smiled. She'd heard nothing from him since Christmas, and he was the only remaining link to her parents. Other than Marcie and her mother, of course.

"The thing is, not only will we benefit tremendously from having you on the team, but it's a fantastic opportunity for you, and... well there's not much keeping you here, is there? It could be a new start for you." He looked awkward. "Sorry, that didn't sound quite how I intended, I just meant—"

"No, you're quite right," she said quickly. "Most people have family, or a partner. Or both. I have neither. You're only telling the truth, Ron." She smiled at him, covering the stab of hurt she'd felt, and he leaned back in his chair, relieved.

"Milan," she said into the silence that followed. "It does sound appealing. What a great opportunity."

Ron nodded eagerly, obviously sensing she might waver. "Of course there will be interviews—a selection process—but being a director, my recommendation will carry a lot of weight." He grinned. "I think you can safely say you have the backing of the other director, too."

She stared at the edge of his desk for a while, lost in thought. "You've given me a lot to think about."

"Yes, and I'm sorry to spring two such very different options on you at the same time. I know it's not ideal, and I'm in two minds myself which one I want you to take! The noble me would love to hand over the fieldwork to you, knowing I'd leave it in such capable hands. But the selfish me—the one that thinks of myself as not only your boss, but your friend—thinks the Milan job is such a great opportunity for you, and that you'd be such as asset there as well as good company, that I can't not want you to go for it."

"Well all I can say is thank you so much for considering me—for both jobs. I'm flattered."

"You're the best person for the job. Both of them, unfortunately." Ron grinned. "If only we could clone you!"

"Now there's a scary thought. I think one of me is quite enough for the world!" She got to her feet. "I think I'll go for lunch early. I feel the need for a strong cup of coffee!"

"Don't go to our café, then."

She shuddered. "I rarely do. I usually go to Tony's, round the corner." She made for the door. "I'll do some thinking and let you know."

"Ah, about that—" Ron rose from his chair and she turned. "I'm afraid you haven't got very long to ponder."

"How long, exactly?"

"They want the new directors to be in place before I leave, so there's plenty of time to hand over the reins, particularly with the new distinct roles. So we're advertising straight away. Application deadline is next Friday, with short-listing by the end of the week after."

"That doesn't give me long."

"I know."

"And the Milan post?"

"If you're interested, I need to know by the end of next week too. Sorry."

"Oh well, I suppose at least my agonising will be short-lived," she said lightly.

He smiled. "There's that."

Her head was spinning as she walked back to her office. Her first instinct was to go and find Kevin; drag him off to lunch and talk everything through with him. Ron hadn't said to keep any of it quiet, and by the sound of it everyone would know by tomorrow. She wanted to talk to him about Laura too. But Kevin wasn't around; he'd gone out to help on a dig. She left him a note and headed out for lunch.

"So you don't mind taking Laura under your wing, the week after next?" Today she'd found Kevin but he was sitting in front of a huge pile of paperwork, which wasn't like him at all.

"No, that's fine." Kevin shuffled things aimlessly.

Rebecca folded her arms, leaning against the bench. "Sure? You're not exactly bowling me over with your enthusiasm."

"Honestly, it's fine. She sounds great." He glanced up at her quickly, giving a very unconvincing smile. "So what about these new director posts then?"

"Kev what's up? Because something is."

He ran his hands through his hair and sighed. "Just the usual."

"Oh dear. Has the course of true love not run smooth?" She sat down beside him.

He laughed humourlessly. "The course of the third date hasn't even run smooth. If I ever manage to get to the true love bit, I'll tell you."

She tucked her arm in his. "Aw, I'm sorry."

"It's okay. I suppose it's better to be dumped sooner rather than later. Less gain but less pain."

"Oh no, it must be bad. You've started torturing idioms." As she hoped, that raised a small smile. "You know what you need," she said, dragging him to his feet.

"A makeover? Inside and out? A shrink?"

"Nope. Cake. Come on."

Chapter Eighteen

"Don't tell me. Butterscotch latte with chocolate sprinkles. Would you like a blueberry muffin with that?" Steve grinned, hands frozen in front of the coffee, just waiting for her to say the word.

"No. I'd like a caramel latte with cinnamon please, and a hazelnut latte for Kevin."

Steve put on what Laura called his 'mock-shock' face. "Ooh... she's living dangerously today. Large?" he slid a bowl-sized cup under the jet and jabbed at the buttons.

She nodded. "Well, what can I tell you? I need some excitement in my life."

Steve felt his cheeks flush a little and was glad he had his back to her. He felt that they were on a new footing now, although he wasn't quite sure what it was. But she sounded tense and cross. He watched the froth come up the top of the cup, trying to work out what to say. He cleared his throat as he gave the top of her latte a quick dusting of cinnamon.

"There you go."

"Thanks. It looks gorgeous." She took a long drink and Steve was mesmerized by her oh-so-perfect mouth on the edge of the cup. When she put her head up, though, he had to suppress a chuckle. He handed her a serviette.

"Here, you've got a foam moustache."

"Oh! That must look glamorous," she dabbed at her mouth.

"So he's not very exciting company then?"

"Who, Kevin?" She looked over her shoulder. "You must be joking!" She searched in her purse. "How much is that?"

"Two pound fifty for Kevin's but yours is on the house."

She looked at him. "You don't have to do that, you know."

"I know. But I want to." He smiled. "Don't get too used to it though. Temporary privilege."

"Great. A new taste experience and I saved some money too." She passed him a £5 note and he scooped change out of the till.

"So what's up with Kevin then?" he asked. "For someone who's not exciting, you spend a lot of time with him." Ouch. Too far. He started to clean imaginary spills off his side of the cake counter.

"Oh no, don't get me wrong. He can be exciting."

Great. Just what he wanted to hear.

"Just not at the moment."

"Oh? Why's that?"

"Actually, hold on a minute." She walked back to Kevin, resting a hand his shoulder as she bent to talk to him. Then she came back.

"I was going to be good and leave the cakes alone today, but he needs a cake and I can't sit there and watch him eat one by himself. It'll kill me." She smiled. "Besides, it would be rude not to keep him company."

Her eyes moved along the counter. "I'll have an apricot Danish and he'll have an almond and pecan slice, please. If that doesn't cure him, nothing will."

"Cure him?" Steve took two plates off the stack and picked up the tongs. "Of what?" He carefully extracted the cakes.

"He's a bit depressed."

"Oh. Sorry to hear that."

"Well thanks, but there's no need for you to be sorry. You're not the guy who strung him along and then dumped him."

Steve's head whipped round and his arm knocked against the cake cabinet, shooting Rebecca's apricot Danish on to the floor.

"God, I'm sorry." He said, tilting the other plate before he lost Kevin's slice too.

"Don't worry. You know I told you about that stint I did as a waitress? I was useless." She took Kevin's cake.

Steve opened the cabinet to get her a fresh pastry, trying to focus on what his hands were doing. Once it was on the plate, he felt brave enough to say what was hovering on his tongue.

"Guy? So he's..."

"Gay. Yes," she said, keeping her voice low.

Steve shook his head, bewildered. "I had no idea. You never mentioned it."

"Well, I wouldn't have done, before. It's Kevin's business, not anybody else's." She took her plate and put it on the tray.

"But you're mentioning it to me now."

She smiled. "I think I know you well enough by now to trust you with that piece of information, don't you?"

"I hope so," he smiled back. She turned to go but he stopped her. "You'll probably think I'm daft, but I'd always presumed you two were a couple."

"Us two? Kevin and me?" Rebecca dissolved into giggles. "Now there's an unlikely combination!'

"You seemed to get on so well, and you spend so much time together, and, I mean, I had no idea that he gay. At all." He shook his head, knowing he was blushing. "You must think I'm a complete idiot."

"No. I don't know anyone who's pegged Kev as gay unless he's told them. Contrary to the stereotype, not all gay men are camp." Her eyes twinkled. "And he doesn't particularly like musicals, either."

Steve spread his hands. "Hey, I don't buy into that attitude either. I just can't believe I've presumed you two are a couple all this time."

"It's ironic really, because I'll let you into a secret. So far away am I from being part of a couple, that I've been using a dating agency in my efforts to become one."

"And how's that going for you?" he asked croakily.

"Disastrously. That's why I'm not doing it anymore."

"Sorry to hear that."

"Probably for the best. I think meeting people naturally is the best thing, after all. It always felt false." She smiled at him and his heart did its usual little flipping over thing. She turned to go again, and Steve felt a wave of panic. For some inexplicable reason, he felt that if he missed his chance to say something now, he'd never get it again."

"Rebecca."

"Yes?"

"Look, er... if I'd known you weren't with Kevin before- "

"You'd have asked him out?" said Rebecca innocently.

He gaped. "No, no! I'm not gay—"

He stopped. Rebecca was killing herself laughing.

"Very funny."

"Sorry. Look, could we talk later? Will you be around? These coffees are going to get cold, and I'd better get back to Mr Cheerful.'" She jerked her head.

"Sure. I'm here until 6."

"That's a date, then." She gave him a brilliant smile and walked off.

Steve watched her go, grinning like an idiot.

At first, Steve couldn't wait to see Rebecca at the end of the day, but as the hours went by, he got more and more worried. Rebecca had been single all that time, but had given no clear signals that she fancied him. Maybe she just saw him as close friend material.

He leaned through the hatch. Good. Neil was standing close by sealing up salads. "You were right. They're not together!" Steve hissed.

He looked up. "Who?"

"Rebecca and Kevin!"

Neil shrugged. "Told you so."

"You said you didn't think they were. I don't why you were so sure." He frowned. "Unless... you know, don't you?"

"Know what?"

"About Kevin?"

He turned away and started to clean the worktop. "What about him?" he asked gruffly.

Steve lowered his voice. "That he's—"

"Gay?" finished Neil. "Yeah. I suspected."

"How? I can't see it at all."

"I saw him leaving a gay bar a couple of times. That was a clue."

Steve glared at Neil's back. "And you didn't think to mention it?"

Neil turned round. It was the first time Steve had ever seen him look cross. "No. I'm not your spy, Steve, and I didn't think Kevin's personal life was any of your business!"

"No, I... sorry. You're right. It's just if I'd known... "

"If you'd known? Dude, you were too tied up with Laura, and of course, you could always have asked Rebecca if she was single," said Neil wryly.

Steve felt like an idiot. He shrugged and went back to the counter. Neil was right, both about Kevin's personal life and his own reticence with Rebecca, but he didn't have to be so bloody touchy. What was up with him lately?

When Rebecca eventually walked in, he felt more nervous than pleased.

"Nearly done?"

"I'll be five minutes. Are you okay waiting?"

"I'll go and tuck myself in the corner."

"Okay. I'll bring you a coffee."

He refilled the chilled cabinet and made sure there were just a few of each kind of pastry and cake. They didn't sell so well in the evening so most of them were best left wrapped.

He carried two butterscotch lattes over to her table and sat down.

She bent over her coffee and inhaled. "Mmm. Butterscotch. Thanks."

"That's okay." He leant back and sipped his coffee. "Ah. That's better."

"Hard day?"

"Very busy, for some reason. This afternoon's been crazy. What about yours?"

She rolled her eyes. "I was on the site with Marcie this afternoon, and she took great delight in arguing with every single thing I said. I think even if I'd just said 'well here we are on a dig site' she'd have said 'no, I think you'll find it's an archaeological excavation. The woman's so petty."

"Sounds stressful."

"I've had better afternoons."

He desperately tried to think of a way to lead the conversation in the direction he wanted. "How was Kevin's afternoon?"

"I hope it was okay. I took pity on him and asked him to do some writing up at the museum. Marcie's not keen on him by association, and I thought he could do without that today."

"What a kind boss." He smiled. "I still can't believe you two aren't together. I can't believe you tried internet dating, either."

"Tried being the operative word. It's not for me, I've decided it's far better to see who crosses your path."

"I crossed your path a while ago," he said quietly, "and of course it turns out you were single all that time, so I guess that I wasn't your type, and you just let me carry on walking." He tried to laugh and make it sound like a jokey comment, but failed utterly.

She rested her elbows on the table and put her chin on her joined hands. "I did decide you weren't my type, as a matter of fact," she said, looking him in the eye. "Because my type is single."

"But I am single!"

"I know that now," she said, giving a rueful smile. "Ever since Tony told me Laura was your sister. Before that, I presumed that Laura was—"

"My girlfriend?" Steve gaped at her. "You're joking!"

"Oh, worse," said Rebecca cheerfully. "When we overheard the police say Laura Reynolds, Kevin and I presumed she was your wife."

Steve put his head in his hands. "This is crazy," he said softly, "If I'd know you were single, I would have asked you out ages ago."

"And if I'd known you were single, I would have beaten you to it," she said lightly.

His head shot up. "Really?"

"Really. I definitely noted you crossing my path." She smiled at him and Steve felt like one of the people on those old Ready Brek adverts who visibly glowed. "But I got involved before with someone whose relationship was in a mess, all but over, apparently, I was the only person he could talk to...." She shook her head, looking embarrassed. "It didn't end well, not for me anyway, and I didn't want to go through that again. Then when I found out Laura was your sister, I figured that if you were single, you'd obviously never shown any interest in me because... well, because you weren't interested in me."

"Never shown any interest in you?" He protested, smiling. "What are you, blind?"

She laughed. "Sorry. You did sometimes. I was getting very mixed signals, and I felt I was being a bit of a strumpet, kissing you on the cheek that first time. Though back then I hadn't heard of Laura."

"Ah. Whereas I didn't think you were a strumpet until you kissed me the second time." He grinned, leaning forward.

"Well you were fair game by that time, because by then I knew Laura was your sister. And you looked like you needed it."

"Ah, I see. It was charity."

"Definitely." Her eye twinkled and she leaned a little closer.

"I don't suppose you fancy donating again?"

"Is it for a good cause?"

"The best." He said huskily.

He must have been convincing because she did kiss him. And this time, it wasn't just on the cheek.

"That's a lot more enjoyable when you're not on the verge of a panic attack."

She smiled. "A lot more enjoyable when it's a proper kiss too."

"All the time we've wasted, when we could have been doing that. You have to see the irony."

"Irony? Tragedy, more like." She sighed.

"Better not waste any more, then. What about dinner?"

"Yes please, but not tonight. Girl's night in, sorry. Do you like Mexican?" She looked at him hopefully.

"I love Mexican, there's this great place, Chi—"

"Chilango!"

"You've been there!"

"Yes, and I'd love to go again. Desperado's is good, but Chilango-

"—is the best," Steve finished.

"Yep. Saturday night?"

"Great." Suddenly an unwelcome thought popped into his head. "Oh no," he groaned. Should he tell her the truth? Yes. Start as you mean to go on. "Rebecca, I really hope you can see the funny side of this, but I've got a date on Saturday. An internet date."

Her eyes went wide. "Seriously? You've been internet dating too?"

"Yes. Look, I'll try and cancel."

Rebecca was laughing. "You don't have to, honestly."

"I want to. Anyway it's not fair on her, when I've got no intention of seeing her again."

She quirked an eyebrow. "Careful what you're throwing away there. She might be gorgeous."

"Not as gorgeous as you." He reached for her hands.

She smiled. "Much as I'd love to stay here for some more flattery, I'm afraid I've got to go."

"Okay. Will you be in tomorrow?"

"Yes, but only for a quick coffee, tomorrow's mad. You can let me know then if you've cancelled your other woman." She made a face and Steve laughed.

As they said goodbye outside, it occurred to Steve that it was about time he took some initiative, so he took her hand in his and kissed her, just long enough to send a tingle down his spine.

He didn't quite skip home – that would have attracted funny looks – but there was a definite spring in his step, and he sang very loudly as he cooked dinner.

Chapter Nineteen

Steve sat at a table in the plush surroundings of the Maharajah's Palace Tandoori Restaurant and wished he was somewhere else. Anywhere else. It wasn't that he didn't like this place; it was cosy and tastefully decorated, with red velvet curtains and subtle wallpaper, and the food had been good when he'd been here before. But he would far rather be waiting for Rebecca, or a friend, than waiting for his Hot Match No.2.

He hadn't been able to cancel the date in the end, because he couldn't contact her. At least, as far as he knew he wasn't contacting her; there hadn't been any response, so unless she was sulking and just not bothering to reply—perhaps she though leaving him sitting there in the restaurant by himself was suitable punishment—then he had to presume that for some reason she hadn't seen his message and still believed the date was on.

If that was true, he could hardly not turn up, could he? That would be unchivalrous in the extreme, and Rebecca had agreed with hi. So they'd delayed their date until tomorrow, and here he was, waiting for Chantelle and wondering how on earth he would explain that he didn't really want to be here, didn't really care if they got on well, and had no intention of seeing her again? As opening lines went, it wasn't a great one. But nor could he think of a subtle way to bring it into the conversation, unless it turned to heartless cads who invited women on dates under false pretences. Then it would fit right in.

The more he thought about it, the more he was inclined to take to his heels and flee. Perhaps standing her up would be nore helpful and more fair, than letting her think this was a proper date, happily anticipated by both parties, that might lead to more dates.

Think positive, Steve, he told himself firmly, filling his glass from the jug of iced water on the table. Perhaps she'll be a really nice person, and understand completely. She might even laugh about it! He might end up with a really good friend.

Idiot, said the cynic in him. Yes, because that's why women sign up to dating agencies, Steve—to increase their circle of friends! And that's a pig flying past the restaurant window. You have to get out of this now. Leave a message with the desk, pretend you were called away on an emergency, and then when you get back in touch explain you've met someone now and won't be using the dating site any more. He was just getting to his feet when the door opened and a slender woman in a red dress walked in. She was grasping her matching clutch bag as though it was a lifebelt, scanning the restaurant uncertainly. He had to put her out of her misery. All thoughts of fleeing were put to one side as he rose to his feet and diffidently held up a hand. She looked relieved as she made her way over, but confident too, looking his in the eye and smiling as she came up to the table. Steve had to admit she was attractive. The red dress flattered her figure and her shoulder-length hair shone.

"Hello." Instead of sitting down opposite him, she leaned over kissed him. On the lips.

Since when had that been usual blind date etiquette? Steve hoped he didn't look as flustered as he felt right now.

"Hi. You must be Chantelle," he croaked.

"And you're Steve. Even hotter than your picture."

Floor, swallow me up now. "Er, thanks," he squeaked. Change the topic! ""I ordered some popadoms, I hope you don't mind. I was starving."

"Lovely." She smiled, taking a popadom and putting it in her mouth in an interesting way, while looking at him quite intently.

Her lipstick really was very red indeed. "Shall we look at the wine list?"

"We can, if you're willing to risk it," she raised her eyebrows, her eyes still fixed on his.

"Er.. risk it?" He frowned. "Why? Isn't their wine any good?"

"No, the wine's fine." She leaned forward, showing more cleavage than Steve was comfortable with. "But I'm dangerous after a couple of glasses of wine."

"Re-really?" He tried to smile casually but he'd never been so uncomfortable in his life. "Do you start to sing loudly? Or will I have to drag you down from the tables to stop you dancing?" Well done. Bit of humour. Keep it light.

"No, although I can dance for you later, if you like." She raised one slinky eyebrow. "Wine makes me horny, and after a couple of glasses, I might let you drag me anywhere."

Oh. My. God.

"Look, I think I should tell you that I tried to cancel this date," he said in a rush.

"Oh, yes, I think I remember seeing a message about that." She winked.

"You saw it?" He was flabbergasted. "Why didn't you reply?"

"I thought you were just getting cold feet. And I might be just the woman to warm them up." Steve became aware of her feet, no longer in their spiky heels, twisting caressingly round his ankles.

He moved his feet sharply away. She looked amused.

"I sent that message because I've met someone. I'm not going to be using the dating agency anymore."

"I see. Set a wedding date, have we?"

"No, but—"

"Then why don't you relax and tell me something about yourself?"

"I can't see much point," he said tensely.

"Charming. I made the effort to come here, the least you can do is have dinner with me and make polite conversation. I promise to leave your feet alone."

He flushed. "Right. I suppose we could still have dinner."

She raised her hand and signalled to the waiter. "So what do you like to do in your spare time?"

"Er,I run, go to the gym occasionally—"

"I can tell." She let her eyes travel down his torso admiringly. "Me too." She moved closer to him and lifted her dress up to nearly hip level. "Look how toned my thighs are."

Steve stood up, pulled some notes out of his wallet and let them fall on the table. "Dinner's on me, Chantelle. You have a great evening."

"Ooh, thanks." She smiled briefly in his direction then eyed the young waiter, who'd just arrived at their table and was looking rather confused. "I'm sure I'll have a very good time."

She turned to the waiter without giving Steve a second glance.

As he walked away, he heard her say, "Hi. Are all the waiters here as good looking as you? I'll have to come here more often. Now, can you sit down and explain the menu to me? I never know what to choose."

Chapter Twenty

Rebecca sighed and leant back in her seat. "I couldn't eat another tiny, single, miniscule thing." Half a Chicken Taco topped with roasted tomato salsa and a small pile of salad lay abandoned on her plate. She pushed it away from her. "Oof."

Steve grinned. "And I was going to take you somewhere for an ice-cream. Cool you down a bit."

She fanned herself with a serviette. "I am quite hot."

He smirked. "Yes, you are. Though you could be a bit more modest."

"Hey!" She glared. "I thought I was being very modest, actually. I only said quite hot."

"Hmm, well…" he ran his eyes over her, pondering. "Some days I suppose you score a 'very'. But not when your face is like a beetroot."

Their first proper date had been delayed by a week, in the end, and in that time they'd found plenty of opportunities for coffee or lunch together. That had been a good thing, thought Rebecca, because they were comfortable with each other now, and she'd felt relaxed as she got ready tonight. It was a world away from the tension and dread she'd felt going on her internet dates. She leaned her head against his shoulder and he planted a kiss in her hair.

"So could you manage an ice-cream?"

"Maybe, once we've walked there. Is it far?"

"Is it far, she says. I thought you were fit."

She batted her eyelashes at him. "I'll have you know, I've been told I'm well fit," she said solemnly.

"What is it about me that attracts all these very forward women?" he sighed. "It's a terrible curse." He pulled her to her feet and she giggled.

"I still can't believe you joined Methodical Matches too. What are the chances?"

"Two lonely hearts," he intoned, passing her coat to her, "just looking for love… quite a high chance, I think."

She buttoned up her coat and Steve kissed her very thoroughly.

"Honestly! In public."

He took her hand and led her to the door. "Couldn't help it. You look too gorgeous to resist."

"Really? In my coat? It's not exactly the most revealing thing I've ever worn."

He opened the door and as she stepped out after her, he stopped and pulled her towards him.

"I love you in that coat."

"Only in my coat? I'd better not take it off, then," she said lightly, very aware that he'd used the l word, even if it was in the wrong context.

"You know what I mean," he said, smiling. "You look wonderful in it. It really suits you. And I used to wait for it to appear every day. If there were lots of people milling about outside the café, I'd still know when you turned up because I'd catch a glimpse of this plum coat—"

"It's not plum, it's auberg—"

She was momentarily silenced in the nicest possible way.

"Sometimes, you know," said Steve as he pulled away, "that really is the only way to keep you quiet."

She pulled his head back down again. "I know. Why do you think I talk so much?" she asked huskily.

Steve tried to be quiet as he opened the front door, even though he felt like being loud. Not just because he'd had a few drinks, but because of Rebecca. They'd had a fantastic time at Chilango's and Steve was buzzing.

Taking off his shoes he padded to the kitchen. He fancied a cuppa before bed. As the kettle started to bubble noisily he took a cup down from the cupboard and then nearly dropped it as he noticed Laura leaning against the doorframe.

"God almighty! How long have you been there?" He leaned against the counter, recovering.

Laura grinned and he thought how good it was to see some sparkle and life back in her eyes. He'd never realised just how ill she had started to look; these days she practically glowed.

"Sorry bro. I've only been here a couple of seconds. I was reading but I must have fallen asleep on the sofa."

"Just waiting to give me a heart attack, huh?"

"Ah, you guessed my cunning plan. The kettle was in on it too, masking my footsteps."

"Want a cup of tea?"

She shook her head and pushed herself off the doorframe. "I'm getting some water then I'm heading for bed." She pushed herself off the doorframe and went to the cupboard. "So where have you been?" she asked casually. "You're back late."

He couldn't help himself. He could feel a daft grin settling on his face. "I went out for dinner with Rebecca."

"Rebecca?" She turned round. "What, my Rebecca?"

"S'cuse me, she'd not your Rebecca."

"She's certainly not yours," retorted Laura, a little sharply. She got a glass and walked to the tap.

"You're right, she's not. I wouldn't want her to be. She's nobody's Rebecca, she's her own woman. That's why I lo— like her."

She filled her glass and turned to face him, grinning. "Are you drunk, Steve?"

"No, just happy, that's all."

"My my, we have got it bad, haven't we. You do know how brainy she is, don't you?"

"What difference does that make?" He frowned.

"Oh, none really, I suppose." She kissed him on the cheek. "I'm off to bed, lover boy, I'll leave you to float upstairs on your little pink cloud."

He couldn't think of a dignified riposte, so he growled and made a face.

"Growling? It must be your sophistication that attracts her." Laura's voice floated back to him as she went upstairs, laughing.

He laughed too, but as he drank his tea he thought about Laura's remark and felt uneasy. Okay, Rebecca was very brainy, very capable and very good at her job, and at the moment, he just worked in a café, which admittedly wasn't a stretch intellectually; but that didn't matter.

Did it?

"Five minutes more. I can see the edge of the bone."

"You said that five minutes ago, Bec."

"So I was over optimistic. Sue me." She grinned at Kevin over her shoulder.

"It's getting dark."

She glanced up. "Barely, and we've got lamps, haven't we?"

"Yes, if you really need them. But we don't, and people want to go home," he said pointedly, jerking his head.

She moved sideways to look beyond him and saw a gaggle of surveyors and diggers, mooching about and casting the odd disgruntled look in her direction. "Well they can go home, they don't have to stay!" she protested. She bent forward again, pushing her trowel into the small hole she was working on and shifting the soil with small, careful movements.

"Someone has to, you know that. Health and Safety," Kevin said huffily. "And it's not going to be me." She turned round, meeting his glare, and stuck her tongue out, but he carried on. "The site needs to be locked down, and we're not the keyholders. It's not fair to keep everyone hanging around, Bec."

She straightened up. "Okay, fair enough."

"It'll still be there tomorrow."

"Yeah, yeah."

When they got back to the tent, she was surprised to find Marcie still there. She should speak to her; that was the professional, civil thing to do, and anyway they were under scrutiny. She didn't want the surveyors or the site security team gossiping, and they would if there was the slightest hint of discord.

She started to wipe off her trowel and wandered casually over to Marcie. "Good day?"

Marcie glanced up. "Yes thank you," she said coolly. "It's looking very promising." Her eyes were down on her finds again.

Rebecca waited, but Marcie obviously didn't intend to elaborate. "Good." She went to the plastic box with her name on, and carefully put her trowel in the tool belt inside. Her parents had given her the tool belt for her birthday before they died and the compact set of trowels and brushes it held all had her name on the handle. They went to every dig with her.

"Not taking your tools home?" Kevin asked.

"No, I need to buy food on the way home. Besides, we've got the luxury of an onsite security guard, haven't we? They should be safe enough."

Kevin nodded agreement and wandered outside. Rebecca closed the box, grabbed her coat and turned to leave.

"You?"

Rebecca turned, startled.

"Sorry?"

"How was your day?" said Marcie abruptly.

Wow. Was she trying to be friendly? Miracles would never cease.

"Good, thanks. I think I'm coming down on some burials."

"Really?" Marcie couldn't disguise the interest in her voice, but when Rebecca looked up, she quickly looked down. "Good," she muttered, and carried on sorting the untidy heap of sample bags in front of her.

"See you tomorrow." Rebecca thought she heard Marcie grunt a reply as she left, but couldn't be sure.

"Thank God!" Kevin exclaimed as she emerged. "I'm starving, woman."

"I didn't make you stay." She punched his arm lightly.

"Oh had to, had to."

"Why?"

"My boss is a complete slave driver." He rolled his eyes. "She would have had me working until dawn if I hadn't stood my ground."

"Really?"

"Yes. You know how it is in these high pressure working environments," he sighed dramatically. "If you leave before the boss, that's it, you're out on your ear in no time."

"How awful for you. She sounds like a nightmare."

"Uh-huh. I have to keep her sweet by wining and dining her, too, and showering her with gifts. It's the only way to hold on to my job." Kevin turned sideways to wiggle through the gap between the security gates. "And on that note—oof, these are a bit close together – forget buying food. KFC, or do you want to share the microwave Indian Buffet For Two that's lurking in my freezer?"

Rebecca slid through after him easily. "Not sure you should have either of those, fatty. Salad for you."

"And I was going to ask what you wanted for you birthday. Shan't bother now."

"Soz." She grinned. "Indian buffet, please, providing you've got wine."

"I haven't."

"We'll stop off and buy some. My treat."

"That's very gracious of you, boss."

"I know." It started to rain and she fished in her bag for her umbrella. "Bugger."

"Forgot your brolly?"

"Yep."

"Shame." He ostentatiously pulled the in-built hood out of his collar and flicked it deftly over his head. "I'll buy you a new brolly for your birthday."

She sped up, resisting the urge to hunch down in her collar against the rain. "No thanks," she called over her shoulder. "I already know what I want."

He jogged a little to catch up with her, and fell into step. "What's that then, m'lady?"

"What I want most of all is another archaeologist to work with who's not uppity," she started to mark off points on her fingers, "or temperamental, or a bit of a slacker, always wanting to knock off early."

"You don't want much, do you?"

She patted his arm. "A nice bottle of Chardonnay will do for now, though."

"Good, because this is no time to be searching for the impossible, especially not on an empty stomach." He stuck his elbow out and she put her arm in his, laughing as they hurried towards the off licence.

Chapter Twenty One

Steve pushed open the door of Methodical Matches and stopped. It said Methodical Matches on the window, so this must be the right place. But this couldn't be their office. It was tiny, just a lobby area really, with a reception desk on one side—currently devoid of a receptionist—and a staircase disappearing upwards on the other. Perhaps all the cogs turned upstairs, he thought, but then he saw the large sign on the wall pointing upwards to Cooper's Insurance.

Steve had presumed they'd moved out when he'd seen the Methodical Matches signage appear on the front of the building, but it looked like they were still operating upstairs. He frowned. Weird.

"Can I help you?" asked a voice that Steve mentally tagged as 'bouncy'. A head had popped up from under the reception desk, belonging to a woman with a scarily intense suntan.

"I am in the right place for Methodical Matches, right?"

"You certainly are." She flashed him a smile and her teeth glowed fluorescently.

"But Coopers is still based here? Have they let out the first floor to you?"

"No, we only occupy this area. They still have the rest of the building, although it's only their admin department and data centre now. Their public-facing departments have moved to different premises." She smiled tightly. "Being an internet-based company with no physical product, we don't need a lot of floor space."

He frowned. "So where do you keep your computer servers, stuff like that?"

Her eyes narrowed. "We have a separate data centre elsewhere. Can I ask what your interest is?"

"It's just that a friend told me you run a very small operation. I can see she wasn't joking." He let his gaze wander meaningfully from one corner of the lobby to the other.

Her smile was a rictus grin now, her cheeks reddening through the tan. "It's perfectly adequate. You know what they say, quality not quantity."

"Ah yes. Talking of quality and quantity, can you tell me how many people you currently have signed up to your service?"

She blinked and leaned back a little. "How many?"

"Yes, you know. Numbers."

"The system can handle—"

"No, sorry," he broke in, "I wanted to know how many people are signed up right now, with profiles that are live on the site."

"Why do you want to know?"

He shrugged. "Isn't that the first question most people ask? I'd have thought that was your most important statistic."

He gave her what he hoped was a disarming smile, aware the atmosphere had got confrontational. It obviously didn't work.

"I hear what you're saying, Mr...?"

"Reynolds."

"Mr. Reynolds, but I'm afraid our policy is to keep that kind of information confidential except to clients."

"So much for the age of transparency, huh?" This time he went for the apologetic grin. And got not a flicker of a smile or thawing of expression in return. "Luckily, I am a client." He pointed to her laptop. "Reynolds, Steve Reynolds."

It was hard to tell, but he thought she went a little pale. She probably recognised the name, if Rebecca was right, because she did everything.

"Could you confirm your date of birth for me please? And your username?" Her tone had completely changed now to embarrassed and conciliatory. She typed in his replies. "Yes, of course, I can see you are a client, Mr. Reynolds. What can I do for your today?"

He raised an eyebrow. "I'd still like to know how many clients you have."

He had to admire her for meeting his eye as she told him, although her tan was now looking more blood orange than tangerine.

"Locally, 27."

He gaped, then recovered himself. "27. When you say locally... "

"In the London area."

"How is that defined?"

There was no term for the colour she'd gone now. She dropped her eyes. "Er, within the M25," she quavered, and then burst into tears.

"Look, er..." He patted his pockets frantically for tissues and passed one over.

"Th-thanks."

"That's okay. I'm sorry if I upset you."

She shook her head, mopping at her face. "No, you have every right to ask. You're thinking the numbers are pathetic, and you're right. It's a difficult kind of business to get off the ground."

"I can imagine."

"But that's not really what's upset me. I've had a bad day, that's all. You're not responsible for all this wailing." Her smile, wobbly as it was, was the most genuine one he'd seen from her.

Steve felt his resentment melting away.

"Anything I can help with? If it's a leaky tap I'm not a bad amateur plumber, even though I say so myself."

A strange hiccupping laugh escaped between her sobs, which thankfully seemed to be subsiding. "No, there's not a tap down here. I use Cooper's staff kitchen when I want a coffee."

"Right."

"And their loo," she carried on disconsolately. "And Marjorie lets me keep my lunch in the fridge up there." She slumped back in her chair and blew her nose noisily. "I have to put a label on it."

There was something so comical about the despairing tone of that final comment that Steve let a small snort escape. Nicola glanced up sharply and then saw the funny side too.

"Sorry," said Steve.

"It's alright. It is ridiculous. This is the only way I could afford office space, if you can call it that. Cooper's don't need a meet-and-greet area any more, now that only back-end stuff goes on here. It's just the employees who need access, and most of them use the staircase at the back. It seemed like a great opportunity, especially when they agreed to let me put signage on the window. But it's pathetic, isn't it. I'm pathetic."

"Not at all. At least you're giving it a go, showing a bit of enterprise. And I'm guessing you're doing that all by yourself..." he asked gently. "Am I right?" He prayed she wouldn't start crying again. Crying women he knew were one thing. Crying strangers were another.

"I wasn't to start with," she said heavily. "That's sort of the problem. I set it up with this guy Andy—he used to work upstairs at Coopers, writing data analysis programmes for them."

Steve's brow furrowed. "Tall? Sandy hair? Skinny?"

"Yes—do you know him?" She leaned forward, eyes bright with hope.

"Not really. I work at Tony's—you know, the café? He used to come in for lunch sometimes."

"Not recently?"

Steve thought for a minute. "He certainly hasn't been in since we did that Mexican day in January. Or at least not when I've been there."

"Oh." She sat back. "You wouldn't know where he's gone then."

"Afraid not. Did he run out on you, then?"

She nodded. "I handled the business and admin side of things, he wrote the client matching program and handled the website. He set it all up, hung around for a week entering the first few clients, and then he left one evening and didn't come back."

"Didn't he leave a message? Or a forwarding address?"

She snorted. "Oh yes. I got an email three days later, from a new webmail address, telling me about the 'new life' he'd decided he had to start. I told him the program seemed to be going nuts—I don't know what it's doing but it might as well be one of those randomiser programs for all the success it's having," she said bitterly. Then she slapped her hand over her mouth. "Forget I said that! I shouldn't be telling you any of this. I'll get it fixed, honestly, and if I can't I'll issue refunds."

"Er... don't worry about me. I know this isn't the best time to say it, but I came in to cancel my membership."

She put her head in her hands. "Of course you have. Why wouldn't you? So will everyone else soon, I expect. All 26 of them."

"I thought you said the 27 people were inside the M25? What about your clients elsewhere?"

She laughed hollowly. "Oh yes. Our other clients. We had 30 applications from the whole rest of the country. Right from Northumberland down to Cornwall."

"Ahhh, I see. Tricky."

"Yes."

"So you turned them away?"

"No, I told them we had too many applicants and they would be put on a waiting list. The plan was to put them on area by area once we had enough people there to make it workable." She tilted her head to look at him. "Can you believe that?"

He shrugged, not wanting to condemn her when she was already down. "I can see the logic."

"London was the only place where we had enough applicants to go ahead and make the profiles live, and even that was pushing it. We only had 32."

"So you've lost a few already," said Steve sympathetically.

"Yes, and I can't say I'm surprised, are you?"

Safer to change the subject than answer that one, he decided. "Did Andy ever reply to your message about the program?"

"Yes. He said he'd access the server remotely—he'd already installed the software to do that on his laptop, so that he could work from home when he wanted to—and he promised me he would get it sorted. But it's not. In fact, whatever he did to it seems to have made it worse. It's gone completely haywire, and the questionnaires it generates seem to get longer every week!"

"Have you told him that?"

"Yes, but I've heard nothing from him since. That was two months ago, and I can't track him down. It's like he's disappeared off the face of the earth."

"And you can't alter the program yourself in any way?"

She shook her head. "Not a chance. I wouldn't know where to start! I didn't take an IT qualification at school, I only did the basics—and I wasn't that great at them, to be honest."

Steve knew he should be cross about this, in a disgruntled-customer-who's-been-misled kind of way, but it was all too much like a farce and, looking at Nicola now, all he could feel for her was pity. Andy was a heel, leaving her in the lurch like this. He wished he could do something to help. Suddenly it occurred to him that perhaps he could.

"Nicola, I think I might be able to help. With the matching program, anyway."

Her head came out of her hands and her eyes brightened. "Really? Do you know about computer programs, then?"

"No I don't, but I know someone who does."

"That would be fantastic!" Nicola beamed. Then her face dropped. "But IT experts cost a fortune. I could barely afford to pay them for a morning, and it might take hours."

"Nicola she's not an IT expert, she's my sister. But she does know her way round computers and programs, she has got an A level in IT, and she won't expect to be paid a fortune. Anything but."

"It's got to be worth a try. Do you think she'll do it?"

"I'm sure she will. But," he emphasised grimly, "when you hear what I'm about to say, you might decide you don't want her within a mile of your business."

Her eyes widened. "Tell me more."

Much to his surprise – something he felt guilty for afterwards—Nicola didn't turn a hair when Steve filled her in about Laura's track record, and she didn't seem to be just taking a chance to save money, either. She seemed genuinely sympathetic and was happy to have Laura, "in my extensive open plan office," she'd said, laughing self-deprecatingly, for as long as it took take.

Ten minutes and a quick call to Laura later, and the details were sorted. Laura would try to sort out the program, or if not, try to create a simple one that would match Nicola's clients with someone compatible. It might not be the scientific sifting of variables that people had signed up for, thought Steve privately, but who was to say something more basic might not work just as well – and on so few people, it would probably make the same matches anyway.

All it was costing Nicola was the price of keeping Laura in coffees and light lunches. She considered she was getting the best end of the bargain.

"I can't thank you enough, Steve. It's really kind of you." She beamed. "It's a shame you're cancelling your membership, a girl would be lucky to have you."

"Why thank you," he grinned. "I should be off. Nearly time for work."

"Oh, before you go... "

"What?"

"I know it's daft but I'm meant to ask you why you decided to cancel. Customer feedback, and all that." She shrugged. "I'll just put 'incompatible matches', shall I, and leave it at that?"

"You could, but that's not why I wanted to cancel."

"Really?"

"Really. I wanted to cancel because I think I've met the girl of my dreams."

Nicola practically bounced out of her chair. "Fantastic! Can I put it on the website? What's her username? Will she mind?" She clapped her hands together. "Is there a chance there might be the first Methodical Matches wedding in the near future?"

Steve put up his hands. "Hate to disappoint you, but I didn't meet her through the dating agency. I only went on two dates."

"Oh." Nicola deflated. "What were they like?"

"Honestly? Awful. Sorry." He smiled. "Although in your defence, I don't think that's got much to do with your matching program. Number one was just after my money and number two, er, was after my body."

"Really? Oh. But there's not a lot I can do about that." Nicola perked up a little. That's something, then. Good luck with the girl of your dreams."

Steve smiled. "Thanks."

He walked out into the street. That was it, then. He couldn't believe he'd said it out loud—and to a stranger! But he honestly felt Rebecca was the girl of his dreams. The One.

He hoped she felt the same about him.

Chapter Twenty Two

Rebecca had only just got to her desk when the phone rang.

"Hello, Rebecca Maynard—"

"Bec, it's Kev. Are you coming over to the site this morning?" He sounded strained.

"I wanted to, but I've got these proofs to check—"

"Leave those until later. The site's been vandalised."

"Vandalised?"

"There's, er, a few things been taken and they've destroyed your trench."

Questions were buzzing around Rebecca's head, but she knew asking Kevin all of them over the phone wasn't the best use of her time. "Stay there. I'm coming straight over."

She didn't even stop to tell Ron. She could call him in the cab on the way.

Rebecca stood at the edge of her trench beside Kevin. All her carefully excavated layers were gone, replaced by a heap of sandy soil, with the bones of the skeleton she'd been able to glimpse yesterday sticking out here and there.

She turned, trying to keep her anger tamped down. Losing her rag would accomplish nothing. "And you say none of the other trenches have been touched?"

"No. Nearly everyone who was here digging yesterday is here today, and they all say their areas are exactly as they left them. It's just yours. None of their tools have been taken either." He added hesitantly.

Her head shot round. "What do you mean, none of their tools?" She saw his expression and then she was running towards the tent. She saw the plastic box with her name on dumped on the floor in front of the others with the lid off. Empty, save for a tatty old pair of gloves.

Kevin came to stand beside her. "I'm so sorry, Becs," he put his hand on her shoulder. "I know how much those tools meant to you. We'll get them back."

"Only my trench. Only my tools," she said through gritted teeth. "Please tell me nobody is dumb enough to think this wasn't Marcie King's doing."

She could hear Kevin swallow. "She hasn't turned up this morning, Becs, but I don't think we should jump to any conclu—"

Rebecca turned and called him a name she'd never called anyone before, and stormed out of the tent. She strode up to the security guard and he took an involuntary step backwards, even before her finger jabbed into his chest.

"And where the fuck were you while this was going on?" she yelled.

"Er, I wasn't on duty Miss, it was Roger—"

Rebecca called him the same name she'd called Kevin.

"Our coffee not good enough for you any more, then?" He leaned on the counter, shoulders squared, and tried to look threatening.

Rebecca grinned. "Dunno, why, has it gone downhill since last time? It's probably the staff. They're pretty useless, so I hear."

He grunted. "So, to what do we owe the honour?"

"Honour?"

"Of madam gracing us with her presence."

"I'm thirsty."

"But you haven't been thirsty for the last two weeks?"

"Oh I have, but as sir knows I've been elsewhere, I'm afraid, working."

"Really. Madam doesn't have a tap where she works?" he asked haughtily.

"Nope."

"And no coffee machines where you work?"

"Oh, we're drowning in coffee over there," said Rebecca brightly. "But it's not as nice as yours." She batted her eyelashes at him theatrically, very fast. "Ow!" She clapped her hand over her right eye. "Eyelid strain!"

"Serves you right," he said severely. "Well I suppose I could forgive you, even though this is barefaced flattery and cupboard love."

"Cupboard love? Hold on. I wasn't offering that. Coffee really has got expensive here."

"Don't go lowering the tone with your lewd remarks."

"You started it!"

"Ahem." He looked at her sternly. "That's quite enough. What can I do for you?"

Her lips quivered.

He glared. "Don't start! What would you like to drink?"

"A butterscotch latte, please."

"Ah. So long away, yet I see madam still favours the latte avec butterscotch a la Steve." He grinned and reached for the butterscotch syrup.

"Oui."

"Ooh, I like a girl who speaks French," he laughed, his back to her as the cup filled with milky froth.

She grinned. "Moi, aussi."

"Oh? Is there something you're not telling me?"

"Non, monsieur. Rien."

"Phew." He slid her latte over to her. "And would madam like a cake too?"

"I imagine you have plenty of tarts here."

"Sorry madam, we're not that kind of establishment."

"I'll settle for a Danish then." She took a sip of her coffee.

"Ah, you prefer tall, blue-eyed blondes, do you?" He sighed sorrowfully.

"Well I used to," said Rebecca. She stared at him very deliberately over her coffee cup, making his stomach flutter. "But I can make exceptions."

"What kind of exceptions?" he asked hoarsely.

She didn't answer for a moment, running her eyes over him.

"Oh, for other shades of hair, towards the darker end of the spectrum. Say, light brown."

"I see."

"And the eyes don't have to be true blue. They could be..." she looked at him meditatively. "Kind of greeny."

He swallowed. "Any other preferences?"

"Definitely. Medium height, about 5'10ish, not too skinny, not too fat."

"I'm beginning to get the picture."

"Looked in a mirror lately?" she asked, raising an eyebrow suggestively.

Get this back on a humorous level, Steve, or else you're going to have a heart attack mate. "Excuse me, madam, but are you coming on to me?" She would laugh now, then he could steer the conversation back to safer waters. "Because if you are, I must warn—"

"Yes."

"— you that you may be charged with harassment..." he trailed off.

"I missed you," she said quietly.

"Good. You seem a lot happier today."

"I'm making a concerted effort. Kevin told me off for making everyone miserable and tense. Sorry if I've done that to you too."

"No. I understood how you felt. What's happening about the site and everything? Or shouldn't I ask?"

"I'll tell you if you let me take you out to dinner tonight."

"That sounds good. Chilango, or would you like to go somewhere different?"

"You choose. It's the company I'm looking forward to."

On an impulse, Steve leaned over and kissed her.

"We'll go to Chilango's again then. Shouldn't be too busy on a Monday. 7.30?"

"Great." She looked down at her coffee. "It's getting cold."

"Shall I get you another one?"

"There's not much left." She smiled. "Can you put my pastry in a bag? I should be getting back, it's mad today. I only came in to see you."

"I'll see you later."

"Bye."

He heard the kitchen door snap back on its hinges as he watched her go.

"About time too, eh? Although if you kiss all the customers, Steve, I get complaints."

"What?" he asked. "I wouldn't, er, Rebecca and I, we're—"

"Going out?" said Tony, wiping down the counter, his back to Steve, "That is why I say, about time. But," he said, raising his voice as he thrust the cloth forcefully into Steve's, "this is work. I'm pleased for you, but save kissing for the break times, not when you're serving, si?"

"Sorry, Tony."

"No problem. I was young man once, too. And skinny man once, also. Is hard to believe now, eh?" He grinned. "Now you wipe down front counter, and refill the coffee machine. The more you are getting done now, Prince Charming, the quicker I am letting you go to see Cinderella." The twinkle in his eye suggested that despite the reprimand—well-deserved, he had to admit—Tony wasn't really cross with him.

He grinned. "Funny. I never thought of you as the Fairy Godmother."

Tony glared. "There's plenty of people wanting your job, do you know? And that counter, still it is dirty."

"Yes, boss." Steve raised his hand in mock salute and set to it. But his mind wasn't on dirty counters and coffee machines. It was on kissed Rebecca, and how things would go tonight. He felt contented and stirred up at the same time.

He had plenty of time for happy anticipation, in the end. At 4.30 Tony declared he wasn't fit for anything with his head in the clouds, and sent him home.

"So the police think it's Marcie?" Steve asked, before biting into his burrito.

"They do now. I never had any doubts, myself."

"Barmy woman. Risking her career to get back at you in such a petty way."

"Oh there was nothing petty about it." Rebecca smiled tightly. "She knew how important those tools were to me. How hurt I'd be."

Steve reached for her hand. "I know, honey. I didn't mean that wasn't important. But she must really be off her rocker. She must know her career in archaeology's probably over."

"Yep."

"So do they know where she is now?"

"No. They know she got on a flight to France in the early hours of that morning. She'd been staying in a cheap hotel since she got back from Italy, apparently. She hadn't bothered to find a flat."

"And the security guard wasn't suspicious?"

"No. She filed out at the back of the stragglers, then as she got to the gate she said she'd forgotten something and she'd just be a few minutes. He saw her go back towards the tent and then stood there a while talking to one of the surveyors. From where he was standing, the tent would have blocked the view of that section of the site. It's quite a way from the gate, so it's not surprising he didn't hear anything, either, especially as he was talking."

"And when she left?"

Rebecca shrugged. "She always takes a big bag to and from the site. She just walked out with her usual bag. When she left, he knew she was the last person on his list, and he'd already done a perimeter check. So he just locked the gate and went to sit in his little box."

Steve shook his head. "Unbelievable."

"Yet unfortunately true." Rebecca gave him a small smile. "Anyway, on to a happier topic. You've got next Saturday off, haven't you?"

"Sure have. I'm all yours," he grinned.

"Great. Fancy coming to a wedding?"

Tonight had been great, Steve thought. Despite the shadow cast by what he'd now termed the Marcie Goes Mental incident, they'd still had a good time. He didn't think he could be any happier. He stopped the car outside Rebecca's flat and leaned over to kiss her goodnight.

"Would you like to come in for a coffee?"

Wow. That had come out of the left field. "Er..."

"Your enthusiasm's overwhelming," she said, raising her eyebrows.

"No, it's just, er..." he cleared his throat. "Is that coffee with a small c, or coffee with a capital C?" he asked, awkwardly.

"Oh I see," she said sharply. "If it's coffee with a small c, you're not that bothered, thanks, you'll go home and have a drink there? Is that it?"

"No, of course not! You know me better than that!"

She had the grace to look guilty. "Sorry, but it was a bit of a direct question."

He kissed her. "I'm sorry too, but I had to ask in case, I, er..."

"What?"

"Needed something from the glove box," he said pointedly.

Rebecca out her hands to her face for a moment. "Oh God. Sorry. There was you trying to be all responsible and caring and discreet, and there was me accusing you of being shallow."

She buried her face against his chest and he sighed theatrically. "I suppose I forgive you. On one condition."

She lifted her head. "What's that?"

"Will you please tell me if it's small c or large C, bearing in mind I'm happy with either?"

"I was thinking more medium c."

"Right." He froze, not sure what to do and not wanting her to take offence. In future, Steve, keep some in your pocket, you moron.

"But a good boy Scout should always be prepared," she said mischievously.

"I was never a boy scout, but what the hell," said Steve, yanking the glove box open. "Get in there and put that kettle on, woman. Pronto!"

Chapter Twenty Three

"Hi! You must be Laura."

Laura blinked. That tan was bright. "Yes."

"Would you like a coffee before you start?"

"Yes please."

Fifteen minutes later she was engrossed. The program was a mess, cross-referencing various spreadsheets and web links. She needed to go for Plan B.

"Nicola, do you have the original information from your clients' profiles?"

"Yes." She beamed then frowned, speaking slowly as if remembering something she'd learned by rote. "Plain text file versions of profiles are saved automatically as a back-up."

"And that's still been working?"

Nicola rolled her eyes. "It's about the only thing that has. I print them out too, so there's something on paper if the computer crashes."

"Great. Can I have your print-outs? It's going to be easier to make a new, simpler matching program and abandon this one. I need to start from scratch."

"Whatever you think best. I wouldn't have a clue."

It took Laura the rest of the morning to sift through the mountain of detail the profiles recorded and decide on sensible parameters, and then as promised, Nicola took her out for lunch.

Once she was back, she spent time designing the program and then began to enter data from the print-outs. She expected to find Steve's details, but her eyes widened when she saw Rebecca's profile. She knew she'd tried internet dating, but had no idea she'd been with the same agency as Steve.

By the time Nicola called a halt for afternoon coffee break—not that there was much for Nicola to be wearing herself out with, as far as she could see—Laura was ready to run the program she had designed and generate new matches.

She began to save the matches for each client in a file, so Nicola could refer to it when she sent out emails. She looked at the next batch. These were from currently inactive profiles but Nicola had asked her to run them through anyway, in case any clients decided to reactivate their profile.

She shifted uneasily. Rebecca and Steve had both come up in each other's top three. She shouldn't be surprised. She'd been dimly aware as she entered the data that they had a lot in common. Laura frowned. She knew they'd only been out once, but thinking about them together made her uncomfortable. They had distinct roles in her life at the moment, and she didn't want that to change. Not when things were going right for a change.

She could change some of their details to make sure they didn't come up as a match. She flushed guiltily, dithering.

In the end she left them exactly as they were. Not because she'd had a sudden attack of integrity, but because she figured it was unnecessary. Their profiles were inactive, and from what they'd both said about their experiences, neither of them intended to try internet dating ever again.

So they'd never know.

"Thanks for meeting me."

"'Meeting me'? That is very formal!" Francois laughed. He had risen to his feet as Rebecca walked over to his table and now he kissed her on both cheeks. "It's my pleasure. I was planning to see you while I was in London, already."

Rebecca settled herself opposite him. Francois never changed, she thought, as he sat down. Still full of old-fashioned courtesy – how many men, these days, would wait for her to sit down before they did?—and still very handsome, even with the grey that was starting to creep through his dark hair. Those cheekbones. That jaw!

"You look well, Francois."

"You do not just look well, you look gorgeous. And so like your mother," he said with a smile.

She laughed, trying to ignore the nervous churning in her stomach. "French flattery already! Nothing changes."

"Indeed. Now what can I do for you, Rebecca? It sounded important."

He rolled the r in her name beautifully. If he were fifteen years younger, perhaps she wouldn't need an internet dating agency. She sighed inwardly, wondering how many women's knees had been turned to jelly over the years by that accent and those looks. And how many men's, too.

"Oh, I just thought it would be nice to catch up," she said lightly. "You're not in London often. I thought I'd best grab the bull by the horns."

"This is charming, I am sitting here for just five minutes and you call me an animal." His white teeth flashed as he grinned. "Is this English hospitality?"

"Sorry," she smiled.

"I forgive you, cherie. Perhaps coffee before we start to 'catch-up'? Even though I am not sure what I am meant to catch."

She raised her eyebrows. "Your English is excellent, Francois, idioms and all. You don't fool me for a second. It's all for comic effect."

He stood, clutching a hand to his heart. "How can you say such a thing?" He rolled his eyes. "Now, what can I get you?"

"A vanilla latte, please."

He shuddered comically. "An abomination. Vanilla is a flavour for ice creams. But I will order it." Another flash of that brilliant white smile, and he was off towards the counter. Steve was serving behind the counter now. She gave him a wave, hiding her nerves behind a big smile, then wondered how she was going to broach the subject that was on her mind.

"I brought sugar, too."

Rebecca jumped.

"I wasn't sure how you took your..." Francois wrinkled his nose, "vanilla latte." He said the words as though he had a nasty taste in his mouth and Rebecca giggled.

He looked over and smiled, stirring his coffee. "That's better. When I walked back to the table, your face—" he shrugged, "I don't know. Angry? Sad? You looked like you were in a black mood, as you English say. If one can still say that?"

"No, I'm fine. Just tired." She leant forward to look in his coffee cup. "Espresso, I presume?"

"Double. What else? It is the only thing they serve in England that gives something close to the, the kick of French coffee. Not like your latte, full of sweetness and froth and strange flavours!"

"I know someone who would agree with you wholeheartedly on that," said Rebecca wryly. "But you'll never meet him, thank God. And I apologise on behalf of England."

"Merci," he laughed. "So, why did you really want to see me?"

"I haven't seen you for ages. Do I need an excuse?" She concentrated on stirring her coffee.

He regarded her steadily. "No, but your tone when you called me—it did not sound like you wanted just a 'catch-up', as you called it." He sipped his coffee. "You knew I was in London at Christmas, Rebecca, yet you did not seek me then."

She smiled. "I was busy at Christmas, and presumed you were too. You weren't over here for long."

His gaze was very direct, and she squirmed under it, realising that she was wringing her hands. With an effort she made herself still, took a deep breath, and met his eyes. She wanted to speak but felt like she was on the edge of a cliff—about to make someone push her over the edge.

"We have known each other for many years, yes? You may say to me whatever you wish. I am your honorary uncle," he said gently. "Your parents would have been happy to know you could talk to me."

"It's about them. When they died. That's what I want to talk about," she blurted.

He nodded slowly. "Yes?"

"I want to know what happened." She couldn't help herself. Her eyes flicked up, wanting to gauge his reaction.

He spread his hands. "You know what happened, Rebecca. There was a car accident and your parents were killed, along with David King. A tragedy, not only for you and friends, family, but also for the archaeological community. You know this."

"I know what I've been told."

"What else is there to tell?"

"I want to know exactly what happened. What caused the accident—"

"Bad roads, an unexpected rainstorm—"

"—and why Marcie King blames my father for her father's death," she finished, her voice quavering.

Francois sat back, putting his hands on the armrests of his chair. "Marcie has never comes to terms with her grief, not in the way that you have, I think." He shrugged. "Whether it is her personality, or how she was supported after her father's death, or the reaction of her mother... who can say?"

"I know that."

"So, she looks for someone to blame. This not new, this anger she has. She has kept it alive all this time. Why is it bothering you now, cherie? Put it out of your mind. It is her problem, not yours."

Rebecca wanted to believe him but she'd noticed how he moved his hands back and forth on the arms of the chair as he spoke, just a little. It flashed a warning signal. Francois was usually so poised and calm.

"It bothers me now because she made it my problem. You must have heard from Ron what happened?"

"I did. I'm sorry about your tools. I know how special they were to you."

"Thanks. But I'm sorry, Francois, I don't believe you."

His eyes narrowed. "Believe me? About what?"

"The accident. What caused it."

"You know what the report from the Thai authorities said. They are the facts. Marcie is a bitter woman, but one we must feel a certain sympathy for, oui?"

"Marcie says my father was drunk that night," she said flatly. "That he should never have been driving." The words sounded abnormally loud in her head, as though they were ringing out. She half-expected silence to fall all around them. But the hubbub of the café just carried on as normal.

Francois said nothing. When she looked up, he was drinking his coffee again. "This is excellent."

"Yes. I come here all the time."

"Most surprising, for an English café."

She leaned forward. "Yes, the coffee's great," she said abruptly. "Is it true? Was Dad drunk?"

After a hesitation that felt like years, he nodded. Rebecca collapsed back into her seat, stunned. She couldn't believe it. No wonder Marcie blamed her father. And her, by default. How had Marcie known?

"But this is not the whole story." He put down his coffee and clasped his hands together, elbows on the arms of his chair. "David King was also drunk. So your mother had to drive," he said slowly. "If there's any blame, that's all there is. Your mother was never a confident driver; she rarely drove abroad." He sighed. "But I believe whoever drove, the end result would have been the same. Nobody could have kept that car on the road once the storm hit. Half the road was swept away."

"How do you know?"

"Because I drove out there the next day." Francois looked pale now under his tan. "I waited while the authorities recovered the car, and I identified the bodies," he said softly. "Your mother... well. Let us say from her position, it was obvious she had been in the driving seat."

"And you've never told Marcie? Or her mother?"

"Oh, but I have," he said grimly. "But you know what you English say about the blindness of those who do will not see."

There was a long silence.

"Was there anything else you wish to ask?"

She shook her head.

"Then, cherie, we shall discuss a happier topic. How can I get you to come and work for me? And if we can arrange it, would a two month trial period in Milan – a sabbatical from your Museum – help you to come to a decision?"

Chapter Twenty Four

Rebecca took her keys from the ignition and smiled at him. "Ready?"

"What, to play Kevin's stand-in? You've got me here under false pretences."

"Don't complain! Thanks to Mr. Grumpy's absence, you get free food and a night in a hotel. With breakfast, might I add."

"Yeah. Free food I didn't choose," he pouted as he climbed out of the car.

"Kevin chose some Italian thing with chicken. You'll love it." She walked round to his side and Steve looked at her admiringly.

"You look gorgeous."

"Oh, now you notice?" she teased.

"I couldn't see you in your full glory before." He grinned.

"Thanks. It's the same outfit I wore for Anna and Jessica's wedding, but hopefully no one will notice."

"Same crowd, then?" he asked as they started towards the church.

"Not by a long chalk, but there's some overlap."

"I see. Hope I pass muster."

"Oh, you'll do. I'm sure you'll cause quite a stir."

"What, with my rugged charm 'n all."

"No. Well, yes, obviously." She grinned and took his hand. "But mostly because you're not Kevin, and usually it's him I drag to these things."

"Drag? Aren't they normally Kevin's friends as well, though?"

"Often, but unless they're close friends, he avoids weddings."

"Why?"

"Doesn't enjoy them. It's because he always gets cornered and asked when he's going to bring a girlfriend along, and when it's going to be his turn. Especially at family weddings.""

"Right. Awkward."

"Yes."

"Why doesn't he just tell them? Are his family all hugely anti-gay or something?"

"Not any more than your average family, I don't think."

"So why not make a stand? Tell everyone and get it over with?"

She shrugged. "Because he doesn't see it as anyone else's business. On a personal level, and on principle too."

Steve slipped his arm round her. "Explain."

"Well, do you think it's anyone else's business that you're heterosexual?"

"Er... no."

"And do you think you should be expected to declare your sexual preferences to everyone? To have to come out as straight?"

"No, and I see your point. It's not fair that people make presumptions." He shrugged.

"But they do, not always because they're prejudiced, but because they're wired to expect 'the norm'".

"And cause misery for the minority."

"Unfortunately, yes, But a wedding would be a great time to come out, that way everyone finds out at once. Done. Dusted. No more awkward questions."

"No, he'd just get a whole new set!" She laughed. "The more accepting relatives would start asking when he was going to settle down with a nice boy, and he'd hate that!"

"Not a fan of commitment then?"

"I wouldn't say that; he's just not found the right person yet."

"Poor bloke. Hope he does, he's a nice guy."

She grinned. "Funny, that. I used to have the impression you weren't too keen."

He blinked at her innocently. "Don't know what you mean."

She raised her eyebrows.

"Okay, perhaps I was a bit jealous."

"Completely without reason."

"I know that now, don't I!"

They reached the back of the queue filing into the church.

"Shh! Behave yourself, we're going in."

"Yes miss." He grinned and swooped for a kiss.

The woman in front was wearing an intricate, bright purple fascinator so huge that as she turned round Steve instinctively ducked, expecting it to either fly off or take his eye out. She glanced at him without recognition, her eyes sliding off him to Rebecca.

"Rebecca! Thought that was your voice! How are you? Where's Kevin? And who is this delightful man?" She moved closer to him, resting a proprietorial hand on his chest.

Rebecca stretched to look at Steve over the top of the woman's head and fascinator. "See?" She mouthed, grinning.

Steve collapsed into the chair beside her and groaned. "I'm bushed."

"No! Really?" She smiled brightly. "What's happened to those dancing feet? Surely they're not worn out?"

He shot her a steely look. "So would yours be if you'd spent the last half hour dancing with Purple Fascinator Woman."

"You mustn't keep calling her that. Her name's Veronica! She's Jason's cousin."

"I don't care if she's Kylie Minogue's cousin. She's got all the grace of an elephant and the charm of a mosquito."

"Better get your net out then, she's headed this way."

"What!" He jolted upright, looking all around. "Where? I can't see her."

Rebecca doubled up with laughter.

"Oh. Very funny." He glared.

"Good meerkat impression. Best I've seen."

"When you're done humiliating me, can we go? That hotel bed is starting to call to me."

"That depends."

"On what?"

"What's all this about Kylie Minogue?"

"She's hot. I'd dance with all of her cousins to get an intro."

"Oh would you now?"

"Wrong thing to say?"

"Not if you're happy to spend all night alone, waiting for Kylie," she said lightly.

He sat bolt upright again. "I didn't know there were other options."

"If you keep talking about Kylie Minogue there won't be, Meerkat Man."

He clamped his lips together and mimed zipping them up. "Shutting up about her right now, ma'am."

"Good. Come on." She pulled him to his feet. "If you're so tired, I'd best get you to the hotel."

He looked down at her. "It's only my feet that are tired. The rest of me is fine. Completely fine."

She kissed him and took his hand. "I'll be the judge of that, thank you."

Steve woke up to find himself lying on his side, curved around Rebecca's back. That was a pretty darn fine place to find himself, he decided. He lifted his head to peer over her shoulder and found her smiling up at him.

"Morning."

"Morning gorgeous. How are you?"

"Marvellous, thanks."

"Good. So," he said solemnly, kissing her shoulder, "Now you've had a taste of my coffee with a capital C, what's your opinion?"

"Hmm, well after experiencing your coffee with a medium c, I had quite high expectations," she said, eyes twinkling, "and I wasn't disappointed. Grande Latte standard, I think."

"Glad madam was satisfied."

Rebecca's smiled. "Oh, she was."

He bent his head and trailed kisses down her side towards her hip, then watched as her knees jerked upwards, her arms flailed and she disintegrated into giggles.

"Oh God, I'm really ticklish! Do that again and I'll kill you!"

"'Do that again and I'll kill you'. Just what every man wants to hear when he's seducing his woman." He tugged her shoulder, rolling her on to her back beside him. "Where are you ticklish?"

"Nearly everywhere, I'm afraid."

He leaned over her, frowning. "Hmm. I'm not convinced." He slid down the bed.

A while later he lifted his head. "You're not giggling."

"No. I'm not ticklish there," she said huskily.

"So you're not going to kill me then?"

She buried her fingers in his hair. "Only if you stop."

Laura stretched and looked at the clock. Nearly ten. She should get up, really, but she was comfy, and it felt so good not to have anywhere she had to be, no deadlines. Though she didn't mind going to the Museum, if she was honest. She loved it.

Still, the day was a'wastin, as Steve would say, and she'd planned to cook him a nice dinner today. She wanted to spend some quality time with him; perhaps watch some comedy DVDs or play a board game, prove to him that she could be a nice person to live with instead of a pain in the arse. There was a lot she had to make up for, and she couldn't do that lounging about in bed.

She opened her curtains and sunshine lit up the room. It was a gorgeous day out there. Maybe she should suggest a trip somewhere instead. She showered quickly, pulled on fresh clothes and bounced downs the stairs.

She glanced round the kitchen as she sat at the table with a bowl of cereal and a glass or orange juice. Had Steve been ultra-tidy this morning when he'd had breakfast, or was still in bed—, which wasn't like him at all? And what was that white thing?

There was a note stuck to the worktop beside the kettle—Steve must have expected her to make herself a coffee first thing. She grinned. She would have, normally, but the sunshine had put her in the mood for something cooler... what? The grin slid off her face.

'Don't forget I'm at the wedding with Rebecca today, I'll be back by lunchtime tomorrow. Ready meals and pizza in the freezer, salad in the fridge. Money in the change pot if you need more milk, this carton's the last. See you tomorrow!'

She dropped back into her chair. Great. She was putting time aside to rebuild their relationship, and where was Steve? Off with Rebecca.

Had he even told her he was staying away overnight? He probably had; she couldn't remember. Didn't he realise that what she needed right now was company? Now the bail conditions were lifted, now that he didn't have to spend time with her, was he not going to bother? Laura's nails dug into her palms. Maybe every weekend would be like this now. Her stuck here alone while Steve and Rebecca were off for romantic weekends, weddings, parties...

She was disappointed in Rebecca too. All that stuff about how she understood what she'd gone through. Had everything—helping Steve out by babysitting her, getting her work experience at GLAM—been to show how wonderful she was and impress Steve?

She stabbed her spoon down into her cereal. She couldn't believe how selfish they were being. They had all the time in the world. Was it so much to ask for Steve, at least, to spend time with her until she was back on track?

She chewed her cereal mechanically. How serious were things, anyway? Had they booked a hotel room together? Soon Rebecca would be staying here all the time; or Steve would be staying at her flat. Before she knew it, they'd be moving in together.

She dropped her spoon into her bowl with a clang. Oh God. Say Rebecca was The One? They might get married. Have kids. Would either of them want her hanging around then? No.

She felt sick now, her mind racing as she envisaged a future where she was either pushed out or simply asked to leave. Who would she live with? She wasn't close enough to anyone else to want to share their home. Steve would never have enough time for her if he had a family, and she'd only just begun to appreciate how important he was to her; now she could only see a future where he saw her as a spare part. She pushed her bowl away from her.

It wasn't fair. She folded her arms round herself, frowning. She couldn't cope by herself yet, she still needed Steve. But how could she stop Rebecca stealing him away?

Chapter Twenty Five

"How are you getting on?"

Laura jumped. "Oh hi. Sorry, I was—"

"—Concentrating?" Rebecca smiled. "It's okay, I just came to see how things were going." She walked over to look at the find Laura had been studying under a magnifying glass.

"Good thanks. It's interesting to see the other side of it all."

"Even the side where you get your hands dirty?" Rebecca grinned.

Laura looked down at her hands and grimaced. "Yeah, that's the one."

This week she'd been working with some uni students, under the guidance of Tasha, learning about cleaning and labelling finds.

Rebecca looked round. "I take it everyone else has gone to lunch?"

Laura smiled ruefully. "I think so. I lost track of time."

"Well if you want to come for lunch with me, I know this great café. Friendly staff."

"Cool! Thanks, I'll just get cleaned up." Laura walked to the sink and Rebecca took her place at the bench, peering through the magnifying glass. Laura had been working on a brooch that Rebecca had tagged when it came in.

"Did you clean this up all by yourself?"

"Yes, start to finish." Laura smiled, going a little pink. She dried her hands and came to stand beside her. "It was so satisfying to see it start to shine. I'd never have guessed it would end up looking like that."

"You've done a brilliant job. This was really caked up." She turned the brooch. Laura had even managed to get the soil out from under the tiny arms of the setting around the stones and that was tricky for a newbie.

As they walked towards the café, Rebecca was glad she'd grabbed her coat on the way out. It was sunny but the breeze was cold. She looked sideways at Laura, only wearing a long-sleeved top, with a thin scarf just visible under her dark wavy hair. "How come you're not cold?"

"Naturally warm-blooded, Steve says."

"Lucky you," Rebecca laughed, pulling her collar up a little. "So how was last week?"

"Great. I thought I'd find all the bones a bit, you know... "

"Gruesome?"

"Yeah," Laura laughed. "But it was so interesting that I just, like, forgot there were bones in the end. Even when Maurice started sawing them up."

"Yes. You do get over being squeamish. Well most people do, anyway!" she laughed.

The café was busy. Laura bagged a table while Rebecca went to the counter.

"And how are my two favourite girls?" Steve asked, smiling.

"We're fine, thank you. But ravenous. We've been working hard."

"Oh yes, I've been hearing about her 'hard work'." He leaned sideway to look past her at Laura, and raised his voice. "If she enjoys dusting so much, perhaps she could so some at home!"

Laura stuck out her tongue at him and grinned.

"Behave yourself and get us lunch or else," said Rebecca firmly.

"Or else what?"

"We'll take our custom elsewhere."

"Right, I'm on it." He scuttled off and returned with two lattes and two wraps. "How's that?"

"Marvellous." She flashed him a warm smile and walked back to the table.

Laura took her wrap from the tray. "Thanks, Rebecca, this is great."

"No problem. Not sure about the staff here though."

"Why's that?"

"That bloke serving behind the counter's a bit forward. He said we're his two favourite girls."

"What a cheek!" Laura grinned.

"I know. He thinks he's funny, your brother."

"That's Steve all over," said Laura lightly. "He's all about the fun."

"He is. I love that about him." She grinned. "Did Steve tell you we joined the same dating agency? He was never one of my hot matches, more's the pity, and he should have been because we've got lots in common. I might have had more faith in it if it matched me with Steve."

"Yeah, the program was a mess," said Laura, "but even if it was working, I don't think Steve would have come up on your hot matches."

"Why not?" Rebecca frowned.

"Oh, don't worry – it's just that the program puts more importance on some factors than others, which makes sense."

Rebecca nodded. "And?" Her heart had started to beat uncomfortably fast. Laura's line of conversation was worrying her

"Like you said, Steve's fun, and, well, that's what he was primarily looking for. Fun. He wanted to date someone, of course –he wasn't looking for a series of one night stands – but he's not looking for anything long-term at the moment."

"I see," said Rebecca faintly.

"See? Nothing to worry about. He hasn't got any strange beliefs or anything. It's nothing you didn't know already!" She smiled at her and went back to her food.

Rebecca looked at her wrap. She didn't think she'd ever felt less hungry in her life.

"Good day?" Steve looked up, grinning, from his newspaper as Laura bounced in the door.

"Fantastic!"

"Coffee?"

"Yes please!"

Steve smiled as he made the coffee. He couldn't believe the change in Laura, though he had to admit to some mixed feelings. He was delighted with this new, motivated, cheerful Laura who was so much more open and so much less hostile. But he couldn't help feeling regretful that he hadn't brought about this change himself. He hadn't had a clue how to help her escape her substance abuse, let alone known how to guide her towards becoming this enthusiastic, glowing young woman. Strangers had succeeded where he had failed so miserably. Whenever he looked at her and felt pride and delight, guilt and inadequacy always came hot on their heels.

He shook himself. This was pointless. He was the first to tell other people you could learn from the past but not relive it.

Laura appeared, stretching up to hang her bag on the hook on the kitchen door. "Mmm, latte!"

"Got to give the working girl some treats after a hard day. I bought some more yesterday, since Rebecca's given you a taste for them. Pair of philistines!" He grinned.

"Thanks." She took a sip. "Mmm. Yummy."

"What did you get up to today, then?"

"Loads of stuff. Kevin made me mirror someone this morning, for a start."

"Don't you mean shadow someone?"

She shook her head. "No, dumbo, I know what I mean. I wasn't copying what they were doing, I sat at a computer and was given all the same information they had, to do the same job. Sooo cool!"

He smiled at her enthusiasm. "What did you have to do?"

"Try to reconstruct a chapel. They've dug the site and know where the main walls were, and there's an old drawing that shows one side, but nothing else in the picture is still there so it's hard to get a sense of proportion. Some of the decorative pieces were salvaged and used on a church three miles away, so we had photographs of those, too, plus an entry in the churchwarden's diary about bell tower renovations."

Steve was impressed. "Sounds intriguing."

"It's amazing! It's like using all these different skills to, to"—she shrugged helplessly—"put together a 3D jigsaw with no definite picture to follow, making sure the inside's right too."

"That's very complicated for a duffer like me."

She punched him on the arm. "You're not a duffer, bro. Haven't you ever watched Time Team?"

"No."

"Nor had I before, but... hold on a sec." She dashed out of the room and appeared seconds later with a slim black case. "Right, sit down. Demo time!"

Steve sat, amused, and sipped his coffee. "Can't wait."

She produced a shiny, very new-looking laptop and Steve raised his eyebrows. "Wow. They let you bring that home?"

She put her head on one side and a hand on one hip. "No, I hid it under my jacket and sneaked out."

He grinned. "Sorry. Just surprised. It looks expensive." kit."

"It is. I'm allowed it because I'm on the intern register now but I still had to sign it out and everything." She opened the laptop.

"So you're all official now."

"Yep." Steve watched her as she frowned at the screen, concentrating. He touched her shoulder. "I'm really proud of you, you know."

She didn't look round. "It's not often you get the chance to say that, is it?" Her laugh was brittle.

"Seriously, I am," he said in a low voice.

She turned round, eyes glistening. "Thanks, bruv," she said huskily. She leant her head against him for a moment and Steve felt the huge knot inside him start to unravel. She's going to be alright, he thought. Crisis over.

Laura pulled away and clicked confidently around the screen.

"These are scans of the renovation bill and the diary entry... "

Steve squinted, trying to read the faded, spidery writing. "Boy, that's not easy to make out."

"No, and the older the writing, the more difficult it is, because the way we form letters and spell words has changed so much over the years."

He nodded. "Can you read what this says?"

"I can now, but I needed help!" she laughed. She read him the documents then brought up photographs of ornate carvings and gargoyles. "These were used when the village got its own church—it's still standing now, see? Our chapel fell into ruin when the family line died out."

"And what's this?" he asked, pointing to a diagram.

"That shows the walls we could definitely place from the archaeology. And this"— she swapped screens – "is a chapel of very similar size, built two years later and designed by the same architect."

"Okay. Have you got the final reconstruction, or isn't it done yet?"

She grinned. "They're not the absolute, final products but I can show you two reconstructions, in fact."

"Two?"

"Yeah. This is mine."

Steve was impressed at how Laura could move the 3D model around and let him view the inside. "Not all the texture work's done, but the structure is all there."

"That's amazing." He looked at her with respect. "You've picked this up really quickly, Laura. You must have a talent for it."

She blushed. "Thanks, and look—I can take you on a tour." She grinned as he watched an animation that 'flew' him inside the chapel and turned him round to view the internal structures before flying him out of a side door.

"Wow. Very clever." Steve clapped. "Is that what you meant by two reconstructions – was the tour the second one?"

"No." She opened another file. "This is Ella's reconstruction."

To Laura's credit, the differences weren't immediately clear, and he didn't spot most of them until Laura talked him through it.

She sighed. "Hers is way better than mine, especially the texturing."

"Hey, come on! I bet she's been doing this for years."

"Ten," Laura admitted."

"You can't compare yourself to someone who's got so much more experience, you've only been at it for a couple of weeks! I think yours is incredible."

"Thanks." She shoulder bumped him, looking embarrassed. "She has got a degree in archaeology and one in Graphic and Computer-Aided Design."

"There you go then. You're up against a talented lady."

"Oh yeah. Everyone is, there. They're all really—"

"Cool?" he grinned.

"Yeah!" she laughed, picking up her coffee. "And really friendly too." She took a sip. "Yuck. Cold."

"I'll pop it in the microwave for you." He got to his feet, then on an impulse leant over and kissed the top of her head. "I'm really glad you've found something you love, Lor," he said quietly. "You deserve it."

To his surprise, she stood up and hugged him. "I don't deserve anything. I've been such a cow to you, and you've taken it. I'm so sorry." And just like that, her smile disappeared and she was sobbing into his t-shirt.

"It's not your fault. Things were so tough for you, and I don't think I was that hot as a surrogate parent." He hugged her tight. "I probably did the wrong thing, fighting to keep you with me. You'd have been better off with someone else."

She tightened her grip, nearly squeezing the breath out of him. "Don't say that. You were fantastic and you were always there for me, even when I cocked up big time."

"That's what brothers are for."

"No, it's not. Brothers aren't there to do your washing, cook your dinner, help you with homework, clean up after you, tell you about contraception... and bailing you out isn't in the job description either." She sniffed. "Can I have a tissue?"

Steve looked at her solemnly. "Sorry, I don't think that's in the description." That made her laugh, just as he'd hoped it would. He passed her some tissues and waited while she blew her nose ferociously and wiped her eyes. "I'm not sure there is a job description for brothers, however old they are," he said quietly. "And when they willingly take on the role of guardian as well, I think it's superseded."

"But I never thought about it!" Laura's lips quivered. "How much you gave up for me and what I put you through. When all your friends were still at uni having a good time, you were working your guts out all day and then spending all evening doing my washing, helping with my homework..." she shook her head and fresh tears streamed down her face. "You gave up everything to look after me and I've never said thank you..."

"Shh." He hugged her tightly. "I think you just did. All I wanted was for you to be happy, and it seems you're finally there, sis. And that's certainly not down to me."

"Is."

"Is not."

"Is." She poked him in the ribs.

"Is NOT." He poked her back and she slapped him.

He moved away. "Right, I know when I'm beat. I'll make that coffee."

"No, I'll do it. And I'll make you another one too."

"Oh well, if you're offering..." he grinned, lying down on the sofa and putting his arms behind his head. "I could get used to this."

"You'll have to. I'm going to start pulling my weight."

"Best start eating cakes then, there's nothing of you." He looked her up and down. "That's worth about one lot of washing up a week."

She put her hands lightly around his neck. "Do you want to drink this coffee or shower in it?"

He laughed. "Back to the kitchen, wench."

"Yes, m'lord."

She reappeared with the coffee and curled herself into an armchair.

"So enough about me. How was the wedding?"

"Good. It didn't rain, the food was spectacular – it must have cost a bomb – and of course I got to spend the weekend with Rebecca." He grinned. "That's a pretty big bonus."

"Yeah, she's great. So friendly, and soooo good at her job. Everyone at the museum thinks she's, like, the goddess of archaeology." She sighed. "It won't be the same without her, but hopefully someone else will take me under their w—"

"What do you mean, without her?"

"Well she's not going to turn down that job, is she, and Kevin said they've offered to let her go out there for a two month trial—"

"What job? Out where?"

"She must have told you..." Laura looked at him, stricken. "Oh God, she hasn't, has she? Steve I'm sorry, I've put my foot in it."

"No, she has told me. There's going to be a restructure and Ron's suggested she applies for promotion. She hasn't got to go anywhere for that, has she?"

"Not that job. Ron offered her that at the same time, apparently. What a choice! But she won't go for the GLAM job, will she, not once she's spent a couple of months in Milan."

"Milan?"

"Sorry. I really thought she'd have mentioned it, but then you've only just got together, haven't you. It's not like it's serious. She probably wasn't intending to tell you until she'd decided."

Not serious? Weren't they? "It would have been nice to know."

"Well she's still young, and she's got a brilliant future ahead of her. Her career comes first at the moment. She was very honest about it on her profile, that's Rebecca all over, isn't it? Said she wasn't looking for a long term relationship at the moment." Laura smiled. "It's brilliant, isn't it? She's going to have a fantastic time in Milan. I'm so pleased for her."

"Yes," said Steve. His heart felt as if it had doubled in size and was trying to escape from his chest. "It's great."

Chapter Twenty Six

She'd intended to go somewhere different for lunch, because Ron was pushing her for a decision and she wanted time alone; time to stop and think about her future and what was best for her. Seeing Steve would only blur the picture and she couldn't let that happen when he didn't want a serious relationship. She couldn't give up what might be the chance of a lifetime for someone who might get fed up with their 'fun' in a couple of months' time. And now that she had the option of a trial period in Milan, the idea was appealing to her more and more. What did she have to lose?

But she was so deep in thought that she walked to Tony's on autopilot, only realising she'd done so after she'd opened the door and seen Steve look over at her. If only she'd known from the start he only wanted fun. Then she wouldn't have let her heart get so involved.

Well it was too late now, for her heart and her peaceful lunch. Just her luck that today, Tony told Steve he could go for lunch straight away, as it was still early and fairly quiet. Steve needed no second telling and he had his apron off before she'd reached the counter.

But as he came round the counter he didn't look overjoyed to see her.

"Hi."

"Hi. Rebecca, can we go somewhere else for lunch?" He didn't meet her eye, just looked out the window, pulling his jacket on.

"Of course," she replied, bewildered at his abruptness. "Lead on."

He didn't take her hand as he led the way to a sandwich van parked near the canal, and barely spoke.

"I thought we could sit outside."

"Fine." A cold feeling of dread was curling around inside her. She'd never seen him like this before. Sometimes he'd been reserved, but never this cold.

He walked to a bench overlooking the water and sat down.

Rebecca sat beside him, automatically leaving a small space between them. Somehow I don't think I'm going to have to worry about breaking my news, she thought dully. I think I'm going to be dumped instead. She closed her eyes for a second, trying to control the tears that stung her eyes just at the thought of it, and took a deep breath.

"Steve, what's wrong?" Better to tackle it head on and get it over with.

"You tell me," he snapped.

The unreasonable retort and his tone made her hackles rise instantly. "If I knew, I wouldn't ask, would I."

"I just wondered when you were going to tell me that you're taking a job in Milan, that's all. Or even that's you'd been offered it."

Oh God. "I meant to tell you—"

"Well, no rush is there? Just because everyone else knows. Lucky me, I found out everything I needed to know from my sister. She thought I knew."

"Steve, Ron told me about the Milan job before we got together. When I still thought you were married."

"And you haven't found time to mention it since? Slipped your mind. Too busy buying a new suitcase and sunglasses?"

"I know I should have told you, but I didn't want to say anything until I'd decided how I felt about it, and I haven't, not yet. I didn't know Laura even knew about it. She must have overheard me and Kevin talking about it."

"Oh because of course, you've sodding well discussed it with Kevin. Why doesn't that surprise me, Rebecca? It must break your heart he's gay, you make such a lovely couple."

"Don't be stupid."

"I'm telling it like it is, that's all. You two are far more of a couple than we'll ever be, because you tell him everything, and your career doesn't stand in the way of that relationship, does it? Don't worry, I know my place. You just wanted some fun. I'm the light entertainment to keep you amused until you bugger off to Milan."

"That's not how it is, you know that."

"I don't know anything, Rebecca, anymore. That's what hurts. I thought we were going somewhere. When we slept together it meant something to me. It was special. But it obviously wasn't significant for you. I guess I must be old-fashioned. It didn't even earn me sufficient status in your life to be informed, did it?

Her eyes flashed. "Oh I'm sorry, I missed that bit in the contract, I wasn't aware that sleeping with you meant I had to instantly report everything that happened in my life!"

"You don't. But this, Rebecca, this was important."

Silence. Rebecca felt like she was going to throw up any minute. Thank goodness they were near the canal, she thought, feeling strangely unreal and detached. "Perhaps we should talk about this when we've both had time to think."

"If you want. But from where I'm standing, the only one of us who's got thinking to do is you. Because it doesn't matter what I think, does it. You've proved that."

He thrust his uneaten lunch into the bin, slamming the lid down savagely when it wouldn't shut, and turned to go.

"Will I see you tomorrow?" She hated her voice for trembling.

"Come round if you want. Laura's out from 7."

He walked away, leaving Rebecca sitting there. She cried so much that after several minutes the owner of the sandwich van came over to see if she was alright, and ended up calling her a cab.

"I'm going to Milan. Just for the trial period, to see how it goes. No definite decisions." She was sitting beside him on his sofa.

"That's it then," said Steve quietly. His chest hurt.

"What?"

He could tell that she knew damn well what he meant. He shrugged. "It's over. Our relationship. If that's what you can call it."

She flushed. "I told you, I haven't decided anything yet."

"Come on, you wouldn't be going for this trial period if you weren't considering taking the job, would you. And that leaves us nowhere."

"That's not true."

"It's my fault, I suppose, for presuming we were heading in the same direction. Of course you weren't looking for anything serious, because—"

"I didn't say that—"

"—you knew you were considering moving abroad. I wish I'd known that was the deal. I thought things were going well, that we'd carry on." Say all of it, the voice in his head demanded. Get angry. Tell her that you thought she cared for you as much as you do her, and that it breaks your heart that she would even consider moving thousands of miles away.

 "I'm committed now, I have to go. All that agonising I was doing went out the window when I got angry." She smiled bleakly. "In the end I said yes just like that. But I don't want us to end like this." Tears were shining in Rebecca's eyes. "I don't want us to end at all."

"What did you think would happen, Rebecca? Did you really think I'd say, 'Great! You're going to live in Milan, we'll have to plan our dates a bit more in advance'? You're the one who's brought this to an end by deciding to move to Italy."

"But I haven't! I'm only going for two months—in 9 weeks time I'll be back in the UK. Are you saying our relationship can't stand 9 weeks without seeing each other? You could come out for a holiday."

"No. I'm saying our relationship can't stand 9 weeks of not knowing if it's the last 9 weeks." He shook his head. "I can't stand to get in any deeper. It's bad enough to know that our relationship – that I – wasn't even a factor when you were considering this, but to wait for 9 weeks, missing you, not sure what's going to happen, and then maybe find out in the end it's all coming to an end anyway... even worse if I come out there on holiday. I can't do that. It's not fair of you to ask me to."

He couldn't look at her. Tears were clogging his throat. He'd waited 9 weeks for something before; 9 weeks of hoping and dreading while his Dad underwent a new form of treatment. And at the end, all it had given either of them was an extra 9 weeks of false hope, pain, and torturous uncertainty. It had made him feel completely helpless and he wasn't going to voluntarily put himself through weeks of that awful dreading and hoping again.

"We've been going out a few weeks – not really long-term, is it? Yet on the strength of that you're asking me not to spend two months trying to find out if my dream job lies elsewhere – and you accuse me of not being fair? "

"Long-term? What chance have you given us to become long-term?" He laughed humourlessly.

"So that's it?" she said, after a long silence. "You don't want to see me again?"

"Only as a friend," he said quietly, and ignored the sob that escaped her. "I still care about what happens to you, Rebecca. I can't just turn that off.. I really hope you get what you want." I just wish the thing you wanted most was me, he thought. That I was at least level-pegging with your career, not scrabbling around at the bottom of your list.

"I hope you get everything you want, too." Suddenly she was on her feet, pulling her jacket on. "Although you already have it," she said harshly. "Your cosy little café and Laura, and that's enough for you. How dare I want anything different, anywhere different, that isn't in your picture? I'm a jigsaw piece that doesn't fit into the gap you've got left, so you're right. Best to finish it right now." She fled towards the door. "Bye, Steve."

"Rebecca—" he was on his feet, wrenching open the front door she'd slammed a second before. "Rebecca!" She didn't even turn, throwing herself into her car. She was crying, but he fought the urge to go over and stop her driving away; what else could he say that would make a difference? It was Rebecca who was ruining this relationship. She couldn't expect him to hang around for a couple of months while she swanned round Milan, only for him to find she was abandoning him for good. Her employers might be prepared to do that; he wasn't.

When her car turned the corner, he shut the front door, feeling dazed. It was over. It couldn't be over. He'd spent so long wanting to be with her; had been so happy when they finally got together. How did it go so wrong, so quickly?

Because you should have known better, that's why. Should have known you weren't good enough for her. Should have stayed clear of someone so career-minded, knowing you'd always come second. He went to the kitchen to make himself a cup of tea.

He'd probably saved himself from a world of hurt. Her remark about him having everything he wanted, with his 'cosy little café', had been telling. She would never accept that he could be happy 'just' working in a café; in her eyes it could only ever be a stopgap. She needed to know he was headed somewhere higher, like her. A good thing, then, that this had ended now, before she left him behind altogether.

Perhaps it wasn't all her fault. She wasn't used to having emotional ties to affect her decisions. Since she'd lost her parents, she'd had nobody important enough to do that. Certainly not Kevin. The poor guy seemed nearly as gutted as he was.

He looked down and realised he was a cup of boiling water, with no sign of a teabag. He threw the teaspoon down and it clanged hard on the worktop. He resisted the urge to throw the cup after it too.

Chapter Twenty Seven

Rebecca put her suitcase down and collapsed on to the bed. She lay on her back looking at the ceiling, waiting to cool down so that she could think straight. Even for Italy, even for April, this was hot. She had a mental image of her head as a red pepper. Her apartment wouldn't be ready for another week but once she'd decided to go to Milan, she'd wanted to get there as quickly as possible; no time for more doubts or arguments. It also gave her a week's holiday before she started work, time she badly needed to clear her head after everything that had happened. Staying at the hotel would make it feel more like a holiday; if she'd moved straight into the apartment she would have started unpacking and buying food in. She relished the idea of eating out all week. Luxury!

Francois had recommended The Ravello to her. It was roughly halfway between the Castello and the Duomo, two of the city's major attractions, and it was reasonably priced too. The downside was that it didn't have its own restaurant, but that wasn't a problem here; she'd be spoilt for choice.

This was her first visit to Milan, but she wasn't going to rush to see everything at once. She wanted to save some trips for the rest of her time here. If she took the job permanently, of course, her 'time here' could be 'forever'. She shivered. Maybe after two months out here, that wouldn't be such a scary thought. She was grateful to Francois for giving her the chance to try out life here before making such a big decision.

Thinking of Francois made her sit up. If she lounged on the bed much longer, she'd fall asleep and waste the afternoon, and she was meeting him for dinner. She hung up her clothes and grabbed her wash kit. Everything else could wait; Milan couldn't. It was out there waiting to be discovered.

Twenty minutes later she was ready to hit the streets, wearing a much lighter dress and low-heeled sandals. She stepped out of the cool hotel lobby into the blindingly bright sunshine, armed with her guidebook and a separate map. First, she needed to find somewhere to eat lunch. Preferably somewhere she could sit and watch the world go by for a while, with a table big enough for her guidebook and map. She wanted to sit in the sunshine and make plans.

She decided to go with the guidebook's suggestions on this first foray. Half an hour later she had walked and window-shopped her way to 'Bagutta', a small restaurant with an attractive terrace. It had felt good to stretch her legs after travelling for hours. She chose Risotto alla Milanese, a rice and saffron broth. It smelt divine as the waitress put it on the table, and tasted even better. Afterwards she sipped a rich, dark coffee and sat enjoying the sunshine on her face. It was great to be away from the stresses that life had piled on her lately.

Not that was heartbreak was one of them, though. How could it be? She hadn't known Steve that long; it would be crazy to be devastated about breaking up with him. If she'd have thought of him as her other half, she would have told him about the Milan job, wouldn't she, so there was the proof. Why else would she have pushed it out of her mind every time she went to mention it to him?

She should have told him though. That's why she'd cried; they were tears of guilt, she told herself. Yes, that was it. It was lucky he'd only wanted some fun, a 'casual relationship', though she'd been surprised to discover that. She'd thought he was the type of man who would see where a relationship took him, not dismiss long-term relationships out-of-hand. Maybe raising Laura, a long-term commitment in itself, had made him shy away from long-term commitment in romantic relationships; that was lucky because it meant she knew his anger was just because his male pride was dented, nothing else. He'd soon get over it.

They'd had a perfectly civil lunch before she left; she'd given him her Easter cactus to look after and he had given her a trowel with her name on it. That's why she'd cried again, of course, not because her heart was breaking. Then he'd given her a kiss on the cheek and left. No hard feelings.

So why was she so miserable? And if fun was all Steve wanted, why had he been so devastated?

She gave herself a mental shake. This wasn't getting her anywhere. She ate a tiny zabaglione for dessert while reading her guidebook, and by the time she'd finished the last light, delicious bite, she had chosen her excursion for the afternoon. The Museo di Milano was just around the corner, she'd discovered; less than five minutes walk.

Fired up at the prospect of her first adventure, she nearly walked away without her sunglasses. She turned back to pick them up and a sudden movement in the restaurant window caught her eye. She was sure the curtain was pulled back earlier, and equally sure it had just been twitched across. She frowned. Someone was rather touchy about their privacy, weren't they! They shouldn't eat out, then. She put her sunglasses on and set off for the museum.

"It's just that I've never been offered this kind of opportunity before."

Steve closed his eyes. He hadn't expected her to ring. He was trying to get over her. "I understand that," he said quietly, keeping all emotion out of his voice.

"It might never happen again."

"I know. That's why I would never ask you to give it up. I wanted the chance to discuss it. Or at least have time to get used to the idea."

There was a long pause.

"Steve, I—I know I've no right to ask this of you, but please could you reconsider coming out here? I've got five days off at the end of the month, and I really need to talk to you. There are a lot of things I haven't said. Questions I need to ask too."

He didn't know what to say.

"I'd love to spend more time with you, Steve. Just the two of us, away from everything else." Her voice wobbled a little. "I miss you."

Away from everything? Not away from Milan, he thought, and Milan was the problem. The elephant in the room. And she was missing him? Huh! Perhaps she should have thought of that before.

And yet.... "I might be able to. I'll ask Tony, although he's not been feeling that well this week."

"What's wrong with him?"

"I don't know. I'll see how things go." He hesitated. "But if I can get a few days off, I'll come out."

"Thank you."

"Thanks for inviting me," he said, then cringed. This stilted politeness was ridiculous. A few weeks ago they were waking up next to each other. He couldn't play it cool. "I miss you too."

"Good." She sounded tearful. "I mean, not good, but—"

"I know what you mean."

"I've got to go. Talk to you soon. Bye."

"Bye."

Chapter Twenty Eight

Rebecca loved Milan. It was vibrant; a fantastic hub from which to explore this part of Italy, which was why when Steve came he would get a surprise. She'd booked a long weekend on Lake Garda, staying in a wonderful hotel in Sirmione.

She was loving her job, too. Loving the lack of red tape, and loving working for Ron and Francois. They'd gathered a great team around them: friendly, enthusiastic, and genuinely the cream of the crop. She felt overwhelmed, sometimes, by the thought that Ron and Francois considered her a worthy part of such an exalted group.

But she hated being away from Steve with every fibre of her being and missed him more than she thought possible. It was like bereavement; that was her only comparison. A constant dull misery that lurked under every laugh, every good meal, every sunny morning... she still appreciated all the good things, but they never erased that ache. It was always there, underneath.

She couldn't wait to see him. She was going to tell him how she felt, lay all her cards on the table and admit that he was more than just fun, to her, and ask him if he felt the same. She hoped he did. She hoped that's why he'd been so hurt and angry at her before.

If he said no... well, she would still be hurting. But she would stay here, because Steve was the only thing to go back for. She missed Kevin, but he'd already been out for a visit and she was guessing he'd be a regular visitor if she stayed here. If Steve said yes, then in five weeks she would go back to England for good. Steve had ties to England, and her heart had ties to Steve—several billion more than she'd suspected.

Now she was only waiting for Steve to phone and tell her was flight he was on, so she could pick him up at Bergamo airport.

"Tony? Are you okay?" Steve stopped in the kitchen doorway, holding a box of syrup bottles.

Tony was sitting on the chair in the corner of the kitchen; Steve hadn't even realised he was there until he turned to push open the kitchen door with his hip. Tony never sat down. He looked grey.

"I'm fine. Fine," said Tony weakly, trying to smile as he mopped his face with his huge red hanky.

Steve frowned. What had been wrong with that picture? "Stay there," he said, pointlessly. Tony didn't look like he was going anywhere. He barrelled through the door and dumped the box beside Neil.

"Great, time for my break—"

"Sorry mate, you're holding the fort, Tony's ill."

He didn't give Neil time to answer. He'd realised what had looked wrong. Tony had been holding his hanky in his right hand, and he was left-handed. He bent down beside him, chilled by the sight of Tony's clammy face.

"Have you got chest pains?"

Tony nodded.

"I'm ringing 999."

"No, do not bother them with this small thing," he said hoarsely, shifting his bulk on the chair. "Is probably indigestion. Perhaps I forget to take tablet."

Steve was already tapping 999 into his mobile.

"Indigestion? So why aren't you using you left hand?"

Tony's eyes slid away. "Just a little pain, probably pulled muscle, is all."

Steve ignored him, asking for an ambulance. He found Tony's GTN spray in his coat pocket and popped an aspirin from the packet in the first aid cabinet, glad of the reassuring voice on the other end of the phone. Tony was weakly insisting that he was always sweaty; "I am a big boy, too big, you know!"

Five minutes later, the paramedics swept in the back door, dealing with Tony kindly and efficiently. Steve only had a couple of minutes to give them as many details as he could before they whisked Tony off to hospital. Steve leaned on the counter in a daze after they left, pulling himself together. The paramedics had said that the fact Tony was still conscious and talking was a good sign.

He began to tidy up things that had been moved out of the way to allow the paramedics room to work. The he stopped. What was he doing? He was meant to be ringing Maria, Tony's wife. He dialled her mobile.

Maria alternately cried and berated Tony, in his absence, for not taking his tablets and losing weight. "Always he is eating, enough for thirty men, Steve! I tell him no but he does not listen."

Steve tried to be reassuring, but in the end he had to cut her short. "Maria, don't you think you should be getting to the hospital now? Tony will want you there." He wasn't entirely sure this was true, from what he knew of them both, but it seemed the right thing to say.

"Yes. I must go. You are all right at the shop, Steve? If you have to shut, I understand."

"We'll try and stay open for the usual hours. Ring me when you have news. Take care."

"Of course. Ciao."

A look of relief swept over Neil's face as Steve came through the door. "There you are. What's going on? Someone said they saw an ambulance pull round the back."

"Suspected heart attack, I'm afraid," said Steve quietly.

Neil gave a low whistle. "God, I didn't think it was that serious. I'd have come through, but I was swamped out here. Is Tony going to be alright?"

Steve shrugged. "I hope so. He was still arguing, and the ambulance got here quickly. Fingers crossed."

"Poor guy."

"Yeah. I know it's short notice, mate, but could you stay until 7? Or even 6?"

"I can stay until 8 if you want."

"Cheers. I'm happy to lock up, but I'd like to cash up before you go, so everything's above board."

"Dude, you know Tony would be totally cool with you cashing up by yourself."

"You're probably right, but I'd feel happier if you at least checked my totals."

Neil slapped his shoulder. "Whatever you want. No problem, boss," he grinned.

Boss? That made him feel uncomfortable, but also, strangely—proud, if that was the right word.

What would happen tomorrow? Would Tony want him to be in charge, or would he pick someone else? Or not well enough to even think about it?

He would take charge tomorrow, unless he heard anything to the contrary. Rinaldo had been there longer than him but it was his day off. But then he'd ring Maria and ask her what to do. He loved working at the café, but he didn't feel happy giving the orders without Tony's blessing; laying down the law and dealing with suppliers was Tony's job.

He wasn't sure he could fill Tony's handmade, Italian, and not inconsiderable, shoes.

The phone rang and Rebecca's heart gave a happy jolt. She didn't get many calls to the landline, and she'd already spoken to Francois thus evening. It must be Steve.

Rebecca curled her legs up under her on the sofa. "Hello, you. Everything sorted? Flights booked?" She couldn't stop smiling; it was so good to hear his voice.

"No, they're not, I'm afraid."

There was a pause. A small cold needle of dread dug into her stomach.

"I'm sorry, but I can't get away."

"Can't? Or won't?" She said harshly.

Steve made no reply.

"Are you telling me Tony won't give you the time off? Or is it Laura?" Rebecca tried to calm down. "Is she okay?"

"Laura's fine. And it's can't, not won't. Thanks for letting me explain."

Rebecca winced at his tone, but knew she deserved it. "Sorry, that wasn't fair. It's just that I've been looking forward to seeing you. And afraid you might change your mind," she added softly.

"I haven't changed my mind. In fact, the more I thought about it..." He took a deep breath. "God, this isn't a good time to discuss this. But I'm not ready to give up on us just yet. Even though I'm probably a fool, heading for a broken heart."

"That makes me feel so guilty." Tears were pricking in her eyes.

"I understand it's not easy for you either, but I'm left waiting to know where my life is going."

"But why? This is what you wanted, isn't it? A casual relationship."

"You said that before. But when did I ever say that?"

"You didn't."

"So I gave you that impression how, exactly?"

"You... well didn't, I suppose, but Laura – never mind."

Steve's voice was sharp. "What did Laura say?"

"Look, I don't want to get her into trouble for giving away your secrets—"

His voice sliced across hers. "What did she say, Rebecca?"

"She said you'd put on your profile that you weren't looking for a long-term relationship."

There was a long silence that Rebecca was too nervous to break.

"Did she now? The lying bitch," Steve spat.

"Steve, don't be angry at her! She probably—"

"Angry? Oh, I'm way beyond angry. How dare she interfere in my life!"

Rebecca hesitated. "So it's not true then?"

"No. I told the truth, which was that I was interested in meeting new people and was happy to see where it went; I wasn't looking for a long-term partner specifically but wasn't opposed to the idea either."

"That's pretty much what I put," she said quietly.

"Really? Because, big surprise, that's not what she told me."

She'd never heard him so bitter, but she was starting to feel the same. "Laura talked to you about my profile too?"

"Oh yes. Said you wanted a relationship, but nothing that would get in the way of your career, because that would always come first. That was when she dropped the Milan job into the conversation."

"She was never meant to know about that. I wanted to discuss it with you properly, although I know I left it far too late." Rebecca's head was spinning, trying to put it altogether. "I know she's done an awful thing, Steve, but she might have a good reason."

"Like what?"

"Maybe she's scared of sharing you, or even worse, losing you. You've always been there for her, and she's always had you to herself. Perhaps she sees me as a threat to that, especially now you two are so close. She's probably not sure where her place would be if we were together. You know," she floundered, "properly together."

"Perhaps." Steve didn't sound convinced. "She could have talked to me about it though."

"How would she start that conversation? Maybe she was afraid you would get angry."

Steve chuckled suddenly. "Do you always have to be so bloody reasonable about everything?"

"Sorry. It's the scientist in me. I look for all possible explanations." She paused. "Steve, I didn't consider the Milan job until Laura told me that. I would never have gone."

"Really?"

"Yes, unless you wanted to try living out here too."

"God, Rebecca, I... what a mess. It broke my heart to think I didn't even cross your mind."

"At least we've found out. When we see each other—"

"Rebecca, Tony's had a heart attack."

"Oh my God! Is he okay?"

"It could have been worse, he was lucky. He hasn't been taking his tablets or looking after himself too well. They're doing tests at the moment, but I get the impression it will be a while before he's back."

"That's awful. Poor Maria, too! Give them my love."

"I will."

"So who's running things?"

"Me, at the moment. His brother, Bernardo, is coming over to help out for a couple of weeks, but I don't think he'll hang around indefinitely. He's got his own business to run."

Rebecca was upset about Tony, but the heaviness in her heart came mainly from disappointment at the thought of not seeing Steve, and disappointment in Laura, too. She'd tried so hard to make her feel part of things at the museum, and to give her a sense of pride in herself and a sense of purpose. Despite the excuses she'd made for her, this felt like betrayal; like having everything she'd done for Laura thrown back in her face. Surely she wasn't that horrible. Was the prospect of her as Steve's long-term girlfriend so terrible?

"Rebecca?"

"Sorry. Just trying to take it all in."

"I know the feeling."

"So you won't be able to come out here at all? Because I might be able to save a couple of days' leave and have a long weekend later."

"I don't know. Neil's off back-packing soon—he was meant to go at the end of last week, he's already giving us an extra fortnight. He's a good lad."

Rebecca laughed weakly. "Good lad? Listen to you, Granddad."

"I know," said Steve ruefully. "It's the pressure of command. It's made me come over all mature."

Hearing him make jokes again made her miss him more than ever. "I can't believe I won't see you for five six weeks."

"It feels like a lifetime." He sighed. "I'll phone when I can, but—"

"You're really busy."

"Yeah, I am. Trying to do Tony's job as well as mine might send me nuts, eventually."

"You're not making the wraps?" She needed to bring some light-heartedness back into this conversation; otherwise she was going to grizzle.

"Sometimes. Neil and I take it in turns."

"Surely they're not as good as Tony's, though?"

"Hey, I've had no complaints!"

"That's because everyone's making allowances."

"Probably. Rebecca, I'd better go. Sorry but I've got orders to look through before bed, and I'm in at 6 to start the breakfasts."

"Ouch. I'll let you go, then. Phone me when you can?"

"Of course. Take care."

"You too. I miss you," she blurted.

"I miss you too. So much," His voice was rough. "Bye."

"Bye."

The tears were streaming down her face before she clicked the handset back into place.

Chapter Twenty Nine

Rebecca was buzzing. The concert had been fantastic, although she hadn't expected it to be so long. There had been so many encores at the end, and when it was clear that all the singers had left the stage and could not be tempted back yet again, the audience was slow to move. Many of them shuffled in long queues towards the two bars, which were aggravatingly between the auditorium and the exits, their queues stretching back and partially blocking auditorium's exit doors.

By the time she escaped out into the cooler, wonderfully welcome night air, she was over an hour later than she'd expected to be. Under the bright lights, the streets glistened after the showers that had drenched them on her way there in the taxi. She wished Steve was here; she'd brought him a ticket. She'd had to cancel the Lake Garda break.

The sky was clear now and stars were beginning to appear. It was a lovely night. She would walk home, she decided suddenly. There were plenty of people around, and although it was late, it wasn't the dead of night. It wouldn't take her more than twenty minutes, surely, and she'd avoid the narrow, curving alleyways. It would be good for her, she thought, burn off some of the calories she'd consumed this evening—some, not all. She'd had three glasses of wine and a generous helping of gelato.

She set off, sticking to the well-lit main roads; easy to do in this part of the city. As she got further from the opera house, though, the crowds dwindled rapidly, and fifteen minutes later there was only one other person in view, taking the left turning ahead. She got to the corner and checked out the turning. She knew it would take her in the right direction, but it was narrow and more sparsely lit. She took out the small, foldaway street map that lived in her handbag and stood under the streetlight.

Good. She wasn't too far away from home now. But the quickest route was through narrower back roads, likely to contain only rows of houses. Rows of houses that were likely, at this hour, to be as quiet and dark as the small streets themselves. Or she could carry on; in half a mile this road ended at a major one, and from there she could take a longer, more circuitous route home.

She debated. The longer route was the safer one, but would take at least another twenty minutes in these heels. The back roads would have her home in under ten minutes. The effects of the wine had worn off along with her sense of joie de vivre. Now she was weary, painfully aware of the burning sensation in the balls of her feet and the beginning of a blister on her right heel.

She dithered a moment, then set off down the turning, trying to set a cracking pace. Her handbag was gripped tightly in her right hand, partly to keep it safe, and partly to keep her safe. She would stay alert, and if anyone tried anything it would be a handbag blow to the head, preferably with the pointy metal crossover clasp pointing towards the attacker's eyes.

Five minutes later she was thanking her lucky stars she'd taken this route. Every step was torture now. The few people she'd passed had either ignored her or smiled.. Ahead of her in the distance, she could see the turning that would take her nearly all the way to her front door. She would soon be home, thank God, because she'd been reduced to a hobble and it had taken twice as long as she'd predicted. She didn't dare take her shoes off because in the dim light she might step on anything.

She heard a noise and stopped. Not the most sensible thing to do, she scolded herself. It sounded as if someone had kicked a can. She looked back behind her but could see nobody. Perhaps the noise had been further away than it seemed. She carried on, going a little faster. Even though this road was only two turnings away from her front door, she'd had no reason to take this route before and didn't know the street at all. She hadn't passed anyone for several minutes and the stillness and quiet was starting to freak her out.

In front of her the road curved and became narrower. There was barely room for a car here and the road surface gave way to cobbles. Another noise made Rebecca glance over her shoulder, but again there was nobody there. Maybe it was just a cat prowling the street. But it made her edgy. She tried to urge her feet to go faster, but she'd reached the cobbles now, still slippery from the rain..

Another noise. Louder. Dark space on the left. A flicker of movement within it. Turning her head. A face. A split second of recognition.

Imploding pain in her head. A scream that resounded inside it, unable to escape. Crushing force driving her to her knees. Joints jarring on the cobbles as she fell. The flashing thought that she couldn't endure this pain, it was too much-

Blackness.

Rebecca was aware of voices, and pain. Part of her brain nagged her to listen to the voices, but another part—and it seemed to have the upper hand at the moment—told her to stay in the easy, hazy state she was in. But eventually the voices seemed to become more distinguishable all by themselves.

She still couldn't move or open her eyes, but now she could hear every word clearly.

"That bitch should be locked up," a voice hissed.

"Steve, I—" Rebecca lost track of what was being said for a moment, trying instead to identify that voice. She struggled to retrieve memory. Ron? Was it Ron? But he had said Steve. They hadn't even met, had they? Why were they talking?

"She could have killed her, Ron. And I'm not convinced that wasn't what she intended!"

"I know you're angry and I understand, but this isn't helping Rebecca."

"I can't help her, I'm not a doctor!"

A doctor? What was wrong with her? She tried to reach out a hand but her fingers just twitched feebly.

"It's frustrating for all of us. If- Steve, I think she's coming round."

She knew he was coming closer. She could feel the warmth radiating from his body, smell his aftershave.

"Bec?"

His voice was gentle but urgent at the same time. With an immense effort she opened her eyes and then groaned at the lightning strike of pain.

"What is it, honey? Pain in your head?"

She only just stopped herself from nodding in response. Pure reflex, but she sensed

it would have been agony, as would moving her jaw to talk she suspected.. She raised a thumb instead. Her mouth didn't seem to be working at the moment anyway, the words forming inside her head but not knowing how to come out.

"I'll go and get the nurse, see if they can give you anything." He looked down at her tenderly. "I'm not going to kiss you because it might hurt. But it's so good to see you awake, Rebecca." His voice broke before he finished, his eyes glistening.

She couldn't do smiling either, it seemed, but a tear prickled in the corner of her eye. He took her hand and stroked it gently.

"Don't worry. Everything's going to be fine. You'll soon feel better."

She tried to squeeze his hand, but something wasn't right. He was speaking but his voice sounded tinny and far away. She couldn't understand the words...

"She's gone again."

When she woke again, it seemed easier to open her eyes, although her head was still pounding. Moving her head and talking still weren't happening.

"Hey, you're awake." Steve was smiling down at her, although she could see the worry lurking in his eyes. He took her hand and she squeezed it. "Ouch. That killer grip is coming back," he teased. He supported her shoulders and got her a small carton of drink with a straw. She managed one or two swallows but it was physically painful and she felt like she might choke at any moment.

By the time he lowered her gently back on to the pillows, she felt exhausted and frustrated.

"Now, you don't have to do this if you don't want to," he said quietly. "But since your hand squeezing is so good, it would be great if you could answer a few questions to help the police." He took her hand. "I thought we could do one squeeze for yes and two for no, keep it simple. What do you think?"

Squeeze.

He smiled. "Brill." He sat down on the edge of her bed. "Do you know I love you?"

Squeeze.

"Good." He kissed her hand. "I daren't kiss your head, it's a bit tender. I'll call the police officer in."

A good-looking Italian policeman cane in and sat on a chair on the other side of the bed, giving her a smile.

"Do you remember anything about what happened to you?"

A lighter squeeze. She hoped he would notice the difference.

"Ah. You remember a bit, but not everything, is that right?"

Squeeze.

"Well done." His voice became more serious. "Do you know who attacked you?"

Squeeze.

"Was it Marcie King?"

Squeeze.

"Did she say anything?"

Squeeze squeeze.

"Had you seen her before, in Milan?"

Light squeeze.

"You're not sure?"

Squeeze.

"Did you think that someone was following you or watching you?"

Squeeze.

She was only squeezing his hand, but it felt like such hard work. She was exhausted now. There was a mutter of voices and she realised there must be other people in the room.

"That's enough for now. You have a rest."

What another one, thought Rebecca wearily. I've only just woken u....

Chapter Thirty

Once Rebecca was out of danger, Steve had gone back to England. He was needed at the café and before he left, he'd already arranged with Bernardo to do another stint at Tony's so that he could come back to Milan in three weeks' time and spend more time with Rebecca. While he was gone Kevin came out for a week, and Ron, Francois or both were in every day. Other members of the Milan team popped in periodically bringing treats and books.

Steve's timing was perfect. Two days after he arrived back in Milan, Rebecca was allowed home. Steve picked her up in the morning and when she got back to the flat, she slept for ten hours. It wasn't until the evening that Steve got his chance to talk to her.

"Tony's asked me to take over management of the cafe permanently," he said quietly, his arms wrapped gently round her.

"I see." Rebecca tried to swallow the hard lump in her throat. "What have you told him?"

"Nothing, yet, other than I would think about it." He looked down. "The thing is, Rebecca, I really enjoy running the cafe. And I'm good at it. I'm not saying I'll want to do it forever, but to me a job is about earning enough to live on and doing what makes me happy. He's offered me a very generous deal, and at the moment I'm in no rush to go back to uni."

He reached out, taking her hands in his and looking at her intently. "But on the other hand, where I most want to be is wherever you are. That's the most important thing to me, Rebecca Maynard. You."

Her eyes were brimming with tears but she couldn't find any words.

"And I'm thinking that if that's going to be Milan—most of the time—then that's where I want to be, regardless of what I do." He smiled, cupping her face in his hands and wiping away her tears with his thumbs. "Perhaps Tony could put in a good word with one of his relatives out here. I'll have to do a crash course in Italian, though."

She held him tighter. "I've been an idiot," she said, her voice muffled against his shoulder. "I don't need this job, or Milan, to make me happy. I only need you, and I want you to be happy." She pulled back a little. "I know deep down you want to stay in London, and I love working at the Museum. I think I'd like the Director's job."

"Haven't they given it to someone else?"

"Only on a temporary contract. Tasha's taken it, but she'll go on maternity leave in a few months. When it comes up again I'll apply." She shrugged. "Or perhaps not. I loved my old job, and that's still open, so I haven't lost anything. Although you're the only thing I couldn't bear to lose, I realise that now." She kissed him. "And you'll be a fantastic manager. And I'll be fantastically proud of you."

His arms tightened round her so hard that she gasped, and he pulled back, concerned.

"Sorry, honey—did I hurt you?"

"I'm okay." She smiled at him. "Of course, I'm only coming back on one condition."

"What's that?" He looked so worried that she felt guilty for teasing him.

"I'll expect all my lattes to be free, of course."

He didn't reply for a while. He was far too busy kissing her. When they finally broke apart, he grinned. "Done. Hell, you can have everything free."

"In that case, I'd better start packing."

"No. The hospital said you need plenty of rest, and there's no rush. You're not going anywhere for at least another week."

She gave in, but by the end of the week she was feeling a lot better and decided she had her own interpretation of bed rest, although it was different from Steve's and he took a little persuading. Rebecca told him you could have too much rest, and after all, the physiotherapist had said she needed regular exercise.

Thank goodness it was Friday. Rebecca sat at her desk waiting for lunch time. She had done her first full week at work and she was exhausted. The journey that, over the last two months, had brought her back here, had been strenuous; happy and heartbreaking in equal measure.

It had taken Rebecca a long time to fully recover from her head injuries. Her fine motor skills had needed a lot of work, and the first time she saw her swollen, shaved head in a mirror, she cried. The other trauma was Marcie's arrest and trial. Rebecca couldn't help feeling sorry for her, even after what she'd done. Marcie's problems went way beyond holding an illogical grudge; she was ill. Even so, when she heard Marcie was safely locked away she cried with relief.

But in the midst of that, there were good things. Rebecca had returned to work in gradual stages, and last week she'd applied for the Director's job. She was up against some strong competition, but she was strangely unconcerned about whether she got it.

There was a knock on her door and Tasha waddled in. That was the only word for it, she thought, as she grinned at her temporary boss.

"Hot?"

Tasha glared. "Hot. Fat. I've got indigestion and an awful suspicion I've got piles coming on as well, and my only prize for all this pain is a future full of crappy nappies, so don't mess with me Maynard."

"Sorry."

"Huh. Anyway, I'm here to tell you to pack up your things and go." Tasha turned to leave.

"What?" She sat bolt upright.

"Go. Depart. Leave. Go for lunch first or go straight home, it's up to you, but I don't want to see you until Monday morning. You look shattered."

"If anyone goes home, it should be you," Rebecca protested.

"Oh believe me, I am. Now get your stuff because I'm sending in the troops."

The troops turned out to be Kevin, who appeared a minute later. "I've been sent to escort you off the premises."

"Okay, okay. I surrender."

Chapter Thirty One

The sun shone as Rebecca and Kevin walked to Tony's for lunch.

"Heard from Neil this week?" Rebecca asked, tucking her arm in Kevin's.

"Yep. He's back in two weeks." Kevin beamed and Rebecca squeezed his arm.

"That's great." She felt a little choked to see him so happy.

Neil had stayed in Milan with Steve and Rebecca for a couple of days after she came home from hospital, before he disappeared off exploring again. Much to Steve's surprise, Neil was intending to cut his exploring short and go back to London after a few months. Rebecca, however, wasn't surprised. She knew he and Kevin had gone out a few times, even before she left for Milan, and also knew that since Neil had left they'd been keeping in touch.

But she did enjoy the look of amazement on Steve's face when she told him. He'd spent a lot of time repeating, "Neil? Neil? And Kevin?" Although when he'd thought about it for a while, he admitted that perhaps he should have put the clues together.

"What about your love life, hmm? All set to move into the love nest this weekend?" Kevin teased.

"Yep. All packed up and ready to go," she smiled. After a tense period with Laura, Steve had finally found it in his heart to forgive her. Laura was applying for uni soon and a fortnight ago she'd moved out, and was now sharing a flat with Sarah, one of the students she'd met at the Museum. Steve had waited a week then asked Rebecca to move in with him. She'd been saying yes before he'd finished the sentence

"Well if you need any help, you know where I am..." Kevin grinned as they both said, "in Australia!"

She punched him. "Lazy sod! Some friend you are."

Tony's looked rather smarter from the outside these days. With Tony's blessing, Steve had ordered some new signage and given the whole cafe a makeover. It was flourishing under his management and Rebecca was incredibly proud of him.

As Kevin pushed open the door, Steve looked up and saw them both walking in. A big smile lit up his face. Kevin turned to Rebecca and smiled. "Happy days, eh?"

She squeezed his arm. "Yep. Happy days," she said quietly.

Rebecca looked at the next box. Her back ached from hours of unpacking and this one could wait. It must be time for dinner.

Steve popped his head round the door. "Are you getting hungry?"

"You read my mind," she smiled, walking over and winding her arms round his neck.

"I thought, as a reward for all our hard work, fish and chips. Unless you'd prefer Mexican," he grinned.

"Fish and chips sounds gorgeous."

"Good, because the chippy round the corner is great. I'll pop round."

"Okay."

"What do you fancy?"

"Other than you?" she grinned.

"Yes, other than me, you insatiable woman! Scampi? Battered sausage?"

She raised her eyebrows suggestively and he smacked her bottom.

"Behave! We've got work to do!"

"Spoilsport. Cod and chips, please."

He disentangled himself. "Your wish is my command." He bent to kiss her, then frowned, looking over her shoulder. He put his hands on his hips.

"Is that an unopened box I see before me?"

"Might be," she muttered.

"Then get to it, wench, while I gather food and drag it back to the cave! It had better be empty by the time I get back, else there'll be trouble!"

She booted him out the room, and heard him let himself out of the front door a few seconds later. She hadn't asked him if he wanted any money, she realised. She didn't suppose it really mattered, though. She didn't intend to count every penny and argue about who spent what and she didn't think Steve did, either.

With a sigh, Rebecca dropped to her knees and stared at the offending box. The scrawl of black marker told her this box was her CDs. She moved it over to the shelves that housed Steve's CD collection. He'd bought another set of shelves but suggested with a grin that she should slot her albums in beside his, since they both liked their CDs arranged alphabetically.

She ripped off the tape and grabbed the first handful of discs, which turned out handily to be A to C. Top shelf then. She let her eyes run along the other shelves that held Steve's collection. Ah, he had the Art of Noise too. Quirky. She was willing to bet that most people who'd bought that album had binned it long ago. Sometimes she'd wondered why she hadn't done the same thing. Bryan Adams. She had most of his, Steve only had a couple. Blur, Black-Eyed Peas... she frowned. Wow. Steve had lots of the same albums she had, A to C. It was probably just a coincidence. When she got the rest out she'd probably discover all his guilty secrets—he probably had a stash of Dolly Parton albums somewhere.

After she'd slotted D to F in, she stood back and started to look, really look, at Steve's CDs. She couldn't quite believe it. Apart from some notable exceptions (yes, he really did have all Mariah Carey's albums. and she didn't think the worse of him for not owning any Laurie Anderson), their CD collections were scarily similar.

By the time a gorgeous aroma announced that Steve had returned with dinner the shelves were nearly full.

"Steve! I've discovered something really strange."

He put his head round the door and grinned. "I told my neighbour has some odd habits."

"Steve, stop mucking about! Honestly, this is weird."

"Can I at least put the food down?"

He deposited the bag safely in the kitchen and followed her into the lounge. "Really? You found something weird in here?"

"Yes." She stood by the shelves, and waved her hand at them dramatically. "Look."

"At what? They're my shelves, sorry, our shelves, and now there's more of them."

"No, look at what's on them."

He frowned. "Er... CDs?" Then suddenly his face cleared. "Oh I get it. Very funny.

www.penrose-publishing.co.uk

You've found my Mariah Carey albums, haven't you?"

"Yes, but that's not it. Our CD collections are practically identical."

"That's not so weird. We're around the same age, have a similar socio☐economic background, we've both lived in London for some time... I bet the majority of people our age have got a couple of Oasis albums, some Robbie, a bit of Coldplay, Blur, ☐asabian, Christina Aguilera—"

"I agree, and if that's as far as it went, I wouldn't think it was odd, but—"

Her mobile rang. "Look at them properly! You'll see what I mean!" she hissed, as she picked up the call, too distracted to check the caller id.

"Hello?"

"Hi, is that Rebecca?" The voice was familiar.

"Yes."

"It's Nicola, from Methodical Matches."

She suppressed a grin at Nicola's 'from'; she obviously couldn't get out of the habit of pretending she was just a cog in a larger corporate machine.

"Hi Nicola. You're working late."

"I know, I've been here all evening generating our new Hot Matches."

"New?"

"Yes. My business partner's finally come back and fixed the crazy computer program, but collating the new results has taken hours."

"Oh dear." She tried to sound sympathetic, but she couldn't see that it was anything to do with her any more, and the smell of the fish and chips wafting in from the kitchen was driving her mad. "Of course, my profile's inactive."

"Oh yes, that's fine. We quite understand. It's just that since we finally got the program to work properly, we're running all our client's details through again."

"Er... good."

"It works really well! The problem was, the program was too intelligent."

"Oh?"

"Yes. It was set up to receive new input from sociological studies on relationships. That's why it started asking more and more questions and there were more variables than it had been made to cope with apparently. I don't really understand it all myself."

"No, me neither," Rebecca muttered.

"It was weighting certain sections more than the others, over☐writing earlier calculations. At one stage it was matching people purely on what books they read. Can you believe it!"

"Funnily enough, I can."

"Anyway, the reason I'm ringing you is because, it's not only generated everyone's top ☐ hot matches, it's generated an ideal match for everyone. Because of the inconvenience, we're telling everyone about these, and letting them have the next three months' membership for free."

"That's very kind, but I'm not interested. I have a partner now—"

"Oh, good for you!" Nicola chirruped.

"—and as I say, my profile's inactive. In fact, I was going to cancel my membership entirely as soon as I had the time."

"Well if you're sure..."

"Yes."

"I'll do that tomorrow for you. In the meantime, I'm sure you're still curious to know who your Ideal Match was—"

"Not really."

"Not even the teeniest bit?"

"Look sorry, Nicola, but my dinner's getting cold."

"Oh." There was a lot of hurt in that one small syllable. Then her voice brightened. "Tell you what, I'll just pop them in the email with the confirmation of your membership cancellation, shall I?"

"□reat idea. Thanks," said Rebecca hurriedly. "Bye, Nicola."

"Bye."

Steve was looking at her qui□ically from the door. "What was all that about?"

"Nicola."

"I thought I could hear her dulcet tones. Are you still trying to pull other fellas? Hmm?" He grabbed her.

"No. I'll explain later! Now let me at the food, I'm ravenous!" She ducked under his arm and ran to the kitchen with Steve chasing after her.

Later, they sat licking sticky fingers—they'd not bothered with knives and forks, they'd just dived in—and enjoying a glass of white wine.

"You're right about the CDs," Steve said, "it is weird." He found a hidden chip in the corner of the bag and swooped.

"What? Oh yes. I'd almost forgotten about that. It's not just the obvious ones, is it? Told you."

"At least we won't argue about what music to play."

"I might, if you insist on playing Mariah Carey."

"Well who the hell is Laurie Anderson? What does he sounds like?"

"She."

"What?"

"Laurie Anderson's a she."

"Don't care. As I was about to say, in that case he—sorry, she—is banned on principle."

"Even though you might like it?"

He nodded solemnly. "Even though."

She sighed. "Fair enough. I'll just have to make sure I boot you out of the house at regular intervals, then."

"Or use headphones. Then I could stay here…" he grinned and bent down, licking one of her greasy fingers, "and still enjoy your company. There's lot of things that you don't need your ears for," he said mischievously.

She kissed him but pulled away. "Fun as that sounds, at the moment I do have a report to finish. Sorry."

He stood up. "Very virtuous. I should be virtuous too because I've got a spread sheet of orders waiting for me on the computer upstairs."

"Okay." She smiled up at him. "What say we meet back down here to finish the wine at, ooh, let's see… □□□□?"

He kissed her lingeringly. "It's a date."

He disappeared upstairs and Rebecca set up her laptop on the dining room table. She needed to check her email first—she was waiting for some last minute results before she finalised her report, and was praying Kevin had remembered to forward them to her.

He had, just minutes before he left work, by the look of it. Good. She scanned down. Wow, Nicola had been better than her word. She really was working late. The cancellation email was already sitting there in Rebecca's inbox, sent fifteen minutes earlier. Rebecca's fingered hovered over the delete button—after all, she knew the important bit already, her membership had been cancelled—but now the email was actually in front of her and her Ideal Match was only a click away, a spark of curiosity was burning in her.

There wasn't any harm in taking a quick look at it, was there? Just out of interest.

The body of the email was much as expected. Two weeks' notice, direct debit cancelled, no refund of registration fee, blah blah. The Ideal Match was in the attachment, and she was surprised to find her heart starting to beat faster as she clicked to open it.

The first page contained the usual hot matches too. "Goodbye Richard, 37, and Barry, ," she muttered.

At the bottom of the page, in large bold letters, was the message 'SCROLL DOWN TO SEE YOUR IDEAL MATCH!'

She took a deep breath. Don't be daft. Rebecca. You've proved already that computers are no good at picking potential partners. This is completely insignificant because you've found your perfect partner already.

'CAUTION!' it said across the top, then further down: 'THIS PERSON COULD BE THE LOVE OF YOUR LIFE!'

Rebecca grinned, relaxing. Ludicrous! "Come on then," she said with a smirk. "Show me my Prince Charming." She scrolled down.

'YOUR IDEAL MATCH IS'

*** STEVE REYNOLDS! ***

She stared, transfixed, for ages, before she realised a tear was running down her cheek. She wiped it away and jumped to her feet.

She would run upstairs and tell Steve, for the hundredth and definitely not the last time, that he really was her ideal man.

Available in English and simplified Chinese
Available in paperback (pocket book size)
Available as an audio book

Please go to our website:
www.penrose-publishing.co.uk

See also books from our other authors:
Devon Volkel
Joshua Mercott
Les Gates
Aaron Smith
Joanne Smith
Grace Harding

www.ingramcontent.com/pod-product-compliance
Lightning Source LLC
Chambersburg PA
CBHW070928130626
46555CB00001B/339